STARCASTER

A Novel of Time and Magic

shana shaheen

Five Rabbits, Inc.
Boulder, CO

www.shanashaheen.com
www.shanaabe.com

Cover Design: The Midnight Muse, midnightmusedesigns.com
Interior Design for Print and ePub: Dayna Linton with Day Agency

Cover photograph copyright © William J. Shaheen

Library of Congress: Pending

Print ISBN: 978-0-9984702-1-4
e-Pub ISBN: 978-0-9984702-0-7

First Edition: 2017

10 9 8 7 6 5 4 3 2 1

Printed in the United States of America

BY
SHANA SHAHEEN

STARCASTER

By Shana Abé:

DEDICATION

For Sean, the sci *in my* fi*!*

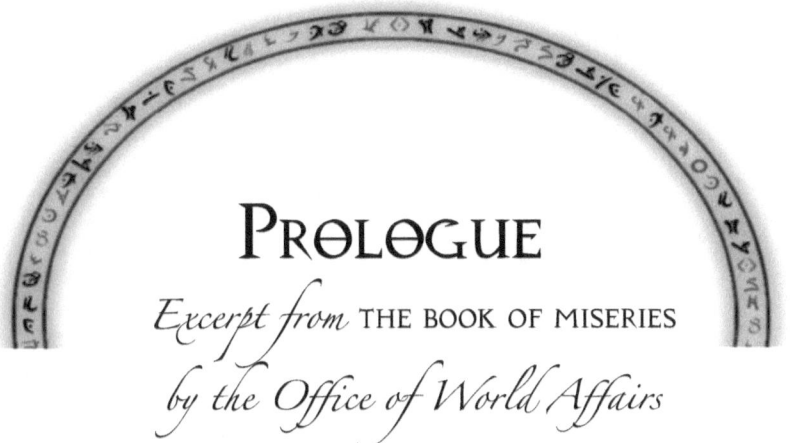

PROLOGUE

Excerpt from THE BOOK OF MISERIES
by the Office of World Affairs

DEATH HAS ALWAYS STALKED us, but back in the Bright Times, the Era of Machines, Death and Man joined hands and did their best to destroy the earth.

They nearly succeeded.

Science was a mad thing then, a rabid dog running loose, and there was no way out of its path. People designed machines, and machines designed ever more lethal robots and beans and peppers and bombs. Elegantly scripted diseases escaped from vials to worm their way into human cells, and turned our population inside-out.

Our waters frothed with poisons. The skies soured. Rain fell either nonstop or not at all. Babies were born withered, missing hands or toes or hearts; mothers and fathers dropped dead in factories or in the dunes. And still the machines burned on.

When the sane few protested, laws were passed to protect not the people, but the technology.

The *technology*.

And that is why now, the only law we have so binding as those from the days before is that of Magic.

Magic will be obeyed. It is our absolute and all.

CHAPTER ONE
Ember

903 Years Earlier

I'M BUILDING A SNOWMAN.

Well, it started out as a snowman. It has a good, traditional snowman base, nice and round and solid, but that part took me about twenty minutes to complete, and I'm not wearing gloves. I couldn't find any in my rush to leave the house and I'm *not* going back inside yet, so my hands are cherry-red frozen. No longer good for packing snow. I keep them tucked under my armpits when I'm not working on the snowman; I sort of forgot my coat, too.

Once upon a Mom-was-still-here, I would have been yelled at for going outside without a coat. These days, Dad or Mason would just bring one out to me. Anyway, none of them are here right now, are they?

Like catching a cold is going to kill me. Ha ha.

I'm building a snowthing. It has a misshapen head and two odd little snow arms (good luck finding twigs or branches buried under three feet of summer snow) that stick straight out from its body, as though it's trying to find its balance.

Its face is blank. I don't have rocks or marbles or anything else to give it an expression, so I use my finger to carve out eyes and a smile. I know for a fact there's a package of carrots back inside the cottage, but God help me if Dad finds out I used one for a snowthing nose.

It's a long trek down the mountain to get more carrots.

Fresh powder dusts my creation, altering its shape yet again, smoothing us both. It falls from the sky in huge static flakes that come and come and come, and everything around me is gray and pearly and mysterious.

If my life were a fairytale, I'd be the banished orphan/princess/misunderstood monster, surviving in a world of hushed isolation, waiting for rescue.

Except I'm not an orphan (only half). Definitely not a princess. The monster question is a little hazier, and *misunderstood* implies that someone's around trying to understand me.

I'm not waiting for rescue. Not any longer. I'm going to spend the rest of my days in the sifting flakes and the pearly light, and there's no surviving any of it. I already know that.

Snowfall coats the empty bone forest that hugs my home. Snowfall devours the high-altitude silence. Our cottage squats smothered in virgin drifts, no smoke sighing from the chimney, no steam rising from the eaves. The path I broke from the front door to the yard is the only visible evidence that anything alive up here still resists the weather.

That, and my snowthing.

We are the final two creatures left standing at the top of the world.

I squint at it, carve the smile deeper. But now it looks more ghoulish than happy, so I blow a frost sigh and scoop up another handful of snow and plaster it over the face, ready to start over.

That's when I hear it—the swoosh of air gliders above the clouds.

Gliders, of course, cross over the Sangre de Cristo Range all the time, but at a safe distance above the storms. Most of the time you can barely hear the whir of their engines, but these don't sound that high. I tip my face to the sky and even as I'm thinking, *Wow, they're cutting it close*, a glider breaks through the bubbly pewter bottom of the cloudbank above me, sinking so swiftly that I instinctively jerk back a step.

It's a personal craft, not a commuter. But even for one that small, the only good place to land is along the crumbled old highway fronting the cottage, so it settles there, *right the freak there on the highway*, and it's followed within seconds by about ten more.

Not like the highway's going to get plowed anytime soon, but still.

I forget about my snowthing. I forget about my deadened hands and the flake-spackled cold. I stand there open-mouthed as the glider doors open and people burst out into the drifts and the pearly gray day and begin to clamber awkwardly toward me.

This is astonishing for a variety of reasons. The only people who tend to venture this far up the mountain anymore are my father and my brother, and only because they live here, too. They go down into town for work and for school; I'm the sole permanent resident of these ghost woods. In all the time we've lived here, not a single stranger has risked getting this close to the house.

I certainly don't know *these* people, yet they seem to know me. Most of them are juggling vid cams and lightrings and mics, and all of them are shouting my name.

"November! November Duval! Are you November Duval?"

I go back another step and my foot meets a hidden patch of ice. I hit the ground so hard my teeth clack together, barely missing my tongue. My snowthing topples and breaks into lumps.

"November! Can you give us a statement, November?"

They're mediaheads. I recognize a woman from the local evening newsfeed; a man who hosts a highly caffeinated morning show. They're wearing heavy cosmetics and wraps too fashionable for snow this deep. There are even a couple of journo bots in the mix. Everyone's struggling to get closer.

A floating mic zooms up to my face, followed by a spinning lightring that blinds me. I want to slap at them but I'm afraid to because floating anythings are expensive and I can't afford to replace them if I break them. So I duck my head and find my feet again—the vid cams are recording my every tentative, achy movement—and when I look up there are cams everywhere, and the mediaheads still hollering questions at me, and at least three holo projections that show a girl with rippling, snow-wet blond hair and red hands and no coat and white crusting the entire left side of her body. She looks stupefied.

This is not happening. How can this be happening? Am I hallucinating? This is not—

A fourth holo of me pops up, this one just of my face. The cam for it must have some sort of special filter: my skin is pale and flawless; my eyes are huge and intensely greenish blue; my hair looks so golden it's almost metallic.

My bottom lip is painfully crimson. I must have bitten my tongue, after all.

I taste it now, too, the unpleasant rust taste of blood, so without thinking I wipe at my mouth and spit.

Everyone gasps. The people nearest me slog hastily backward.

"Ember!"

One person is rushing toward me and my blood, not away. One person here calls out my true name. Mason is supposed to be in class right now, but apparently, he's not. I see him on his solar skis, slipping easily through the strangers crowding our yard.

(My brother has always been able to move like that, even without the skis. Like water, or the wind. In this way, he's my opposite; someone who knows how to flow around impediments instead of ramming through them.)

"Ember," he says again, quieter now because he's reached me. He jabs his poles into the snow and grabs my shoulders. I barely feel it; I think I'm made of cold.

"Ember, you *won*," Mason says. In the holos he's ruffled and smiling, slightly winded. He towers over me because I'm still up to my knees in drifts and he's not.

He bats away a lightring and says, "You won the ticket to the Time Train. You're going to *live*."

And I think, *Oh, hell no.*

Two and a half years ago, I woke up and got dressed for school and ate lukewarm oatmeal for breakfast and Dad gave me a curt nod goodbye from his chair at the table, and everything smelled like oatmeal and beer. Mason was already out the door so I had to hurry to catch up with him; even though we're the same age, he's always been taller. He has long legs, crane legs, that eat up distance.

We'd lived out on the plains then, hearty fields of wheat as far as you could see, and I had no trouble running to his side. I wasn't even out of breath. It was nearly Christmas and the temperature had finally dropped from scorching to reasonable. The morning air felt wonderful, crisp as an apple, tangy as leaves. The sky blazed with that perfect sapphire sharpness that only came with this time of year. Sapphire sky; golden wheat. I loved autumn.

We caught the school tram together, found seats in the back and strapped in. Mason was instantly joking with one of his buddies, but I'd pulled out my LitPad and was busy finishing my assignment on *The Tempest* because Shakespeare always gave me a headache and I'd put it off until the last possible moment.

I didn't even notice the girl sitting next to me until the tram stopped in front of the school; we both stood up at the same time and bumped shoulders. I threw her a *sorry* look, but she only kept her face downturned.

It's funny how your memory can play tricks on you. Later on, I kept thinking about all the things about her I must have missed during that ride. Obvious things, like what she was wearing, or if she was reading or listening to music or just watching the mud dry on her shoes. If she smelled. My mind would fill in those blanks for me (*she was looking down at her lap; she was tapping at her homework; she was staring out the windows; her dress had cat hair on it, or dog hair, or rabbit; she was pale and listless and never moved*), but none of that was real, I think. Just my mind, being tricky. Nervous about the blanks.

I *am* certain I remember her hair right. It was lavender and frizzy with mousy brown roots. She needed a trim.

We were the last two leaving the tram. I was ahead of her, distracted because I was trying to shove my LitPad back into my pack. I'd made it all the way to the door when I heard this deep, gasping cough erupt right behind me, *right* in my ears. It didn't seem possible it could even come from the girl, it was so huge and wet.

I hunched my shoulders and hurried out to the curb. Paisley Goodwin from the class ahead of mine pointed at me and squealed, "Gross!" and at first I thought she meant *me*, because her dad was a lawyer instead of a farmer and she was cute and popular and basically an overall bitch.

But she didn't mean me. Not *just* me. The lavender-haired girl had hacked up pink foamy blood and chunks all over my hair and back.

All over.

The tram driver caught the falling girl in his arms, and then she was flat on the floor of the tram and not coughing or convulsing or doing anything at all any longer, or ever again.

Turns out you need to breathe to stay alive, and you need your lungs to breathe.

It was about a month after that when the mediaheads—so calmly at first, so pleasantly—began to mention the words *TB-3*.

Caffeinated Morning Host comes over first. He ignores the splotch of crimson tainting the snow between us, leaning near (no touching!) while at the same time angling his face and shoulders toward his vid cam. We're not even breathing the same air.

He speaks to the cam in a booming, jolly voice. His teeth are mercilessly white.

"November Duval! The Brain just chose *you* as the winner of the sole free ticket to Time Train Three, TimeTech's most revolutionary and *exclusive* new spacecraft! Tell us, how does it feel to know that in one week, you are going to board that train, head to your very own luxurious compartment and *then*,"—he pauses for effect; this guy is so hyped it's like *he* won the ticket—"travel forward in time to your very own *cure?*"

I shake my head. I don't know how it feels. I don't how to say anything. I've brought both hands up to cover my mouth and I'm holding them there hard because I'm not sure what might happen otherwise. I have a maniacal urge to laugh, but my eyes are stinging.

The light from the 'rings splits into prisms through my tears; for a moment, I can't see the cams or the forest or anything else. All I see are rainbow smears.

"She feels honored," my brother covers for me, still by my side. "She can't believe it yet."

A journo bot has picked its way through the snow to end up right in front of us. It has five shiny cam eyes and a mic antenna that comes close enough for me to kiss. The logo pulsing across its front indicates it's from the Total World Newsfeed, *Total News for Your Total World Today!*

Someone back at the Total World Newsfeed headquarters—many thousands of miles removed from me and my pesky disease—uses the bot to ask the next question.

"According to the TimeTech Corporation, there were over six million final entries for the ticket to the Time Train. Ladies and gentlemen, that's six million certifiably sick people from all around the globe who met the rigorous criteria for the lottery, all vying for that single slot. November, are you surprised you beat them all?"

Mason gives my elbow a sharp squeeze. I drop my hands and force my lips into an upward curve.

I will not say:

This is not happening.

I will not say:

This isn't what I wanted.

And I won't say:

Why do you think I'm out here freezing my ass off, instead of inside my house watching the live lottery draw on our holofeed? Why do you think I'm standing out here in the snow, dumb and numb and speechless?

Because I couldn't stand to win, and I couldn't stand to lose.

Mason crushes my elbow again and I pull free of him, flick my fingers across my eyes. Maybe it's the last of the tears, but in the holos now, my smile appears dazzling.

"Sorry," is what I say, and I feel that crazed laughter climbing back up my throat. I shove it down again. "Sorry, I'm just . . . I'm amazed." This seems like a safe word to offer to the audience, to anyone at TimeTech who's watching. "Awed," I add for good measure, but my voice cracks.

I wipe my mouth with my sleeve again.

Caffeinated Morning Host nudges the journo bot out of the way. He has a wide, fleshy grin. "And would you say that you're very, very lucky to win the TimeTech lottery today, November Duval?"

"Yes," I agree immediately, understanding his prompt. "I am very, very lucky." I blink into the artificial glare of the lightrings; my eyes won't stop watering.

All around me, the fat flakes fall. I am a smiling liar against them.

"I'm the luckiest girl in the world," I say.

Even though we're almost seventeen, Mason and I share a room. The cottage is an ancient two bedroom/one bath speck of brick and wood, and neither of us was willing to share with Dad.

At first, we solved our privacy dilemma by stringing a pair of blankets on a rope down the middle of the room, but then Mason made this folding wall at shop class out of scrap metal. Every piece he salvaged was damaged or rusted, or both, so the teacher just let him have it, but he hammered everything out and shined it all up. He used solder and invisible hinges to hold it together; it fits perfectly from the floor to the ceiling. So now it's like we each have our own compact, incredibly narrow bedroom. The only significant drawback to it that you have to turn sideways to get past the door.

I etched butterflies and tufted wheat on my side of the wall, and a beaming sun. Mason cut out a window for us that opens and closes with a latch. I etched shutters around that.

I'm in bed, staring up at my half of the ceiling, which I've painted with constellations—Lyra, the Big Dipper, Cygnus, the Herdsman—that glow at night. They're glowing now because it's well after midnight.

A tiny green dot of light appears at the open window in our wall. It hangs there, suspended in the air, until another little green dot joins it, and then another, and another, until there are eight of them total.

These are Mason's robo fireflies. In this forever-winter home, using scrap and supercapacitors and phosphorus and paint, we've created our own version of an old-fashioned summer.

The first firefly swims silently through the dark to land on my stomach. It has practically no weight; it took Mason almost a year of tinkering to get the 'flies light enough to defy gravity with their miniature solar wings.

A second one lands on my arm. I turn my head to look at it and I can't help but smile, and then I don't smile.

I have only six more nights of robo fireflies. Of etched wheat and

Cygnus and what's left of my family, who mean more to me than any cure.

I can't believe I won that stupid ticket. I didn't even want to enter.

"*Eeeem*-ber . . ." warbles an extremely creepy falsetto from the other side of the wall. "*Eeeem*-ber . . . we *wuv* you . . ."

One by one, the other fireflies join the first two, landing on my legs and arms and chest. The last one loops circles within circles until it ends up precisely on the tip of my nose. It clings there, wings open, and green fills my vision.

Carefully I raise my hand and present a finger to the 'fly, letting it hop up.

"They don't talk like that," I say to the darkness. "They have normal voices."

"They do?" Mason's voice drops an octave. "How do you know?"

"Because they're beautiful."

"Beauty isn't a reliable indicator of phonetic quality," he points out, all scientist again.

"I'm still right."

Mason is prepared to indulge me. "Okay, Queenie, you're right."

The robo 'fly tiptoes delicately up the back of my hand, stopping at the joint of my wrist. I am bejeweled in emerald lights.

The house is quiet. It feels empty and echoing after the cacophony of the day. There's a creek that traces a baby canyon through the woods out back, but it's frozen, noiseless, overpowered by the snow. I can't even hear my dad snoring.

He'd shown up not long after Mason; I still don't know if the factory foreman let him go early or if he'd simply walked off the line. Either are very possible. Dad doesn't talk much but when he does, you tend to listen. There's a baritone to him—not just his words, but to everything about him. He resonates. He's tall and brittle and can terrify people with just a long, unyielding look. It's an excellent quality that I wish he'd passed on to me, but it's clear I don't terrify anyone.

I don't. My disease does. It's not really the same, though.

Dad had parked his snowcar in the middle of the gliders, climbed out of the cab and told all the mediaheads exactly what he thought of them for trespassing on his property and harassing his kids *and for chrissake, Ember, where's your coat?*

Every second of it was captured by the cams. I expect a few children around the world learned some new words today.

As soon as we'd retreated inside the house, the calls began. More mediaheads, plus neighbors from the plains, neighbors from the mountains, long-lost cousins a thousand times removed. Even some of the kids from my old school. I hadn't had any real friends there (I'd thought), but suddenly I was famous and I guess that equates to popular, because Paisley G. herself actually activated her fone to gush at me about how mind-blowing it all was, and how I hadn't looked *too* gross on the holofeed, and that she hoped I'd come find her in the future once I was all better.

I told her I definitely would.

The TimeTech people had called, too, but only to say they'd be in touch soon with the details of my upcoming fate.

"Mason," I whisper.

"Yes?"

I finally speak aloud the words that have been squirming at the back of my mind.

"Six-million-to-one. Six million other people who went through the same TimeTech tests as me, the same physicals and all those questionnaires. What are the chances that *I'd* end up being that one?"

It's a rhetorical question because of course I already know the answer. Mostly I just want confirmation of the improbability of it all. The absurdity of ordinary me being handed this great and awful gift.

There's a pause. The fireflies begin a unison march across my body, zigzag patterns that mean something to them but look arbitrary to me.

"Who cares," Mason says at last. "You won, so who cares?"

"I care."

"Listen, Ember." His voice has changed again; he sounds like someone I don't know. Someone I will never know, probably. Older, adult, low and stern. "This is an opportunity for you that isn't going to happen more than once. You're going to *live* because of this. So, don't—don't go around questioning things, especially in public, all right? Just do what they say. Be what they want. Smile and look pretty and try to keep your mouth shut."

I suck in a breath.

"Sorry," he says before I can respond. "I'm sorry. But just . . ."

I hear him get up to stand at our window. I turn my head and by the luminescence of my stars I can see, barely, the lean, pale suggestion of his face. His hair is black, so I don't see that at all.

"Just be happy about it," he says. "I am."

I sit up. All the fireflies take off, swirling about.

"I don't want to go," I say.

"I know."

I cross my legs and pull my blankets up tight around my waist. I knot my fingers into their folds.

"I'm afraid to go," I admit, something I would never, ever utter to anyone else in the world.

But Mason is my twin. We don't engage in lies.

"I know," he says again.

We fall into silence. The fone in the living room begins to chirp;

it goes on for about two minutes before whoever's calling gives up. Dad disabled the message system after dinner but apparently forgot about the ringer. I'm considering abandoning the relative warmth of my bed to go take care of it when Mason speaks again.

"I keep thinking."

I wait. Without the chirping of the fone, the cottage sinks into an even more profound lull than before. I imagine I can hear its skeleton creaking.

"What if it had been me right in front of her on the tram? Why you, and not me?"

I shake my head. *What if*s had been plaguing me for the past two and a half years, and I knew they offered no peace.

What if I'd stayed home that day?

What if I'd run slower, been late, missed the tram?

What if I'd sat somewhere else?

What if I hadn't listened to that woman in the school med center, who wasn't even a real nurse, I bet, who'd told me that it was all so, so unfortunate, but once I rinsed out my hair I'd be fine?

What if I had been stronger, smarter, psychic? Could I have avoided catching this disease that's going to melt my lungs into mush?

"Why not me," I finally say. "It was random. That's all."

Mason grunts, either in agreement or disagreement, I don't know. The fireflies have settled in a dotted line along the foot of my bed, their lights blinking. I flop back against my pillows. It's been a long day and I'm tired of all the drama.

I try, "At least you'll get a bigger room."

"At least you'll get *your own luxurious compartment.*" He mimics Caffeinated Morning Host perfectly.

"Luckiest girl in the world," I murmur, closing my eyes.

"Yes," says my brother. "You will be."

Chapter Two
Ember

H ERE'S MY OTHER TRUE recollection of that girl from the school tram:

A scrawny arm flung past the door out into the sunlight, a palm to the December sky.

Ropy blue veins. Chipped black nail polish.

Dead fingers clenched.

CHAPTER THREE
Taza

I T WAS WIDELY ACKNOWLEDGED that Taza Sullivan had been born with a hole in his heart. Not a literal hole, but the shadow imitation of one; it stretched the breadth and depth of that unspoken space, the seat of his soul. The hole remained despite the many blessings sprinkled like rose petals, like cherry blossoms, all through his life: firstborn of a sovereign, alight with power, handsome and charismatic and smart. Even as a child, all that he touched appeared to prosper with the luxuriant ease of the innately adept.

But the emptiness inside him never ceased gnawing; quietly, cunningly. As he grew older it compelled him to dark, silent places—hollow lands, parched fields, deep deep spells—where he knew no one else could or would follow.

His grandmother declared it to be the price of his gifts. His father publicly agonized that this *lack* would *become* his son. That Taza would spend his mortal life incomplete, forever yearning for the ineffable *something* (even the most accomplished scryers could not foresee exactly what) needed to fill him.

But no one could argue that Taza could cast as others could not. Taza crafted sorcery as others did not. And that, at some point in his twenty-third year, Taza was destined to rule in his father's stead.

He was clever, he was calm, and he could be kind. As he had not yet reached his eighteenth birthday, it was thought that there was sufficient time still for his heart to become whole.

All in all, matters might have been worse.

And then, one morning, they were.

In the Fortress of the Sky, there was only one rule: don't look down.

Actually, there were many more rules than that, but *don't look down* was the only one Taza bothered to follow since it was the only one that would have a potentially permanent outcome should he forget it.

If he looked down, he might fall.

He was not a bird, he could not fly, so he had no desire to fall.

The base of the Fortress was, of course, solid. Solid as could be, in fact, made of granite and pine and a sort of rosy-pink brick forming all the arches. The Fortress had been born of these densely forested hills and it showed; the uninitiated seldom even glimpsed it between the trees. It took at least three years of hard study before the Fortress would suggest its own outline. Another two before the door could be found. And even then, all that got you was an invitation to roam the bottom floors. If you fell there, no one cared.

It was the clear ladders at the top—the complex, invisible spires composed of hexes and enchantments and the essence of falling stars—that offered not only the best view of the universe imaginable but also the most perilous. Only the most advanced casters (the most harebrained, Imogen would say) even attempted it.

Taza was not harebrained. He never looked down when he

climbed the spires. He looked outward. That was what they were for, after all.

For seeing into the Beyond.

He clung with both hands to the top of the spire he'd climbed in these small, dark hours before dawn, his feet hooked firmly into a faintly humming lattice. The magic up here was so thick it raked through his hair and prickled along his skin. Occasionally it gathered into sparks, which would crackle and float like dying embers down to the living earth.

The sparks hurt, much like a rubber band snapping back against your skin would hurt. Usually he ignored them, but he'd only been up here a few minutes so far and already his hair danced on end and he glimmered with light.

Nature was the text and subtext of his existence. Nature was birth, death, and the sorcery that thrived in between; it did not give without taking. And so, for every power, there came sacrifice.

Taza understood that as far as sacrifices went, this one wasn't too bad.

He focused his attention upward, scanning the heavens, the rhinestone ribbon of the Milky Way. A pinprick of yellow crept a slow path across it: one of the Remnants of the Bright Times, a derelict ship or satellite doomed to orbit the planet until gravity decided its end.

There were clubs of spellcasters (mostly scions of the First families, bored and boring) devoted to pulling the machines downward until they burned, but he didn't belong to any of them. Privately he thought them frivolous, which worried him some since it seemed like the sort of opinion his father would approve of. But the truth was, the destruction of the long-dead technology of a long-dead people held no interest for him.

Taza lived for the now. For the power and potential of today.

For revelation, not destruction.

He released the knob of the spire he'd been clutching and lifted his hand, fingers spread. Sparks arced between them, pink and green and orange and gold. Mostly orange, that rarest of colors, which meant a twisting of paths. Travel. Unintended consequences; unexpected fates.

Strange. He hadn't been planning to go anywhere.

He heard a *clap!* above him, sharp as thunder. A deep, sizzling *whoosh* that shivered like gravel down through his joints.

Taza looked up.

A shooting star ripped toward him, a major one, searing a line of flame and smoke across the heavens. It was so bright it obliterated the Milky Way and the stars and the amethyst bleed of eastern light that preceded the sunrise. He was thinking he'd never seen one so big when he realized it wasn't a shooting star.

It was . . . something else. Something long, snake-like.

From far, far below, he thought he heard a horse begin to scream.

All the spires of the Fortress lit to fire, all the ladders, every enchantment suddenly, astoundingly visible. The matrix supporting him went cold as ice against his body. The wind tasted scorched on his tongue.

The snake-star tore overhead, still sizzling, and vanished beyond the black line of the western hills.

He felt the destruction of its landing ricochet through him. The lattice supporting him trembled.

As omens went, it could hardly be more portentous.

Taza Sullivan did not look down. He began, instead, to descend hand-over-hand, returning back to the solid floors of the Fortress of the Sky as rapidly as his aching arms would take him.

CHAPTER FOUR
Ember

EVERYONE KNOWS THAT TIME travel is possible. Not in the way that people used to imagine it, popping miraculously back and forth by means of some type of stationary transporter or whatever, but through the science of speed. Relativity. Time dilation.

Time slows down as we speed up. Go fast enough, and your time tears away from everything slower. At about 87 percent of the speed of light, your reality moves at half the speed of Earth's. At about 97 percent, you're at a quarter of the speed. And so on. The faster you go, the farther into the future you can go—and all in what is, to you, a relatively short amount of time.

(We can't travel into the past. Too many paradoxes. My elementary school teachers explained the concept of paradoxes over and over again, but the example that made the most sense to me was this: Suppose you travel back in time and encounter your younger self, and kill your younger self. Then older you never existed to travel back in time in the first place. Get it?)

But the future is wide open. Paradox-free. That's where Time-Tech comes in.

Nine years ago, they built the first Time Train. A lot of people were sure it wasn't going to work. Time travel still sounded like fantasy, like one of those fluttery, fever-dream possibilities that never quite fully evolve into fact, and people continued to think that even after the science behind it was published. There were all sorts of logistical problems TimeTech had to overcome, such as the path of the train, its energy source, starting and stopping and running it and who was going to be brave enough, or deranged enough, to be its first passengers.

Space travel was one thing. People had been shooting themselves into space for over a century. But shooting yourself into space—much, much farther into that vast scary dark than anyone had ever ventured before; much, *much* faster—just so that you could circle back to our solar system and lift your face to the yellow rays of the future sun?

Think about it. Suppose the train didn't blow up, or careen off course, or get pummeled by asteroids or space junk. Suppose it did *exactly* what TimeTech said it would. In that case, every person aboard was going to abandon the civilization they knew and understood, abandon probably everyone they ever knew or loved, only to end up in an unknown civilization at an unknown point in time. Who on earth would want to do that?

Pretty much everyone, as it happened. The tickets the TimeTech owners were afraid they weren't going to be able to *give* away were snatched up in the blink of an eye. They were cheaper then, not the soul-wringing expense they are now, but they weren't cheap. If your average person worked her entire life as, say, a vid producer, or a police officer, or a librarian, and she saved up every credit she'd ever earned for the payment, she could afford maybe a quarter of a ticket.

Even back then, the Time Train was for a certain kind of wealthy.

At the last minute, TimeTech decided to hold back a token free ticket, which was to be given away via lottery as a gesture of goodwill, in support of the belief that *all mankind deserved to benefit from this magnificent technology blah blah blah.*

One ticket, out of forty. A retired stockbroker won it.

The first train was deliberately slow. The scientists and owners were being careful; it was, after all, the first human experiment with time, and there were a *lot* of rich people on board.

Time Train One traveled its skinny loop through the universe at approximately 99.98 percent of the speed of light. One month for them had been four years for us. It departed and came back without incident.

And everybody was so, so happy. The holofeeds of the passengers exiting the train showed them laughing and showered in confetti; it gave the impression they'd just attended a giant, month-long cosmic party, with champagne fountains and gourmet feasts and galaxies floating gloriously past their windows.

Time Train Two came soon after. It was the same train, but they gave it a different name for its second trip because it was going to go farther and faster than One. It's still not back.

And now there's Time Train Three. It's a brand-new train, brand-new everything, sleeker and even faster (and posher, if that's possible) than One and Two.

Only, here's the thing. Rich people get sick the same as the poor. Rich people want to live as much as the rest of us do. There are so many diseases with treatments that always seem to teeter at the edge of a breakthrough, and rich people have figured out that all they have to do is wait it out. Wait for the inevitable discovery of their cure.

On Earth, that's a risky proposition. On a machine that hurtles through time, however . . .

Barring a few sanity-challenged, obscenely affluent daredevil types, the Time Train has become a repository for the terminally ill.

People like me.

THE FINAL SIX DAYS of my ordinary life wing by so quickly I can barely grasp their shapes and colors. I try desperately to lock images inside me (the chip in the bathroom sink shaped like an otter; the dull polyester weave of our carpet; Mason's crooked smile; my father's fingers, bent and scarred, wrapped around the spatula as he burns the scrambled eggs). I want to memorize everything, every little thing, no matter how trivial, so I won't lose myself to whatever happens in the future. So I'll still be me.

But I can't keep anything straight. I forget to pour milk on my cereal, then forget we're out of milk. I forget if I filed my calculus assignment, then remember it doesn't matter because I won't have school, then forget if I filed it again.

I walk into rooms and only stand there, trying not to break down at the sight of Dad's empty beer cans, or the dirty dinner dishes left out from the night before, or the pile of laundry that never seems to diminish and always needs to be folded. It's ridiculous.

My father watches me with brown worried eyes, and my brother with our peculiar greeny-blue, and I smile back at them and pretend that I'm fine with all of this, really, and oh, boy, aren't I lucky?

Lucky, lucky, lucky.

I don't think anybody's fooled except possibly the mediaheads, who still show up occasionally trying to land an interview before I blast off into the void. Dad shoos them away. If they're insistent, he leans against the doorjamb with his arms crossed and tells them that

I've entered a contagious stage but hell, if they're that damned brave or that damned foolish, he'll just go ahead and call me out to the porch right now to give them their holobyte.

No one ever stays.

I pack the night before. TimeTech has informed me I'm allowed up to three cases and a trunk (a *trunk*?), but all I have is my mother's old hardcase—the one she didn't take with her—and it's not even full.

I ponder it morosely, spread open and offering up its innards atop my bed. Underwear, pajamas, pants, socks. Shirts, thermals, sweatshirts. My favorite sweater with its hole in the right elbow.

If I lean down close enough, I get a whiff of Mom's perfume, still stubbornly clinging to the fabric lining the case. It bothers me on some churlish, unforgiving level, that all my stuff is going to smell like her.

"Take more sweaters," advises Mason, standing beside me, surveying the mess. If he notices the perfume, he doesn't mention it. "It's cold out there."

In space, my mind finishes for him, and I have to stop myself from giving in to that appalling, crazy laugh.

But he's right. I might as well grab a few more, even though the rest of my sweaters are even rattier. At least they're bulky; they'll fill up the case.

"Here," he says, and yanks his own up over his head, revealing a worn gray shirt with a grease stain down the front. "Take this one, too."

"Mason—"

"Take it. A souvenir of me."

I've been coveting it, I admit. It's chocolate-colored and super soft, not a hole in sight. Mason's blood is Clean and so he isn't as bound to our house as I am; he works part-time after school as a custodian. Most of his income goes to either the kind of food Dad won't buy (pizza, candy, salt) or else the clever bits and parts he needs for his inventions. But this sweater is new. I know he saved up for it.

I test the weight of it in my hands. It's real wool, not our usual cheap synth, and downy light, still warm from his body.

He sees my face and gives a shrug. "It was getting too small for me, anyway."

It's such an obvious lie, I have to bite my tongue not to call him on it; I know he's only trying to make me feel better. He's always been generous, far more so than I am. He's the boy who'll give you the last cookie in the jar, or pull the sled uphill the whole way so that you only have to ride. When we still lived on the farm he did all the heavy chores and the truth is, he doesn't even *like* pizza, he only brings it home because I do.

I'm holding his sweater and thinking all this when it hits me again, that awful, sucker punch realization.

I'm going away tomorrow. I'm going away forever.

Forever might be an exaggeration. But it feels like the truth.

"Hey," he says quietly, and touches my shoulder—firm, reassuring, like he'd done when he'd told me I won the ticket. "Don't forget to pack your toothbrush, because in about a hundred years your breath is going to really, really stink."

A laugh escapes me, but thankfully it's not the crazed kind.

"They have that there on the train. All the—hygiene stuff. They supply that."

"Rich folk toothpaste," Mason says. "Maybe it's got gold flakes in it."

"Maybe it's made out of angel tears."

"Or the very last tiger."

"The last vestal virgin."

"What *is* that?"

"I don't know, but she's got to be endangered."

We're both smiling now.

He reaches out a hand and messes up my hair. I shake him off.

Fireflies dance between us, exuberant, oblivious.

WE SAY OUR GOODBYES in the waiting area of the shuttle station. Only ticketed passengers (plus a few company executives and workers) are allowed on the shuttle that will carry us up to the Time Train platform that orbits the planet. I'm already red-eyed and exhausted from having to get up so early to take the mag-train to the shuttle. From our mag-line station in the Sangre de Cristos, it was a two-hour journey to the East Coast, but we still had to leave our house before four in the morning. I honestly can't remember if I slept.

It could have been worse, though. Because there are so many TB-3's living up high in the mountains, we finally got our own station. All of our magnetic lines go straight to hospitals, but once you pass a blood test to prove you're not infectious, you can connect to the main lines. If we'd had to take our old truck down to the Queen City station on the plains, it would have added an extra half a day to our trip.

But now we're here in the moist, heavy heat of the Atlantic seaboard, being escorted by a pair of security guards to the waiting area. My inhaler's in my pocket, but so far the humid air slips fine into my lungs. It makes my skin feel sticky but I enjoy how it tastes a little like salt.

It's not yet noon here; the sun is burning hard and high above us.

I realize for the first time how much I've missed being warm without layers and layers of clothing. How nice the sky looks without a constant lid of gunmetal clouds.

Mason carries my case and Dad walks slightly ahead of us, but that only works until we're spotted by the mob that's come to gawk at the passengers—who are, aside from me, some of the most powerful and secretive people in the world.

Then it's chaos.

A few of the mediaheads seem to remember my dad's lie about me being contagious, but far more of them swarm close as we push our way toward the area doors. The security guards try to keep them back, but there's no chance. It's two men against an avalanche of cams and mics and waving hands.

"November! November! A word! Tell us what's going through your mind!"

"Are you excited?"

"Are you nervous?"

"Did you leave a will, November?"

"Are you looking forward to your cure?"

"How long do the doctors say you have left, November?"

The cams track our struggling progress and someone manages to hook a floating mic in my hair, which hurts, but I untangle it without comment and we finally get past the doors. Even once inside, we're not concealed. The waiting area is flooded with light and walled in glass. All the chairs face outward. There is no hiding.

And really, I seem to be the only one who wants to hide, anyway.

Knots of people are standing around or seated, all of them acting as if the commotion outside does not exist. They're elegant people, discussing elegant matters in melodious, elegant tones. Some of them have got to be with TimeTech, or friends or family, but the majority are going to be my fellow passengers.

I'm surprised at how . . . *fit* they all look. Sure, four or five are on hover stretchers with attendants nearby, but most of the rest appear ordinary. Ordinary for wealthy people, I mean.

By and large they skew older, but there's a pair of twenty-something guys in blazers who look as if they've escaped from a country club; a sullen-faced boy probably around my age, glowering down at the floor; and even a young girl, redheaded, eight or nine maybe, holding tight to the hand of the nurse beside her. Everyone's attractively dressed and groomed and I'm practically the only person here without a lovely glowing tan.

A tan. Seriously. Because we're going to need that in space.

As the doors swish closed behind my dad and Mason and me, it seems the entire group turns to take us in. They look us up and down and then—like they'd rehearsed it—they all turn away again.

"The charity," someone whispers, but I have no idea who.

Mason sets the case down by his feet and flanks me to the left. Dad takes my other side. We form a line of stiff-necked uncertainty; of strangely blessed, scruffy yokels, knowing we're supposed to be here but still lingering by the potential escape of the doors.

I begin to comb my fingers through the snarls in my hair.

"Ladies and gentlemen, if you please."

The amplified voice that washes over us sounds so much like a computer program that it takes me a second to grasp that it's a real woman. I scan the room until I find her, a TimeTech executive in a tailored suit standing unobtrusively by the other set of doors. The ones that lead to the tarmac, to the shuttle.

"Thank you," the woman says, smiling, because of course everyone has angled in place to offer her their tanned, elegant attention.

The TimeTech lady has her own floating mic. It goes nowhere

near her gel-frozen curls.

"Welcome. We are honored to host you here today, and honored to be able to host you into the future. You are the leaders of our time, women and men who have carved your mark into our world and transformed it into a better place for all. You are titans. You are the hope of our tomorrows. We are grateful indeed to stand in your presence."

The blazer guys both nod solemnly, as if this is their due. Glowering Boy rolls his eyes, which warms me to him marginally.

"Your trip from here to Time Train Three will take no more than fifteen minutes. Your voyage into the future, however, should not be measured in minutes or hours. It will be measured in days for you, in years for us. It will be measured in scientific accomplishments. In new technology. In cures for the incurable. When you return to Earth, you will rejoin a world transformed. And we at TimeTech have no doubt—none at all—that you will carve your mark into that fresh new world as admirably and decisively as you did this one. You will summon forth a brighter future for all mankind."

She pauses, and the crowd breaks into restrained applause.

Right outside, the vid cams are still monitoring us. They're equipped with settings to read the microscopic vibrations of the glass walls and translate them into sound. Even in this sealed chamber, every word spoken is being live-transcribed.

"And with that, ladies and gentlemen, I bid you farewell and good fortune. Shuttle boarding commences in five minutes."

She smiles again, everyone applauds again, and this time when conversations resume, they're a touch more animated than before.

This is it. Five minutes for farewells and final wishes of good fortunes.

Both Mason and Dad look at me, but it's Mason who reaches for me first. I hold him tight. I can't do this too long; it hurts too much. He's been beside me my whole life, my constant north star. I can't imagine walking away and finding my seat on that shuttle without him right there, cracking bad jokes, finishing my sentences. I know people talk about how someone is their other half, but Mason actually is. Always has been. How can I leave my twin?

I want to say something, anything, but my throat's locked up and the only thing I can think of is *See ya around*, which sounds too flip in my head and is very likely untrue anyway.

Oh, but I want it to be true. I press my lips shut so I don't blurt out the words and jinx it.

"Don't worry," my brother whispers in my ear. "You'll see me again." He's not afraid of jinxes.

He releases me. I wipe at my cheeks and turn to my father. He stands there awkwardly for a moment before realizing that I'm not going to move (*because I'm made of lead; I'm made of stone; I am solid and impenetrable*), so he steps closer.

His arms feel thin and strong. He sighs against me and it's that, merely that, that breaks the dam inside me.

"Daddy," I say, but nothing more. I feel his hand stroke my hair, his palm following the curve of my skull, falling to rest against my upper back. He hasn't had a drink since yesterday and his scent's kind of stale, but achingly familiar too.

It's the scent of working in fields, and of cold mountain wind, and of dusty summer wheat. It's the scent of all my days before this one.

I press my face to his chest and think about how I'm not going to cry now because it'll go live and be the last image of me anyone sees for years and years.

"Be safe, girl," my dad murmurs.

I nod. With my face still hidden in his shirt, I scrunch it up hard, then deliberately relax my features and draw back. I hope I look serene.

"Glad I made you enter for that ticket," Dad says, and I nod again.

"Guess it worked out," I reply.

Serene. Serene. I feel like my insides are dissolving.

Dad offers me a nod back, squares his shoulders, and walks away. Just like that, he's out the doors and gone.

Mason and I watch him become swallowed by the mob.

"You'd better go too," I say. "He'll take the wrong mag-line and end up in Tasmania or something."

I'm not really kidding. All three of us are strangers to this place, but I know that at least Mason will read the signs pointing toward home.

He glances back at me, tall, disheveled, right on the edge of handsome.

"See ya around, Queenie."

"Yeah," I lie, and try to smile.

He presses a kiss to my forehead, gives me a smile that's much more honest than my own, then follows Dad.

So now in this naked, crowded chamber, I stand alone.

CHAPTER FIVE
Ember

H ERE ARE THE ANSWERS I didn't give to the crowd shouting at me outside the waiting room:

Tell us what's going through your mind!

Kind of a dull, constant panic.

Are you excited?

No.

Are you nervous?

I'm about to go live with a bunch of pretentious strangers in a long metal tube that rips through space and time. *Nervous* doesn't quite capture it.

I feel sick. Weary. Frayed.

Did you leave a will, November?

Wills are for people who have stuff to leave behind.

Are you looking forward to your cure?

How is that even a real question?

How long do the doctors say you have left, November?

Four months, give or take.

Only four more months.

CHAPTER SIX
Ember

I HAVE A WINDOW SEAT on the shuttle. Next to me is a middle-aged woman with a beehive pile of improbably platinum hair, who for some reason won't make eye contact with me. At first I think it's coincidence, but then, when it's obvious she means it, I stare at her fierce and hard until she just turns her entire head the other direction and keeps it there, and all I see is fakey bright hair. I debate with myself about leaning in close and whispering that it's good she's avoiding my gaze, since looking at me would absolutely give her TB-3, but by then the thrusters are igniting and the shuttle is lifting off.

I'm smushed back into my seat. My stomach hits my spine and my hours-ago breakfast is rising back up and I claw my fingers into my armrests as if that's going to help.

It doesn't. But what does is the view.

Blue sky engulfs us. It darkens into lapis, into navy, into ink. If I cut my eyes all the way to the left, I can see the hazy surface of the planet below us. The green and brown jigsaw pieces of land, the turquoise waters. Earth retreats farther, farther, and then mostly what I see are vortices of white over oceans—future storms brewing, patches of cotton pushed and molded by winds, and I wonder if anyone below is looking up and following our contrail.

Goodbye, I say without sound. I don't want the woman beside me to hear. *Goodbye. I love you.*

The shuttle tilts and I lose Earth; now all I see are stars and shiny, lumpy objects that are satellites and space stations and construction facilities for the ships that travel to the moon and Mars and back. We burn past one of the stations close enough that I glimpse a man silhouetted in a porthole, watching us.

The man waves a hand. I wave mine in return, but within seconds we're beyond him.

The shuttle slows. Without the pressure of acceleration, there's an unpleasant minute or so of free-floating (which doesn't help with my breakfast). My hair lifts. My body bounces against the straps securing me to my seat, and then the gravity controls kick on and I drop back to the cushions.

Gravity feels like being suddenly coated in cement.

The intercom chimes. "Passengers and crew, prepare for docking."

My hair's long and loose and some of it has fallen to rest on Beehive Lady's shoulder. She jerks forward, dislodging it, and I barely have time to pull it to me before she pushes back into her seat again.

"Sorry," I say, but she only keeps staring straight ahead. Her lips are dyed a perfect smoky gray, matching her fingernails and stilettos and skirt.

"Great updo," I add. "You hardly look seventy at all."

I go back to gazing out my window.

The Time Train platform isn't much like the mag-line platforms on Earth. It couldn't be; it's a marvel of propulsion and momentum, of self-contained oxygen and gravity that holds its steady course around the planet. It's a compilation of boxy metal structures that mostly resembles the space stations, but longer, with docking anchors on opposite ends: one for the shuttle, one for the train.

On clear nights, back on the plains, Mason and I would sometimes stretch out in the front yard and watch it slowly trace its long, fat arc across the heavens. Mason would point out the flashes of light that he said would be a solar array adjusting, or a laser zapping a piece of junk in its path. Mason loves anything to do with technology and I never question that he's right; we joke that he's the brains and I'm the brawn of the single person we would have made up together. He'd leap at the chance to be where I am right now.

But I'm the one seeing the platform through the shuttle window, surrounded by stars. I'm the one holding my breath as our craft gently bumps against the bridgeway that will connect us to the safe interior. The engines power down and everyone stays in place, waiting for the command to get up and go out and begin our new lives.

The command comes. I remember to breathe again.

"Ladies and gentlemen, as you exit, you will each be greeted by your personal TimeTech guide, who will brief you on our boarding procedures and escort you to your private quarters. Thank you for your patience."

Everyone begins to stir. Soft chatter rises and seat straps click open and necks are cracked and purses and briefcases are pulled out from padded bins.

I find myself reluctant to leave my seat. It's dumb, because I can't stay here, and I certainly can't beg TimeTech to take me back home (right?), but my fingers feel frostbitten almost. Numb and clumsy on my own straps. Beehive Lady is up and away before I even finish unlocking the first one. I duck my head and blow air past my lips and finally manage the other three only to look up and find Glowering Boy watching me. He's standing in the aisle—not glowering any longer, actually—with his hands shoved deep into the pockets of his vintage leather jacket. He has tousled gilded-brown hair and a hint of unhappiness still sketched around his mouth.

Our eyes meet. His are hazel, surprisingly lucent.

"What?" I say. He's attractive in an abundantly tanned, surly sort of way. I'm embarrassed that he's witnessed my air raspberries.

He raises both eyebrows and frees a hand to make a sweeping gesture that might, or might not, be mocking.

"Ladies first."

I hesitate, but again, I can't read him. It's been a long while since I've had a face-to-face conversation with anyone my age besides my brother; maybe I've lost my grip on the subtle nuances of ridicule. Either way, I stand up and push by him and make my way down the aisle. My hardcase was taken from me before I boarded so I don't have anything to carry except my inhaler, which I keep in my pocket. I don't want anyone to see it and think I might be spreading my disease. For all I know, my *own luxurious compartment* locks from the outside.

The boy's boots are draped in rings and chains that make a silvery, rattly jingle with every step. It's a sound verging on festive, and I smile to myself because I bet that's the last thing this tanned-surly-rich-kid meant for anyone to think when he picked out those boots.

I walk out of the bridgeway and onto the platform, then slow. I'm unsure of where to go next. It's more cramped in here than I'd thought it'd be, noisy, with every inch of space, it seems, taken up by people or machinery. The light falls harshly from above; my shadow splinters off in odd directions. The other shuttle passengers are standing around in claustrophobic clusters or else are heading toward a set of double doors that have an illuminated sign above them that shines To the Train.

I position myself close to a wall covered in pipes and screens and levers and wait for my guide. I'm careful not to lean back.

The boy behind me is corralled nearly at once by a man in a bronze-colored jumpsuit. They brush past me without a glance. I stand where I am, my arms crossed, as the people around me gradually, inevitably, vanish behind the double doors.

Glowering Boy, gone.

Beehive Lady, gone.

The little redheaded girl, gone.

An old man who catches me staring and gives me a wink. Gone.

There are no windows to gaze out, nothing to look at but computer consoles and workers ignoring me and more well-lit signs above firmly closed doors.

To the Train. Yellow Team Only. Blue Team Only. Brain Team Only.

I'm tired again, chilled. I'm beginning to think I might need to beg a ride home after all when finally I'm discovered.

"November Duval." A woman in a spangled sari approaches. She carries a plastic computer slip in her hand that flickers with colors.

"Just Ember," I sigh.

"Welcome. I am Doctor Sengupta." She punches some information into the slip, then looks up again with a smile that I can only describe as pitying.

The charity. And right now, I'm sure I look it.

But all she says is, "Please come with me."

The interior of Time Train Three isn't white and sterile, like a hospital. I'd been expecting that. Yet it's warm, tasteful, with gleaming brass fixtures and lots of glossy wood, like a set from a very old movie.

The clutches of passengers who had seemed so tense on the platform now circulate through the corridors with an air of deep satisfaction. Some of them are already carrying martinis. This world, all sumptuous and plush and polished, is familiar to them. This is what *they've* been expecting.

Doctor Sengupta wants to take me directly to my compartment. Since the entrance to the train is somewhere near its middle, and my quarters are in the back, we walk for quite a ways. I have plenty of time to appreciate the intricately tiled floors; the high, arched ceilings and recessed doorways that all have passenger names engraved on plaques beside them. The passageways are wide enough that we never have to squeeze by anyone. It seems less like a train to me than some grand, floating-in-outer-space hotel.

Just when I'm starting to go numb again we stop before a door with a plaque that reads *N. Duval*. Doctor Sengupta instructs me to place my palm upon the identity pad (it's spongy and cold), and the door glides open.

I enter first.

Wood paneling the color of maple syrup; thick rugs patterned in sage green, cranberry, plum. More brass in the bathroom, plus a beautifully carved marble bowl serving as a sink. Wing chairs around a low-slung table, and another one before a desk. Long, saffron curtains made of what I think is real silk, but I've never touched silk before, so I'm not positive. The air is fragrant with a scent that reminds me of honey, or spice.

I glimpse my hardcase at the foot of the bed—which is huge, much larger than my skinny one back home, and layered in satin and down. Everything here is lustrous, a masterpiece of textures and jeweled tones. There's even a hover lamp with a stained-glass shade above the nightstand.

The only thing looking noticeably out of place amid all this old-world lux (besides my case) is a tube-shaped container that's been fixed horizontally along one of the walls. It's long as a person, a burled wood bottom with a see-through top. There's a control pad on the side that strongly suggests you need a doctorate to even touch.

It's a coffin, I think, and just as quickly try to unthink it.

"Your cryogen pod," explains Doctor Sengupta, who's noticed my stare. "For when you're ready to sleep."

I glance back at the bed.

"Sleep for weeks," she clarifies. "Months, if you wish."

"Months?"

"We can give you all this, Ember." She gestures to the room. "But we cannot predict the timetable of your cure. At some point, you might decide it's better to address your situation in stasis. Several of your fellow travelers will be spending their entire journey this way."

I know next to nothing about cryogen pods, but one thing I do know is that they're supposed to be dangerous for extended use. You don't really *sleep* in them; you're flash-frozen. And over time, that isn't so great. Tissues degrade. Synapses malfunction. Some people never wake up.

I've forgotten to mask my expression. Doctor Sengupta grants me that pitying smile.

"Naturally, TimeTech has installed the most state-of-the-art models, but we still don't recommend cryogen for longer than three months. Yet that's a staggering amount of Earth Time when it comes down to it. You'll be quite safe."

"Sure," I say, because even though her tone is cordial, her eyes are cool and calculating.

Be what they want. Smile and look pretty and try to keep your mouth shut.

I have appeased her. She turns away. "And the Brain will, of course, wake you when it receives the Stop signal from Earth regarding your remedy."

The Brain is not only the computer that conducted the lottery that landed me here, it's the entire master system that will run the train. It's the engineer, the navigator, the troubleshooter. The ultimate guardian of all our lives. Researchers from around the world slaved over it for decades, atom by atom, code by code, and when it was finally ready to be revealed to the public, the media went nuts. TimeTech claims it's the most sophisticated quantum computer ever to exist.

Yet all I can think right now in this stylish, pleasant-smelling room is *I hope so.* The tech in my life up until now has been spotty at best; we could never afford anything really new, not even back when we still owned the farm. The Brain is going to be the only thing between me and a fiery, mid-space collision with a moon or a comet or something. There won't be any other human beings on board besides me and the paying customers.

Not one single executive from TimeTech.

Not one single TimeTech programmer or scientist.

Not even a janitor.

Time Trains One and Two had a handful of salaried human workers, but Three is automated in every way possible. In addition to the Brain, there are roaming cleaner bots and maintenance bots and some nearly humanoid medical bots. There are even chef bots stationed in the Dining Car. Between them all, our every possible need has been allegedly anticipated, our every future problem potentially solved.

But I'm cold in my room. I'm cold inside. I wish abruptly for

Doctor Sengupta to leave; I want to crawl into that bed and pull the covers over me and close my eyes until I can go home again.

She's crossed to one of the walls. Her fingers skim a panel, which slides back to reveal shelves stacked with supplies.

"Your medicine chest." Another panel. "Linens. Towels. Sundries." Another. "Storage for personal items." Another. "And your holo display." She touches the bottom of a small, inset wall pad, which is gray and subtle and in every way the opposite of our bulky old display back home. Instantly a handsome, fair-haired man is standing in front of the bed.

"Good afternoon, Miss Duval. How may I serve you?"

"Uh . . ." I say, stepping back.

"Program test for November Duval," says Doctor Sengupta. "Sengupta Omega Twelve. Confirm standard mode."

"Confirmed," the man agrees.

"Confirm emergency mode."

"Confirmed."

She's looking down, adjusting the pleats of her sari like she's gone through this too many times before. "Confirm access to channels two through forty-seven, and all subchannels therein."

"Confirmed."

"Confirm facial and body recognition." She glances at me. "Don't move."

I'm washed in lights, blinded. I have to force myself to keep my eyes open.

"Confirmed," says the man.

"Program off," Sengupta says, and he vanishes.

"Wow," I say, and I mean it. I've never seen a holo so real before, not even back in school. There was nothing blue or static-y about it. I could practically count the whiskers on the man's chin.

Doctor Sengupta nods. "That was your avatar for the Brain. He will assist you as necessary. Unless you'd prefer a female?"

"No. He's fine."

"Your psychological profile indicated a slight predilection for a male authority figure. The team will be pleased to hear we chose correctly."

I'm standing there trying to decide if I'm offended or not—I don't even remember taking a psych test for the lottery—but she breezes on.

"Do you wish to have the robots unpack for you?"

"No," I say quickly. No one handles my stuff but me.

"Very well." She consults the computer in her hand. "It appears that we're on schedule for departure, so I'm going to leave you now, Ember. In the nightstand, you'll find an InfoSlip. It has train schematics, meal times, service times, a listing of the holo channels, command codes, and so forth."

"Should I—do I just stay in here for the launch?" I'm thinking about the slamming speed of the shuttle liftoff. The state of my stomach. I don't see any chairs with harnesses.

"If you like. The Observation Car is right behind yours, and several other passengers are, I believe, already in the Dining Car. You'll find it a very smooth departure. Should you decide to remain in your quarters, you might not even notice your journey has begun."

She comes toward me and offers her hand. I take it. The sequins edging her bodice glitter in the maple light.

"*Bon voyage*, Ember Duval. I truly hope we meet again."

I DECIDE THAT I DON'T want the story of my future to begin without me noticing. I'm going to go to the Observation Car since it's close. The Dining Car is much farther up the train and I don't think I'll be able to eat anything when we start moving, anyway.

But I'm still cold, so before I leave I open my case and grab the first hoodie I see on top. Only after I pull it on do I notice the small metal box that had been nestled beneath it.

I don't recognize this box. I didn't pack it, and it's not mine.

I pick it up warily. It's light, hardly bigger than my hand. I thumb the latch and the lid pops open.

Inside the box are eight little robo fireflies, resting in the shape of a heart.

CHAPTER SEVEN
Taza

WHAT DO YOU SEE?

The blood in the bowl was black, not red.

But that was merely the poor lighting: a single candle burning near the center of the table, the night shadows devouring everything else. When Taza leaned over the bowl, the blood smelled coppery fresh, and he had to close off the part of himself that was revolted by that. That wanted to get up and escape this stinking, sweltering room. He couldn't even open a window; scrying worked best in the suffocating dark, which was only one of the reasons why he hated it so much.

He tried not to breathe too deeply. He reminded himself that he needed only to look. To See.

The liquid surface of the bowl was a flat black coin. It reflected nothing. It revealed nothing.

Damn it.

He sat back, rubbed his eyes and gusted a sigh, then leaned forward and tried again.

Empty your mind. What do you see?

It was the first lesson of scrying, taught to schoolchildren before they ever touched tentative fingertips to their very first bowl. Allow the emptiness that needs to be filled to exist. Allow the blank void of that surface of blood to bloom. Without emptiness, there could be no truth.

He was trying too hard. That was probably the problem. Also, if he was being strictly honest, scrying wasn't exactly his best skill. Taza's mother's mother was the famous Seer; if he'd inherited anything from Imogen beyond pale blue eyes and a propensity for picking apart the impossible, he couldn't tell.

He should have asked her to look. He should have asked anyone else.

But that was the other problem, wasn't it? He already *had* asked. Not his grandmother, of course—since she was no longer speaking to him—but all around her. And, as incredible as it seemed, no one else here had witnessed the snake-star falling from the sky yesterday morning. No one else, *no one*, had been searching the stars, that particular quadrant of the universe, as Taza had been. No one remembered the smoke, the fire, the sizzling hiss dividing the heavens. The meteorite that had stripped bare, at least temporarily, the strongest magical turrets mankind could construct.

No one from the Fortress of the Sky. No one from the surrounding hills. Not even the groom managing the screaming horse. The man had told Taza the mare was in heat, had been lunging at an anxious stallion.

All the facts together tangled into such an improbable situation that it could only lead to the impossible. And that was why Taza was spending his Friday night *not* out casting, not submitting himself to yet another lecture from his father, not even in reluctant meditation . . . but secluded in the smallest room of the sovereign's West Lodge, scrying to See.

He hadn't imagined the shooting star. It *had* happened.

His candle's flame guttered, muttering riddles. The scent of melting wax mingled with the coppery-rich stench of the chicken blood. Beyond the closed windows of the room, beyond the feathered grasses and wildflowers lapping his home were the August woods, and summer in New Mexico tended toward hot and loud, even after dark. Birds cried out for missing lovers. Night creatures stalked the grounds. But it was the crickets chanting from the trees, ardent and strong, that had trapped the flame in their small incantations. It bowed and straightened in time to their calls.

Empty your mind.

He placed both palms flat upon the table. He gazed down into the bowl.

What do you see?

The black of the blood was nearly complete. There was only a slim of reflection of flame, a subtle slick of light that wavered over the surface . . .

. . . which grew and changed color, shifting from yellow into green. Misty green, like a forest. Purple luminous beneath it, perhaps from a rising or setting sun. A face appeared amid the colors. A girl. Her lips were moving but try as he might, Taza couldn't hear what she said. She was turning away from him, then looking back, her hair a sweep of gold down her shoulders, her eyes the color of the sea.

Those eyes held his with unrelenting intensity; reddened, tear-swollen.

Bruises colored the left side of her face.

He felt the passion of her sorrow as awfully and clearly as if it was his own. He felt his heart clench with it.

She was walking away from him, heading into the misted gloom. He scrambled to follow—

But the vision faded.

Taza sagged back in his chair. His breathing had gone ragged. His muscles had tightened into an extravagant ache. When he pushed a hand against his cheek, he smeared away a tear.

He'd been crying for her. With her.

His chair rocked back; he shoved from the table. For all his vaunted talents, he could not scry. He never could, and here was ample evidence. He'd been looking for his fallen star and had gotten a girl instead.

He found the nearest window, opened it wide. The fresh air lifted his hair and cooled his skin, sweet as a mother's caress. He could take a deep breath at last.

A girl, not a meteorite.

And she'd touched his heart.

Who *was* she?

CHAPTER EIGHT
Ember

THE INFOSLIP INFORMS ME that we're leaving in four minutes, so after I gently replace the box of fireflies inside my case, I don't bother to do anything but risk a quick look into the bathroom mirror. Yet once there, I'm confronted by two things: a haggard, smudgy-eyed girl gazing back at me, and a set of ceramic combs and brushes in the top drawer of the vanity. A hurried check through the rest of the drawers tells me that TimeTech supplies not only things like lotions and toothpaste (spearmint flavor, no tiger or angel tears), but also mascara and lip dye and a whole bunch of other cosmetics I have no clue how to use.

I don't wear a lot of makeup, but that's mostly because I haven't had anyone to impress in a few years.

I consider all the little bottles and needles and pots for a moment, but I'm running out of time so I skip all that and use just the hairbrush. It helps.

Look pretty, Mason said.

"Yeah, well," I say, judging the girl in the mirror, "this is about as pretty as we're going to get."

The Observation Car is the last car of the train, which means that mine is the second to last. Someone has the compartment across the passageway from mine (*J. Castaneda*, proclaims the plaque), but their door is closed and there's no one else out here but me. I look left, right, realize that left leads to the rear of the train, so I head that way. There's a sliding door separating the cars. It opens without sound when I near.

I step into a bubble of darkness and stars. It's confusing enough that I have to pause to get my bearings again, but that doesn't help. There are stars above me, below me, all around. Earth is a huge radiant swirl of colors overhead, bright and wondrous. The moon hangs, a speckled gray orb, beyond it.

I slink forward and bump into something. It's an armchair, and there's a woman in it. She throws me a distracted glance but then goes back to watching Earth. I look around more carefully and see now that there are lots of chairs and people scattered in front of me, and all of it—everyone—seems to be floating in space. Suspended amid the stars.

The Observation Car's made almost entirely out of some type of glass; the only illumination we have is from the outside. It *feels* like a real floor beneath my feet but it looks like nothing. When I peer straight down into infinity, I'm instantly dizzy.

Crap. I notice I'm holding my breath again and force myself to exhale. Inhale. There's breathable air in here and no reason for my lungs to close up, for me to be thinking about gasping and choking (*just like that bony dead girl*) but I have to wonder if this is what the designers intended when they made the car invisible. Every step forward feels like a dare.

I gulp down my fear and grope my way to an empty chair, sinking into it with relief. Part of me wants to hide my eyes but the lure of the view is too strong to resist.

Inhale. Exhale.

"Less than a minute," says someone.

The small fragment of my mind that's still grasping at logic tells me that the reason I can see daylit Earth must be because the sun is behind me. I twist in my seat to find it; the glass has tinted it dark. It's a deep mellow orange, a pumpkin, safe to stare into.

But I don't. I twist back and do what everyone else is doing: I gaze up at my homeworld, and it makes me forget about breathing and dying.

I didn't know it would be so beautiful.

"Over there." A man seated ahead of me lifts a glass of red wine to point out one of the cloud-dappled lands. "There's France."

"Adieu, ma maison à Paris," says another man.

"And Spain," trills an elderly woman.

"Adiós, mi castillo hermoso en las colinas," says a different woman.

"Switzerland," points the first man.

"See you soon, lovely compound-interest credits account," calls out a lady with an Australian accent, and everyone laughs.

Okay, not everyone. I didn't, and neither did the boy two chairs away. He shifts in his seat and crosses his legs and I hear the muted jingle of the chains on his boots. When I look at him all I see is his profile, sharp but still attractive, even though his glower is back. The messy tips of his hair catch the light. If he feels my attention, he doesn't show it. The one eye I can see looks glittery.

I turn away. If Glowering Boy is going to cry, that's his business. I don't want to witness it, and I don't want to cry with him. Not here. Not in front of these people. My bathroom has a shower, and I already know I'm going to shed my tears in there.

A faint vibration begins to hum through the floor. I feel it through the soles of my shoes, almost like a tickle. Light erupts from a pair of cones I hadn't noticed before affixed behind the car.

The thrusters are coming online.

The light flares bright white for a second, smarting my eyes, but then the glass tints it down to violet.

"So long, life," says Glowering Boy, very soft. His eyes dart to mine. I guess he'd noticed me noticing him, after all.

A bell sounds three times, pleasant and ringing. The train begins to move. Several people clap.

Doctor Sengupta had been right. Time Train Three glides smoothly away from the platform; it's nothing like the shuttle. I'm not forced back into my chair. I don't feel any gravitational pull at all, beyond the regular kind that's keeping me seated. It's even smoother than the mag-trains. We're sailing without effort out of the platform's orbit. I could stand up and roam around if I wished.

Some people do, but most of us remain as we are, watching the world shrink. The farther away we get, the less real it becomes. Our planet is a child's bouncy ball. A marble. The head of a pin.

From the InfoSlip I know it's going to take the train about an hour to reach our cruising speed, an astonishing 99.99973 percent of the speed of light. But we're going so fast already. Earth becomes lost to me, one more anonymous dot in a background of stars.

I don't know how long I remain in my chair. Now that I'm seated, my body doesn't want to move again. The darkness that had so disoriented me at first now feels comfortable. I close my eyes and when I open them again, the dots have shifted. People have, too.

"Look," cries a woman, and we all crane our heads to see what she does.

A creamy striped globe travels a line in the near distance, ringed with perfect hoops of tan and brown and beige. It's Saturn.

Everyone stops talking. We all watch in silence as it whips past.

Fewer and fewer people decide to stay in place. Most of them stroll a leisurely lap or two around the car, then exit. Some are lingering in pockets of conversation, taking sips from their glasses. There's no shortage of alcohol on the train, I can tell that already. We might be at some voguish cocktail party, mingling beneath the stars . . . except that there is no ground beneath us. No home or loved ones to take us in afterward.

I sit up straighter as my stomach rumbles. Breakfast was oatmeal and a slice of dry toast and so, so long ago it's like a memory from another year. I'm beginning to tremble from hunger. Or fatigue. Either way, I've got to move.

Glowering Boy gets up and leaves and I tell myself to wait a couple of minutes before getting up too. I don't want him or anyone else to think I'm following him. But the crowd is definitely thinner now, and I'm beginning to attract attention. The majority of it comes from the pair of country club guys loitering near the thrusters. They chortle to themselves and down what looks like whiskey.

I rise to weave my way through the chairs. Only after the Observation Car door slips closed behind me do I feel the knots in my shoulders begin to relax. As I walk by my quarters I consider simply going inside and collapsing until morning, but even as I'm thinking it, my stomach curls in on itself. Growls extra loud. So, I keep walking.

I pass through eight more cars (including the Bar Car, which explains all the drinks) before reaching the Dining Car. I can tell that I'm near, though, because the aroma of hot food (steak, potatoes, fresh bread) wafts over me and my mouth begins to water. I have no idea what time it is—Earth Time, Train Time, whichever—but this smells like dinner and I'm ready to demolish pretty much whatever they have to offer.

The door opens, and I'm standing at the threshold of the nicest restaurant I've ever seen.

There's more of that warm wood paneling, of course, but also a sequence of chandeliers dripping with long, icy ropes of crystal pendants, shimmering with light. Tables are draped in layers of artfully angled linens, ivory over blue over slate. Every place is set with goblets and paper-thin china and heavily scrolled silverware that looks almost medieval next to the delicate plates. Orchids with thick, showy petals arc from sconces adorning the walls. I hear music, too, playing quietly in the background. It's exactly the kind you'd expect. Lots of violins and harps.

Most of the tables are smaller and already occupied by either singles or couples. But there's one longer, community table near the middle of the car that's almost empty, so I find a chair there.

Nearly at once a server bot coasts up. It's carrying a tray of soup bowls (red or green) and baskets of fresh rolls. I take a red soup and an entire basket and dig in.

As I scoop up my last spoonful of tomato bisque, another bot approaches with the next course, which looks like a choice between either Caesar salad or sliced cheese. I don't know if I'm supposed to pick one of them or both. A furtive check of the other tables nearby proves useless, since the bots clear away the empty dishes as soon as you're done.

So I take both. Why not?

The cheese is moldy and I regret wanting it, but the Caesar is crisp and wonderful, about a hundred times better than the sad, wilted greens they used to serve us in the school cafeteria. Better even than anything I could have made for myself at home. I'd never have the patience to crack the peppercorns, shave the parmesan, concoct the dressing. And forget about convincing Dad to spend precious credits on genuine anchovies, even if he could find them at the local mart. If it's not cow or soy or beer, he's not interested.

I'm so lost in the flavors that I hardly notice when one of the chairs beside me is scraped back. But then so is the one on my other side. I look up, and I've got the country club twins to my left and right.

"November," hails the beefier one. He looks like a model from a yacht promo. A pseudo-skipper who'd be steering into the wind while wearing starched shorts and a whale-patterned tie.

"You," I say, flat.

"Didn't feel like dressing for dinner, November?" asks the other one. He's more of a first mate sort, not quite so square-jawed goonish, but still with a mean, practiced grin.

It's true that everyone else here looks a lot fancier than I do. Most of the women are swishing around in glitzy, clingy gowns and all of the men are in suits or tuxedos. I'm still more or less wearing the same wrinkled outfit I put on this morning before dawn. In the dark. My socks probably don't even match.

Dress for dinner. Is that something rich people actually do?

"Why *should* she dress, Corbin?" drawls the skipper. "She's her own woman! Look at her!"

"I *am*, Royce," leers the first mate. "Looking *good*, Miss November."

His leans too close and his very pores reek of whiskey, which I suddenly hate. I angle away and close my fingers around the handle of my fork. I attempt to sound as glacial as possible. "Do I know you?"

First mate shrugs, unfazed. "Everyone knows *you*, November. Congrats on winning the lottery." He says it like *lot-ter-raaay* and both of them sputter with laughter like it's some priceless inside joke.

"How old are you again?" asks Royce.

"Eighteen," I lie.

They exchange smirks. "Old enough," Corbin says.

The bots are attempting to serve them, but my new best buds pay no attention. The soup-and-bread bot circles the table and comes back, still trying.

"And what are *your* diseases?" I stab at my salad. "Something that's going to finish you off soon, I hope?"

"Ha! A wit!" Royce barks another laugh.

"All the more fun," says Corbin.

Bullies are nothing new to me. My final few months attending public school were particularly enlightening when it came to understanding the pecking order of the healthy versus the sick. I still have a scar under my right eye from the captain of the softball team, a girl who'd had especially good aim and a rock.

So, here are my choices now:

I can leave.

I can continue to insult them and hope that *they* leave.

Or I can ignore them.

I decide, in a flush of indignation, on the third option. This is my table. I'm starving and I was here first and there's definitely steak being served that I haven't gotten yet, so screw them.

I take another bite of salad, but the dressing that was so delicious before now tastes sour. I force myself to chew and swallow.

"Say, November, have you ever tried—" begins the skipper, but he's interrupted by a new voice.

"Miss Duval. I beg your pardon for my tardiness."

All three of us raise our heads. An old man rests his hand upon the chair across from mine. (Is it the same man who winked at me on the platform? Maybe.) He's *old* old, his skin freckled with brown spots, an oxygen clip beneath his nose. He has wispy white hair slicked back into a ponytail and a cane in his other hand. And even though he was addressing me, his eyes are on Corbin and Royce.

He smiles a small, narrow smile that isn't friendly at all.

"Sims. Knox. I don't recall inviting you to my dinner with the young lady."

His words are slow. His accent is southern and buttery, nothing like the clipped, nasal inflections of the skipper and his mate.

"Castaneda," says Royce. He looks uneasy. "Nice to see you again."

"Well, now, that's very kind of you. But as I mentioned, this is my date. A gentleman does not intrude."

"'Course not." Royce stands. Corbin follows. "We were just on our way, as a matter of fact."

"As a matter of fact," the man named Castaneda echoes, and the other two stagger off like drunken rats bolting from a trap.

I watch as the old man hooks his cane over the back of the chair, pulls it out, and slowly settles into the cushions.

"Castaneda," I say, remembering. "You have the compartment across from mine."

In light of my day so far, this seems an incredible piece of good fortune. At least this guy is unlikely to try to ambush me every time I step out of my room. Still, there *was* that wink . . .

He nods, taking a soup. "That's right. Please call me Javier."

"Why did you save me?" I ask, blunt.

"Oh, from those weasels?" He smiles at me and the edges of his eyes fold into about a million crinkles. "I've no doubt you could have handled them yourself, but sometimes rude little boys need to be reminded of their place. It'd be a pity to let them spoil your first night on the train."

What I've witnessed appears to contradict the rules of bullying. Mr. Castaneda—Javier—is obviously not physically stronger than either of the younger men. Nor does he outnumber them. So, either he shamed them (unlikely, given their boozy smirks), or he pulled rank.

"Are you a teacher?" I ask, and he laughs, a big belly laugh, like Santa.

"Who, me? Nah. I'm just an old hacker, Miss Duval."

"Ember," I say, then add, "And, um, thanks."

"You are most welcome. Fine rolls, don't you think? Just the right touch of oregano and thyme. I always thought that bread was best made by human hands, but I believe I'll get us another basket."

AND SO, THE REST of my dinner is nice. The food is great, and once the steak arrives Javier doesn't talk much, so mostly we eat in agreeable silence. I can't help but notice the other passengers in the Dining Car watching us but pretending not to.

I learn that Javier is ninety-four. That he has blood cancer. That he likes songbirds and pecans and computers.

"My brother is good with tech, too," I say.

"Is he, now?" Javier responds amicably. "That's fine."

Lots of things are fine with Javier, as it turns out, even his cancer.

"Can't live forever," he says. "To have a vigorous mind imprisoned inside a failing body, everything falling apart? Each morning more difficult to embrace than the last? Who'd want to stay like that? We are bags of meat and bones. Finite for a reason, I fear."

I pause over my scalloped potatoes. "Then . . . why are you here? Why did you buy a ticket for the train?"

"The science," he answers at once. "The journey." He waves an arm to the windows. "To *see*."

"You're not waiting for your cure?"

This shocks me, I admit. Javier Castaneda is not how I imagined an obscenely affluent daredevil would look.

He goes back to slicing his sirloin. "A cure would be a remarkable outcome. But let's just say that I'm not dying for it."

We walk each other back to our car. Javier greets by name many of the people we pass, who (when they notice us together) tend to have the same quickly smothered expressions of incredulity that our fellow diners did. Between the cane and all the formal *good evening*'s, it takes a while to reach our doors.

"It's too bad for you," I say, as we face each other in the corridor. "That they stuck you all the way back here at the end of the train."

"Not at all. I requested these quarters. Endings are more comfortable for me these days than beginnings." He winks; it was absolutely him on the platform. "Anyhow, there are too many jackasses up in the front."

My door seals behind me. The big bed looms soft. I search for a light switch but can't find one, so I try, "Lights off," and the compartment plunges into shadow.

I should unpack. Shower. Clean my teeth. But with bands of stars frosting the universe outside my windows, all I do is I fall into bed.

At least exhaustion is good for something. Even though my last waking thoughts are of my family, I suffer no dreams.

CHAPTER NINE
Ember

MORNING DOESN'T ARRIVE WITH sunlight. Or even cloudlight, or snowlight. Morning looks exactly like the night before: a compartment filled with unfamiliar shapes and shadows. Black space and silver stars outside the windows.

I sit up. I'm tangled in the satin comforter and the top sheet of the bed; that's as far as I got covering up, it seems. There's a clock with an antiqued dial on the nightstand, its face inscribed with Roman numerals. The hands point to nine and twelve.

I *hope* it's morning. I suppose I might have slept through an entire day.

I yawn. The inside of my mouth feels gummy and parched. I remember Mason's comment about my breath stinking (which makes me cup a hand to my lips to check), and then I remember the fireflies.

I tumble out of bed. I go to my knees beside my case and find the metal box. When I open it they're still there in their heart shape, their golden wings slowly lifting and falling, their bodies barely glowing. I stand up and scan the chamber, but of course, there's no strong natural light. No warm yellow sun to convert into energy in the solar cells covering their wings.

I go to the nearest window and hold the box up to the glass.

"Try this," I tell the 'flies. "Is this enough?"

They stir. A couple of them rise up, bumping against the glass, but they're sluggish. I don't think the stars are of much help.

"Lights on full," I say, and the hover lamp and the light tiles overhead warm to brilliance. I lift the box above me.

A few more of the 'flies loft upward. They circle the tiles clumsily, but this seems to be working better than the window. Soon all eight of them are drifting around the ceiling, bobbing up and down in the light.

I imagine it's steak and scalloped potatoes to them.

I observe them long enough to be certain they're not going to hurt themselves against the tiles (they're supposed to be smarter than that, but I'm cautious), then head to the bathroom. The shower comes on in a burst of satisfyingly hot water.

I strip out of my grungy clothes and step inside. The interior of the stall is made up of small, colorful marble pieces. A mosaic of a landscape covers three of the walls. It's got green grass and trees and an azure stream that ends in a pond studded with cattails. A dragonfly perches, iridescent, on a blade in the foreground. The sun shines down on it all, and a flock of black marble birds appears to be winging off into the distance.

Even though logically I know the mosaic is only here because it's exquisite, because it's unique and costly and took some artist who-knows-how-many painstaking hours to complete, I want there to be a message behind this scene. I want it to be: *Don't forget this. You're far away now, but don't forget this is what you're made of. This is where you belong.*

I trace my fingers over the birds. Steam curls up and veils the wall but I can still feel the pointed tips of their wings.

Shampoo, soap, and a hard bristly sponge equals a new me. Only after I'm done does it hit me that once again I've forgotten to unpack, so I'm wrapped in my towel as I rummage through my case, my hair dribbling water down my arms and onto the floor. I also forgot to ask Doctor Sengupta if my compartment's door locks automatically. I assume it does but still dress as quickly as I can.

As I'm shimmying into my khakis I notice a bruise on my left hip. I frown down at it. How did that happen?

Oh, yeah. That's where I landed when I fell in the snow and broke my snowthing—another memory that seems to surface from a murky, long-ago year. Was it really only last week?

No, I realize. I'm on the Time Train. I don't know precisely how many hours have passed since I've come aboard, but we're moving at practically the speed of light. My bruise is now much, much older than a week.

I push the thought away. I take in the jumble of my unpacked clothing flung across the bed and chairs, and then consciously, deliberately fold it all up again as neatly as I can and stack it inside the storage bay. I shove the old case under the bed.

I'm dressed. I'm clean. My fireflies are drowsing beneath the hover lamp and I have on Mason's chocolate sweater for courage. If all the rich folks glam up for breakfast as well as dinner, at least I can be assured that nothing I'm wearing has holes.

I walk over to the 'flies.

"Stay here," I tell them. "Charge up. I'll be back soon."

I get a series of lights blinking and wings buzzing at me in response.

I cross to the holo pad, touch the base, and my avatar appears.

"How may I serve you, Miss Duval?"

"Are there going to be bots coming in here to clean today?"

"Certainly," the Brain says. "Cleanings are scheduled for twice daily."

That seems a little excessive. I'm not that messy.

"Make it only once a day, all right?"

"Certainly."

"And—" I point to my 'flies. "Make sure none of the bots touch these guys."

The avatar cocks his head, examining the fireflies. A lock of virtual hair falls across his forehead in an almost eerily natural way. I have to stop myself from rubbing my hands up and down my arms.

Probably I'll get used to it, but right now it's plain spooky how real he looks.

"Robotic insects," the Brain announces. "Family *Lampyridae*, genus unknown."

"Right. They're solar mostly, and they need to recharge now."

A beam of light shoots out from the top of the holo pad. It must be the same one that mapped me yesterday. It sweeps up and down the fireflies and shuts off, and the avatar continues his recitation.

"Quantum logic processors. Collective intelligence. Supercapacitors powered by photovoltaic and kinetic energy harvesting. Fascinating." He looks at me. "If I may ask, how did you acquire these devices, Miss Duval?"

"They were a gift. I don't want them harmed, do you understand? They're not really insects. They're . . ." I think about this for a second. "They're my companions."

"I understand. Instructions have been transmitted to all service bots regarding your companions. They will not be touched."

"Thank you."

"It is my pleasure to serve. Is there anything else I may do for you now?"

"No. Thanks."

"Very well. Good morning."

"Good morning."

He blips out.

I rub my hands up my arms anyway, warding off goose bumps. He's just so . . . tall. Smoothly spoken. Maybe I should have requested a female avatar, after all. Maybe a woman, even a teenager, would have been less unnerving.

Oh, well. I'm not going to have to deal with him forever, am I?

The Dining Car is emptier than last night, which means I'm able to claim a small table near a window. I don't see Javier or the bullies, but the young girl is here, eating alone nearby. I find myself watching her because the view from the window looks exactly like the view from the windows in my quarters, which is to say, somewhat boring. If there are galaxies floating gloriously past the train, I don't see them.

Anyway, she's interesting even without the view. She's dressed from neck to toe in an elaborately folded tunic, like the kind you'd imagine an ancient Greek or Roman would wear. There are giant, sparkly brooches topping both of her shoulders, presumably holding the whole thing together. I can't tell if it's a costume or just what rich little girls are wearing these days.

She takes apart her breakfast with surgical precision. Every ounce of ham, of poached eggs, of bagel, is cut into perfect cubes. I don't know how she manages it so well with the eggs (they're runny), but she does. She then puts down her knife, shifts her fork to her right hand, and tastes each cube with the sort of thoughtful intensity I'd expect to see on the face of a gourmet chef. Like she's mentally deconstructing the recipe. This kid is the slowest eater in the world.

But the breakfast *is* delicious. I help myself to the fried ham and eggs and slather my bagel with cream cheese. There's a finely sliced smoked fish that goes with it that melts on my tongue. I eat about four times as much as the girl and I'm still finished before she is.

A pair of women in heavy geisha face powder and a lot of lace are lingering over coffee at the table between us, both of them marinated in perfume. They're watching the girl, too.

"The Roxborough daughter," one of them whispers loudly to the other. "I heard she's contagious."

"I cannot fathom why she's allowed out," the other one whispers back. "If you ask me, *none* of the TB-3's should be allowed to leave their rooms." She gives a sniff. "Honestly, what about the rest of us? Are we to be constantly *exposed* to them like common lab rats?"

The girl never glances around. But she's fair-skinned and her hair's pulled back. Her cheeks burn.

She closes her lips around another cube of ham.

I toss my napkin to my table. As I'm passing by the women I pause to clear my throat, then let it deepen into a cough. Their perfume is saccharine strong and the coughing sears my lungs, but it's worth it to watch them cower in their chairs.

I try to catch the girl's eye as I exit but she won't look up, so I leave her to her meal.

I haven't explored any part of the train past the Dining Car; I might as well now. I know there are more than just passenger cars up near the front. There's a Quiet Car, and the Brain Car and something called the Diversion Car, which is what I come to next.

It's crowded, with people standing around or seated on the row of velvet-covered benches lining the corridor that divides the car into two long halves. Each half holds three separately enclosed, glassed-in chambers. I—and everyone else—can see into them.

One chamber has a man skipping around inside, swinging his hand. I step closer and realize that the man is playing tennis. I can see the court, the net, the spectators. I can see his opponent, much farther away than the physical reality of the area would permit. It's virtual tennis, but it looks real to me and it's definitely real to the man. He grimaces as he flubs a serve.

Big surprise, the paunchy old guy in the chamber next over is playing golf. He's standing on a green amid a sunny day, wiping the sweat from his forehead.

I half expect the third chamber to show me someone competing in a polo match, complete with three-dimensional thoroughbreds thundering past, but instead, it's only a woman standing motionless on the brink of a cliff. It appears that she's on top of a mountain; clouds glide behind her, tendrils of white threading a cobalt sky. She's gazing emotionlessly into the distance. When I go on tiptoe to see what she does, I'm faced with a vista of more mountains. Sky. Clouds. She's really high up.

She's barefoot, wrapped in a fawn-colored dress that flutters in a wind I don't feel. Her hair is long and bright and fluttering too and that's when I recognize her. She's Beehive Lady.

She tilts forward and plunges off the cliff.

I gasp in spite of myself. I surge toward her but she's not falling—she's—

Floating?

She's head-down, arms to her sides, suspended in the air. The mountain is rushing past her (*she's falling, right?*) and her dress is flicking wildly around her legs, but she wears the same stoic expression that she had before she fell. She doesn't even close her eyes.

"Time-controlled gravity release," says a voice at my shoulder.

I look over, and it's Glowering Boy. Like nearly everyone else, he's watching the woman plummet.

"She jumps, and the controls adapt by microdegrees. Along with the plastic glass and the wind, it's a good effect. Very convincing."

It is. What looks like a suicide jump becomes a lesson in physics, in the amazing technology built into this train. She's not truly falling at all. Once you strip away all the effects, she's basically levitating in place.

Her arms spread and she seems to slow slightly. Her hair begins to bunch behind her; her dress billows. The ground rises up to meet her and she goes from head-down to upright, arms still wide.

Her toes touch the grass. Her heels lightly follow. She's a doe landing in a meadow of wildflowers, graceful and sure.

People are exclaiming over the jump, eager to try it for themselves. The woman presses a hand to the wall facing us and it becomes a door that angles open. She slips through without acknowledging anyone. A name appears in large scripted letters across the front of the glass—I assume the person next in line—and a man with a grizzled beard and a scarf limps into the chamber.

I turn back to watch the woman. She makes her way through the crowd to the end of the car and vanishes beyond the sliding door.

"I'm Drew," says the boy beside me.

I look up at him. He's offering me his hand, unsmiling. His hair is slightly tamer today than it was yesterday, but he's still got that unnatural, perfect tan.

"Ember," I say, my palm meeting his.

"Not November?"

"No."

I keep forgetting that I'm famous. Infamous. Whichever is more appropriate for someone who's been featured by chance for a few minutes on news holograms around the world.

He tips his chin toward the chambers. "You going in?"

Do I want to commit fake suicide in front of all these people? Or worse, publicly attempt some lame sport I don't know how to play? "No, not now. Maybe later."

Drew reads my mind. "You don't have to do what they're doing. Golf or whatever. You tell the Brain the scenario you want, and it produces it."

"Oh." I try to think of a scenario I'd want that would still be okay to have everyone here watch, but can't come up with anything. "Maybe later," I say again.

The boy nods, nonchalant. He's observing the man with the scarf negotiate what appears to be a Gilded Age ballroom, with couples dressed entirely in black and white twirling to silent music. "The waiting list's gotten too long now, anyway. You'll have better luck as the days go on."

"I'll keep it in mind."

As the days go on. He's right, of course. The novelty of the Diversion Car will wear off for everyone in time. But how many weeks, months, will that take?

How long am I going to be here?

I haven't let myself think about this before. Not in depth.

At full speed, every hour that passes on the train is approximate to about 430 Earth hours. Eighteen Earth days. So a week here is going to be over eight *years* back home. Even if researchers were discovering the cure for TB-3 right this minute, Time Train Three still has to complete its first loop through space before approaching Earth again and receiving the Stop signal from the TimeTech platform.

That's going to take two weeks for us. But it will take sixteen years and six months back on Earth.

And there may be no signal after this first loop. Not for me, at least. It's supposed to come if there's been *any* cure for *anyone* aboard, though, which means that we may stop at the platform in a couple of weeks after all, and some lucky passenger (or passengers) will disembark and the rest of us won't. Then the train will just start up again and we'll travel on. More loops.

The man with the beard and scarf has ascended a dais to become the ballroom's conductor. He stands before an orchestra that stretches on and on, scowling happily, his hands jerking in the air. All the couples dip and sway to his tune.

What scenario would I ask the Brain for if I had the chance? If all these people weren't here?

Not the cottage. The Brain would have no way of knowing what it looks like, and it would be too strange, anyway, to just walk around a facsimile of my house without my brother or father there.

Not the mountains. Too bitter cold. Too snowy.

Perhaps the plains. Perhaps I'd ask for a field of wheat under a summer sun. I could walk through it like I used to when I was a child, skimming my palms along the tops of the stalks. Letting them tickle.

"I'm going boating," says Drew.

I'd forgotten he was next to me. He meets my startled look with a level one of his own. This near, the hazel of his eyes clarifies into an amber/green/caramel mix. His lashes are brown and thick.

"Want to come?" he asks.

"What, boating?" I'm not even certain what that might be. For me, *boat* is a noun, not a verb.

"Yes."

"Like, on a yacht? A sailboat?" What other kinds of boats do wealthy people have?

Drew smiles and maybe it's that I've finally slept or had food, but for the first time I feel comfortable gauging his sincerity. It's a good smile, not vicious. Not like Royce or his fellow goon.

"Something like that," Drew says. "Come on. It's more fun with another person and I'm up next."

I hesitate but then the tennis guy is done, and the name *Andrew Jensen* is scrolling across the glass.

Drew makes his way to the door. I hesitate a bit longer, then follow.

"Excellent," he says, as the door closes behind us.

All the noise and babble beyond this chamber are gone. We're standing in silence inside a clear glass cube, but only for a moment, because then Drew says, "Jensen Diversion Program Two, please," and now we're standing beside a streambed. With willow trees. And sparrows. And patches of pink and periwinkle flowers trailing leaves along the glossy water.

I can *smell* the stream. The flowers and the grass beneath my feet. The birds are chirruping; they sound heartbreakingly authentic.

A sparrow flits from tree to tree. I'm following it, marveling, when I hear Andrew call, "Ember. Over here."

I turn to find him seated in a rowboat. Not even a nice rowboat, but one all grimy and peeling paint.

I start to laugh.

"I'm not much for yachting." He looks defensive and then sheepish, and then he smiles again and it's all still okay.

Before I leave my spot, I bend down and touch a blade of grass. It doesn't feel real, exactly. It's undoubtedly not grass. But it's thin and pliant as grass would be.

Plastic glass, Drew'd said, and I've heard of it, though I can't recall how. Probably from Mason. It's glass with programmable memory. Self-healing. Glass that can bend and change colors and shapes.

"I promise not to capsize us," Drew says now, waiting for me, and I climb cautiously into the boat.

He picks up the oars and shoves us off. We leave the banks of flowers behind (*not really*, I remind myself, *not really because we've got to be staying mostly in place, don't we?*) and drift past more willows, their branches braided in leafy buds the color of new spring. I know there are eyes on us beyond the walls, but all I can see is this lovely day.

There is no Time Train. No loops through the black eternity of the universe. Just a boat and a boy and me, all three of us rocking gently with the current.

It's warm. I take off my sweater and bunch it on my lap. Andrew rows leisurely, gazing all around. A breeze comes and ruffles his hair.

"You don't have to do that, do you?" I indicate the oars. "Row?"

"Probably not. But I enjoy it." He lifts both oars into the air and watches the water drip down the blades. "There's no other place on board to exercise. Have you noticed?"

"No." I suppose that's not too astonishing on a train designed for sick people.

"I rowed in school," he says pensively, and the blades dip back down. His strokes are slow and even. "Before my diagnosis. I miss it. So I guess it's either this or else sprinting through the corridors. How many laps up and down the train before it's a mile, do you think?"

"Depends on how many drunks you'd be dodging."

I get another smile.

"So, what's Jensen Diversion Program One?" I ask, because inquiring about his diagnosis seems rude, even though the whole world knows mine.

"Competitive rowing. It's the only sport my father considers worthy of the family name." He holds my eyes. "This is more pleasant. Less splash."

The water's only an illusion so there's no splash at all; I wonder if that's his point.

A giant 25:00 appears in the sky above us. It counts down to 24:59, 24:58, 24:57, and then fades into the blue.

"What was your diagnosis?" I ask anyway.

"Brain tumor. Inoperable."

"Oh. Sorry."

"Yeah," he says.

We skim through a smallish marsh of cattails, a lot like the mosaic in my shower. A blackbird with red shoulders clings sideways to one of the stems, serenading us as we go by.

"Where is this place?" I ask. "I mean, is it modeled on somewhere real? Or did you just imagine it?"

"Both. It's based on one of our west coast estates. The stream, the flora, the birds. I described it to the Brain, and this is its interpretation of what I said." He pauses rowing. "It's decent, actually. Closer than I thought it'd be."

It's obvious that he's trying to be cordial, so I refrain from getting into how many estates his family owns. I probably wouldn't be able to ask without sounding sarcastic. And without the glower, Drew's a lot easier to look at.

"It's very peaceful," I offer finally.

"I told my family I want my ashes scattered here." He catches himself and gives a shake of his head. "There. You know what I mean."

The blackbird follows us a while, hopping from cattail to cattail, singing all the way.

"What about you?" Drew shifts the oars so that they rest inside the boat. Virtual water darkens the virtual wood. "Where do you want to be buried? Or scattered?"

I stare down at the brown winter sweater on my lap. "I don't know."

"You haven't thought about it?"

"Not really."

His silence is skeptical.

"I've been more focused on living," I say. I bend over the edge of the boat to touch the stream; my fingers poke through the surface without meeting resistance. All of this beauty is only fantasy. "I'll be dead. I won't care what happens."

"Rational, if unromantic."

Anger jabs through me; I squash it down. "I don't see what's so romantic about my lungs dissolving inside me. Death is—gruesome. Disturbing. I don't want to dwell on it."

"Death is only the next adventure," Drew says.

"Right." My anger is bubbling back up.

"Look, there's no point in getting upset about it. Everyone dies. We're just the interesting few who know how it's going to happen."

I don't know why this makes me madder, but it does. Maybe it's that he's so casual about the whole thing. My world flipped upside down with my diagnosis. My dad had to sell the farm he'd inherited from his parents just so I could live in the right kind of air for my fragile, damaged lungs. My brother had to leave behind all his friends and tech work on the plains. My meds eat up all our credits and then some and *this* boy acts like it's all no big deal.

People live, people die. So what.

"I'll get upset if I want," I say. "Pardon me for not being so Zen about my inevitable conclusion."

He returns to rowing. "Zen's better for your blood pressure."

"Just shut up for a while, all right?"

"Sure thing."

And he does. But not for long.

"Sooo . . ." he begins, ignoring my narrowed gaze, looking up at the sky. "New topic. What do you want to be when you grow up?"

"Alive," I snap.

"Conventional answer. Why would you be on the train if you didn't want to be alive?"

"I didn't *want* to—" I begin, but without warning, I run out of air.

I'm *out* of air.

Drew glances down at me. His expression transforms from smug into alarmed. "Hey, Ember, I was only—"

"No—I need—"

But it's too late. The attack is already taking over, a cinching hot band closing around my chest.

I shouldn't have coughed at those ladies in the Dining Car. I shouldn't have sucked in so much perfume.

I press one hand over my heart while the other digs at my pocket and all I can think is, *Oh my God, where's my inhaler? What did I do with it? Where is it?*

It's in my compartment, all the way back in my compartment.

In my pants from yesterday.

Somewhere on the floor.

The lovely spring day shrinks before me as the edges of my vision go black. My heart is exploding. My chest is collapsing. A terrible, tragic gasping consumes me; I can't draw anything into my lungs at all.

I'm caught between the panic of my seizing body and the absurdly humiliating knowledge that all of this is happening on an open glass stage.

I don't want them to watch me die, I don't want them to—

The last thing I see as I fall backward is Drew Jensen reaching for me with both hands, instead of recoiling away.

CHAPTER TEN
Ember

TUBERCULOSIS TYPE THREE, OR TB-3, was invented in a Nebraska lab by a group of pharmaceutical scientists who were (irony!) actually attempting to construct a cure for Tuberculosis Type Two.

TB-2 had been thriving for a decade in some of the world's more crowded nations. Impervious to the antibiotics that had worked on previous generations, Two targeted the weak, the malnourished, the already compromised—and was transmitted easily enough that it had jumped several continents. No one was able to identify its exact point of origin (or even how it came to be), but since it was first diagnosed in the South Pacific, it got the nickname *the Tiki Bug*. Which made it sound cute and kind of harmless, more like a bad hangover than a disease. I'm sure that was hysterical to all the people it killed.

TB-3, however, was entirely known. Controlled. It was created, taken apart, created again, its DNA celebrated and investigated down to the last atom. TB-3 was going to be the key to unlocking the remedy for Two. Somebody—lots of somebodies—was going to make a fortune from it.

But before that could happen, Three got out.

Somehow, *somehow*, it escaped the lab. There was no wishing it back.

TB-3 proved once and for all that man could improve upon nature's appetite for destruction. It attacked anyone: healthy or sick, young or old. And once you got it, you were done.

No cute nicknames. No cure.

No chance of long-term survival.

All you could hope for was a sliver of time before you left behind the grace of your earthly life.

Chapter Eleven
Ember

"T HIS . . . SSS . . . CONTAGIOUS."

These are the first words I hear. They're being spoken in a peculiar, monotone voice, and the spinning whirlpool of darkness that is me can't make any sense of it. *Contagious* is usually a word that invokes all manner of inflections.

Fear. Revulsion. Horror.

I hear the voice again; this time it's more intelligible.

"This patient is non-contagious."

I sigh, and it hurts. Even though everything's still dark there are other people talking now too, and *they're* emotional enough. There are ladies hissing and deeper bass tones muttering and then one more voice, very near me:

"But is she going to be all right?"

That last person was . . . boy. Rich. Eyelashes. Boat.

Drew.

The monotone answers.

"This patient will recover from this episode."

I still don't know who said that.

I open my eyes. I'm flat on my back, staring up at a slick glass ceiling. There are blurs between me and it; when I concentrate on them, I see Drew's face and—and another something I can't understand. It's like a face, but not. It's gray and round and has a suggestion of eyes and a black slit for a mouth.

I take a deeper breath, which hurts even more. The gray-thing shifts and something touches the base of my nose. I swipe at it weakly.

"All patients are required to accept emergency medical attention," the monotone says.

My nose is touched again. I feel pressure there; when my fingers flutter up, they discover a small plastic clip, like the one Javier wore at dinner. It's a medical device, better tech than my old inhaler. Clips make you look like an invalid but they deliver more powerful doses of whatever medication you need. Right now, that sounds pretty damned fantastic.

I can breathe better, and my heart's no long trying to erupt out of my chest. I struggle to sit up. Drew helps.

We're still in the cube but the stream program is gone. It's all only glass again. The door's pushed open and there's a cluster of people gaping at us, but no one ventures too near. I suppose they're not quite convinced the med bot is right about my non-contagious status.

That's the other thing I saw. A humanoid medical robot. It has arms and legs and a torso along with its head, but you'd never mistake it for a real person, not even from a distance. It's covered in a gray, translucent membrane. Vials and syringes and more ominous scalpel-like objects are dimly visible beneath its skin.

I don't have to ask what happened. It's obvious, it's embarrassing, and my first instinct is to jump to my feet and go hide somewhere. But when I attempt to get up, my body lets me know loud and clear that that's a bad idea.

Nope, no way, Ember, you dope.

I have no muscle strength; convulsions will do that. So I sink back down to the slick cool glass and remind myself about how great it is to breathe.

The clip pinches inside my nose and Drew is still lingering above my head. Beneath his tan, his skin has gone nearly as gray as the bot's.

"Take it easy," he instructs, very serious.

This, for some reason, strikes me as hilarious. I want to laugh but all I manage is to say, "Okay," in a husky smoker's rasp.

The bot angles nearer. "Does this patient require assistance to quarters?"

"No." My voice is still raspy but I mean it. "I'll get there on my own."

"No," counters Drew. "I'll take you."

He helps me up and then keeps his arm around my shoulders. I have to lean against him more than I like, but without his support, I'm going nowhere except to a hover stretcher. And this morning has been ghastly enough already.

As we approach the glass door, all the other passengers creep back. Waaay back. We don't have to push past a single person as we exit the Diversion Car. I have officially sealed my status as Outsider to Be Avoided at All Costs.

The lone person who doesn't shy away is the redheaded girl, who only watches somberly, shoulder brooches sparkling, as we stagger by.

What does she have to fear, after all? She's not going to catch TB-3 twice.

We're through the Dining Car (mostly empty), the Bar Car (mostly full), and into our third passenger car before Drew admits, "I don't know where your quarters are, come to think of it."

"Second to last. Right before the end of the train."

He looks thoughtful. "You're with Castaneda."

"Everyone knows Javier." I try to say it lightly, but it comes out merely thin and winded.

"Well, of course." Drew notices I'm having trouble and slows more. We're inching along. "Javier Castaneda. Haven't you heard of him?"

I shake my head.

"He's a wealth management guru. A tech guru. A computer guru. Guru all around. He designed the programs that control the credits accounts of nearly everyone on board. Very high-end, high-tech quantum computing packages. I think he still runs most of them, too. Or did, at least until yesterday."

"He told me . . . he was a hacker."

Now Drew laughs. "I wouldn't be surprised. All I know is, you don't want to make him mad. Bye-bye, trillions in credits. Hello, government attention."

"Every rich guy's nightmare."

"So I'm told."

We reach my door. Drew pulls his arm away, and I'm relieved to find I'm strong enough to stand on my own.

"Oh," he says. "Here's your sweater. You, um, dropped it in the rowboat."

I hadn't even noticed he was carrying it. I take it and it's warm and springy in my fingers.

"Thanks."

He ducks his head and rubs the back of his neck. "Ember, I want to apologize about before. About making you angry."

Now I feel stupid; when I replay our conversation in the boat—what I remember of it—it's clear that I overreacted. I wonder if living trapped inside my home for so long has forever warped any social skills I once possessed.

"It's fine," I say. "I'm sorry, too."

His lashes lift. "I swear I didn't mean to upset you."

"I know." I brush a hand discreetly beneath my nose because it itches, but it's only the clip and that makes me feel even more stupid.

Drew nods and turns away, but doesn't leave. He appears to be studying the wooden panels composing the wall beside us. It's that warm golden wood, throwing a warm golden glow. With his hair and complexion and the color of his eyes, he looks perfectly . . . correct here. Perfectly *right*. Like he could stroll through these corridors until the end of time and no one would ever, ever shrink away.

I can imagine him strolling with the same golden confidence through all those estates his parents own. Directing servants. Ignoring tutors. Pretending that liking grimy rowboats evens everything out.

"I don't," he begins, and pauses. When he starts over, his words are measured. "I do not wish to leave you with the impression that I want to die." He scrapes a nail down the long, swirly fingerprint of the wood. "That any of this is easy for me."

I'm not sure what to say to that since it generally *was* what I'd thought.

"When I said that death is the next adventure, I meant . . . I hope it is. I want it to be." He smiles at the wall. "Very much so. Because otherwise, this all just really bites, doesn't it?"

He glances back at me. I'm struck once more by the strange clarity of his gaze. The misery shining through.

It makes him human again.

"At least the food here is tasty," I say.

He doesn't laugh, but some of the sadness leaves his face. The door to the Observation Car opens and a man walks by, throwing us a curious stare.

"Thanks for the boat ride." I step back. "Maybe I'll see you later."

"It's not like I'm going anywhere else." Drew pushes his hands into his pockets and ambles off after the other guy.

I SLEEP FOR THE rest of the day. As I'm stripping for bed I notice a pair of red dots inside my right elbow that weren't there this morning, fresh bruises forming around them. They're puncture wounds from syringes, ones the med bot must have used on me when I was unconscious. I flex my arm and it's sore—but then again, so's the rest of me. Which is why it's such a relief to get back into bed.

No schedules to obey. No school, no job. No chores. I am a lady of leisure now. I don't even have to feel bad about still wearing the clip since there's no one to see it and point fingers and laugh.

I lift my voice.

"Play music," I say.

The holo comes on; the air before me fills with a list of choices. I think of the bearded man in the Gilded Age ballroom. The graceful, twirling dancers.

"A waltz," I decide, and my compartment is instantly suffused with gorgeous sound.

The fireflies hear it, sashay upward. They dip through the air two-by-two, weaving to the tempo just as those couples had done. I watch them, green lights spinning, my lungs softly crackling, until I drift off.

When I awake I'm once again struck by that uneasy sensation that no time has passed, because everything's the same as when I closed my eyes. There's still music playing; it might be a different waltz, but I'm not completely sure. My 'flies are still dancing. When I sit up, they spin apart to different corners of the room, perfectly in synch.

Only the clock has changed. The dial indicates that it's after eleven.

I'm really going to have to ask the Brain for something more modern. I need a timepiece that tells me a.m. or p.m., at least.

I'm sitting there with a hand against my chest, testing my respiration (not quite so crackly), when I hear the knock on my door.

I look around a moment. Did that actually happen? If a cleaning bot wanted to come in, wouldn't there be a fancy doorbell alert or something?

The knock comes again, slow and uneven.

I get up, grab my clothes, and cross to the door.

"Who's there?"

"It's Javier," says the voice on the other side.

"Hold on."

I dress and open the door. He's standing there with a tray in both hands and his cane over one arm.

"Heard you had a bit of bother this morning," he says by way of a greeting, and I wonder if the art of understatement is a southern thing or purely a Javier thing.

I push my hair out of my eyes and shrug. It's no big bombshell that what happened would be all over the train by now, but that doesn't make it any less mortifying.

Javier hoists the tray higher. It's holding a variety of covered dishes, plus some glasses. "Dinner?"

I'm famished and I've only now realized it. I take the tray from him and (after a quick check to ensure I didn't leave any underwear in view) move away from the door. Javier follows me to the long, low table in the sitting area and sighs his way into one of the wing chairs. I guess this is dinner for two.

"I didn't know we could do this," I say, placing the tray on the table. "Get meals to go."

"I find that many seemingly insurmountable tasks are more readily accomplished if attempted with a degree of panache."

"Panache works on robots?" I say, doubtful.

"Oh, the robots. No, brute coding works best with them."

"So . . . you hacked our meal."

He raises both snowy white eyebrows. "But with *panache*."

I lift the domed lid nearest me and discover a grilled cheese sandwich and—my mouth starts to water—real, thick-cut french fries, speckled with coarsely ground salt. French fries are about as welcome in my house as pizza, and I haven't had any in at least two years. For a man who scorches nearly everything he cooks, my dad's remarkably stubborn about bringing home healthy groceries. I've eaten a *lot* of sliced apples and carrots.

"Is this what they were serving tonight?" I can't imagine someone like Beehive Lady or even Drew enjoying a plain grilled cheese.

"Not in the least," Javier replies, unfolding his napkin.

I pick up a fry and devour it, forgetting all about the napkin and fork and rules. My dinner companion is busy sprinkling what looks like hot sauce from a slender bottle all over his own food.

"Blame my mother," he says, holding out the bottle. "A Tejana down to the bone. Nothing tastes quite right without it."

I shake a drop onto my finger. At first, I taste nothing; then I'm panting and desperate for my water glass. Javier nods to my sandwich.

"The cheese will help."

I take a big bite. After a minute, my head no longer feels like it's going to blow up.

"You're insane," I gasp, when I can speak again.

"Ember, I must tell you how much I enjoy your candor. I imagine you're the only person on this train who wouldn't just simper at me with her lips closed and her heart afire and keep on eating."

I'm recovering enough to laugh as I dab away the tears in my eyes. "But I don't have any credits accounts to worry about."

He nods, genial. "There is that."

The music ends; it must have been changing all along. A new waltz begins, and the 'flies swoop out from their corners to etch fresh patterns into the air.

"I see you have some friends," Javier says. He's watching them with a half-eaten fry forgotten on his fork, his eyes bright. For a second, he almost looks like a little kid.

"Yes. My brother made them."

"You weren't exaggerating when you told me he was good with tech."

"No."

One of the 'flies comes to circle my head. All the others follow. I tilt my face upward and watch as they spin themselves into a ring of lights, gradually descending. I straighten my head because I know what's coming next.

"You have a crown," Javier says. He sounds delighted.

"They do that sometimes. They like to be around me." I hold my head as still as I can and reach cautiously for my sandwich; I can't feel the 'flies on my hair, but I know they're there. "Not really *like*, I suppose, since they're machines. They're programmed to be around me. So we're sort of attached."

Javier sits back in his chair, folds his hands over his stomach. He taps the fingers of his top hand against the back of the other. It's a repetitive movement, meditative, one that suggests he's sat like this many, many times before as he contemplated the creation of wealth and sums and the indignities of cancer invading a long-lived life.

"Protective intelligence wrapped in a truly innovative design. Your brother sounds like a very interesting character, indeed."

"My twin, actually." I look down at my sandwich; the bread is warm and crusty and oozing cheese out the sides. The only thing my own hands suggest is that I need my napkin. "But he'll have had a birthday by now. Two, in fact. He'll be—I mean, he *is* eighteen."

Believe me, I've considered this logically. I've done the math and looked at the facts and understood, from the moment I won that ticket, that this was going to happen. The instant the Time Train reached its full speed, my twin's age and mine split apart, as sure and certain as nuclei cleaved by a collider. Conceived in the same womb at the same time, we'll never be the same age again.

But logic can't prepare me for how my throat closes up as I speak these words. Logic can't fix the soggy, abandoned feeling inside me that threatens to bring back tears. And I don't think I'll be able to blame them on the hot sauce.

I wonder if Mason and my dad are still putting my name on the birthday cake. I wonder what my brother wishes for as he blows out those candles alone. I wonder what both of them think when they gaze up at the stars. At that empty TimeTech platform circling the planet.

I can't believe I'm this homesick already. It's not even been two days here.

"Time is a slippery conceit," Javier muses. "Few people understand that as well as we do, or as we inescapably will. You know, I have an idea. Would you like to join me tomorrow for a tour up front?"

I'm still tasting tears so I take a bite of sandwich, chew, and swallow before answering.

"Up front? The Brain Car?"

"The Main Controls Car, we call it. But yes, it's about the same thing."

"Are we allowed to do that?"

There's nothing like a police force (human or otherwise) on the train, not that I know about or have seen, but I suspect there's *some* way to shut things down if the passengers get unruly. Door locks. Med bots. Sedatives. I've never been exactly docile when it comes to official power and I hate to sound like the girl who always goes along with the rules, but I've already had a close encounter with needles and a blackout today. I'm not eager to repeat the experience.

"I might have played a minor role in the Brain's quantum algorithm," Javier says modestly. "It allows me a smidgen of privileges not afforded the other passengers. Don't worry, child. It won't be necessary to hack us in."

"Oh, great. That'll be great." I try to sound sincere, even though the thought of having to face all those people who watched me this morning turns the few bites I've eaten into a greasy lump in my stomach.

"Wonderful." He points a french fry in the direction of my head. "And do bring your friends. I think they'll enjoy it."

CHAPTER TWELVE

Excerpt from

The Book of Exploration: Approved
and Unapproved Lands

by the Office of Terrestrial Affairs

A LONG WITH OUR POPULATION, many of our natural resources were destroyed in the Bright Times. Woods, heartlands, canyons, clean water, wildlife: all savaged with toxins or burned to ash. Through generations of effort, through complex magicks and a great deal of sacrifice, we have managed to rebuild and reclaim much of the world.

Yet there are still Forbidden Zones.

This book is the complete compilation of Approved Lands for habitation. It will cover topics such as food sources, water sources, and magical hotspots for any sovereign-approved pioneers searching for new territory. Locations are sorted by both accessibility and Spellcasting indices.

A brief note: Although this book includes the boundaries of many of the Forbidden Zones, it is not in any way meant to encourage consideration of settlements upon these lands. The Forbidden Zones are designated ruins of the Bright Times, and as such, are wholly prohibited from exploration or even prolonged exposure to boundary lines.

Crossing into any Forbidden Zone will result in incarceration, execution, or Irreversible Binding of all powers.

Chapter Thirteen
Ember

I'M GOING TO MEET Javier in the Quiet Car, which is the last car (or the first one, depending on your point of view) open to the passengers before the train becomes nothing but sealed doors and tech. Everyone I pass on my way there sees me and more or less sheers out of my path. There is a power to my illness, it seems. All the nose clips and non-contagious proclamations in the world aren't going to overcome the image of me struggling for my life on that floor. The cavernous, wordless fear that one day soon, it might be one of them instead.

Anyway, I'm not wearing the clip this morning. My lungs are hardly aching and I've got my inhaler back in my pocket. That's good enough.

The fireflies are riding safely attached to me; I didn't want anyone swatting at them in the air, thinking they're real bugs. They've arranged themselves in a line down the middle of my sweater, like a row of fanciful green buttons.

I enter the Quiet Car. It's bright and charming. The walls are painted a soft, lemony cream; there are potted palms scattered about and drapery of long gauzy teal. Card tables and satin chairs dot the rest of the space, with hover lamps floating above heads. People are playing games or watching movies on eyepieces or chatting over cups of what looks like tea.

But it's the *Quiet* Car. I can see razor-thin reflections of the movies in front of faces; I can see mouths moving in conversation. But I hear nothing.

There are noise dampeners throughout this car, canceling any sound waves produced within their range. Each chair or table exists within its own pocket of audible sound, but everything else is dampened. So I could stand where I am and shout my head off all day, and no one, not even the silver-haired lady playing a combat game two feet away, would hear a peep.

One of the blazer boys spots me from above his eyepiece. I can't quite remember which name went with which guy, but this one is the skipper. Royce, I think. I stare back at him, undaunted, and his mouth makes an ugly twist, but he gives up and goes back to his movie.

Redheaded girl sits alone, again, in a corner. She's wearing a dress composed entirely of what I think are purple plastic butterflies and reading what appears to be an actual book—I mean a genuine, antiquated book, the kind made out of paper, which I've only ever seen in library archives. There's an image of a young woman on the cover, a magnifying glass held up in one hand. Red's expression is utterly engrossed; she turns a page. Her tongue pokes out to wet her lips and I wonder why she doesn't have a LitPad, like everyone else. Maybe paper books carry more prestige with this crowd.

I glance around but I don't see Javier anywhere. Or Drew.

I wend through the clusters of chairs and tables to the girl, lean in close.

"Hey," I say, but she doesn't look up.

I step nearer. "Hi."

She flinches and drops her book, which falls to the floor in a flutter of pages. I stick out my right hand.

"Red Roxborough, I'm Ember."

She looks at me as if I'm crazy, then down to her book, then back at my hand. Finally, hers lifts in return, and we shake.

"Haven," she says, her voice piping but firm. "Not Red."

"Okay, Haven. Listen, do you want to take a tour with me?"

She gives me a slow, owl blink with both eyes. They're brown, big and dark, with bluish crescents underneath. "A tour to where?"

I lean even nearer. "To the *locked* part of the train."

Another blink. She's processing me, weighing my pros and cons. I'm known to her from the lottery and from the fact of our shared disease, and unknown in practically every other way. I'm a risk, a promise—and I can tell already that she's not the kind of person who's going to take a risk without good reason. Not the kid who dissects her meals with such carefully measured precision. Not the child who wouldn't meet the eyes of the grown women tormenting her.

But her dress is made out of butterflies. She's reading that book. Surely someone so far beyond the mainstream is up for a minor adventure.

I realize, to my surprise, that I really want her to come. Maybe it's her wary demeanor or just the small, curled up C-shape of her in the overstuffed chair, but something about Haven Roxborough rings through me with complete familiarity. She's an outsider here, nearly as much as I am. She's lonely, and alone.

Another few seconds go by, and she's decided against me. She squishes down even lower into the chair, one foot prodding at her book, when her eyes go wide.

The fireflies are switching places down my front. They don't leave the surface of my sweater, but they're arranging themselves into a necklace now, legs delicately climbing, wings flashing gold.

"They're coming, too," I say casually, and pull away.

Haven slants forward like I've tugged her with a string, mouth agape, fascinated by the 'flies. Javier enters the car and I give him a wave, then point to Haven and make an exaggerated *can-I-bring-her?* motion. I suppose I should have asked him first, but he only nods, so it's fine.

I'm outside her sound pocket now, so I send her a look and mouth, *Are you coming?* And she picks up her book and follows me.

There is no knob or handle on the door that leads to the front of the train. There is, however, a sign above it that reads AUTHORIZED STAFF ONLY in those same gently glowing letters as the signs on the platform. There's also an identity pad, like the ones outside our compartments, but I have no doubt that if I were to place my palm upon it, absolutely nothing would happen. Well, maybe not *nothing*. The Brain would take note of it, record it, perhaps react to it later. But I wouldn't get in.

Javier puts his hand on the pad. The door slides open.

He waits for Haven and me to enter first, and as soon as he crosses the threshold behind us, the door closes. Only this time, I can hear it whisper shut.

"Welcome," Javier says. "Ember, Miss Roxborough."

"Thanks."

"Thank you," Haven says, looking uncertain once more.

It's dark inside, humming. Since the Main Controls Car is the lead car of the train, I'd been expecting it to be more open than this, perhaps with a series of big windows at the very front, but instead, there are only a couple of small portholes way up high—not especially useful for seeing out. Most of the room is crammed with consoles, screens, switches. There's a bulky black chair bolted to the floor in front of one of the larger banks of screens.

Many of the displays are scrolling numbers or codes. A few show only shifting bars of colors. I see data for the sensor arrays, climate controls, gravity controls. Aft lasers, food supplies, sanitation tanks, star charts. It goes on and on.

This is the truth that's been hidden beneath the superficial splendor of the rest of the train. This car is functional, not beautiful. I look around and all of a sudden it's a real train to me. A masterpiece of advanced thought and machinery.

The overhead lights warm up.

"Doctor Castaneda. Greetings."

The Brain's disembodied voice speaks to us but it's not until Javier replies that the avatar appears.

"Greetings, Brain."

The blond man pops to life right in front of us. Haven gives a squeak and jerks back.

"You have brought guests," the Brain says, looking at me and Haven.

"I have indeed."

"That is not standard protocol, doctor."

"Protocol override, authorization Castaneda Delta Sixty-Two."

"Authorized," concurs the Brain, with a bow of his head.

"Who is that?" Haven whispers nervously from behind me. I feel one of her hands clutching the back of my sweater, pinching it tight over my stomach.

Javier answers. "It's only the Brain. But that's right, I forgot. You know it as this." He moves to one of the screens and his fingers fly through a series of commands. The blond avatar vanishes, and in his place stands a round-cheeked, dark-haired woman of about thirty.

"Hello, Haven," says the woman in a tranquil voice.

I'm not certain why, but I'm not any more comfortable with this avatar than I was with the man. It's evident that someone put a lot of thought into her, though. She's attractive, but not *too* attractive. Feminine, but not in an oversexed way. *Motherly* is the word that fits her best. Which makes sense, given that she's Haven's avatar.

But she's still too perfect. Her green eyes meet mine and all I see in them is emptiness.

I'm glad I didn't get her instead of the man, after all.

Haven relaxes. She inches out from behind me and says, "Oh, okay," like this was all she needed.

"Here it is," Javier is saying, his hand sweeping the crowded chamber. "A palace of dreams. The unruly offspring of too many minds and too much ambition."

"Hardly unruly," the Brain murmurs.

"I meant it as a compliment, I assure you. Every good parent hopes for more for their child than they themselves were given. As one of your many parents, my hope for you is that you never cease to outperform us."

That doesn't sound like a particularly wise wish to me, but the woman bows her head exactly as the male avatar had done.

"I shall do my best," she says.

"But just in case . . ." Javier glances back at me, smiling, and points his cane at the single chair. "The manual command center. A good, old-fashioned failsafe. I tried to get them to install an authentic captain's wheel in here too—imagine how it would have looked!—but no one went for it."

I take in all the screens in front of the chair. "So, someone would sit here and drive the train?"

"If necessary."

"Who gets to do that?" asks Haven. She's running a hand along the back of the chair. "You?"

"No, child. I'm a programmer, not a lunatic."

"Then, who?" I persist, curious. I thought he was the only person aboard even remotely affiliated with TimeTech.

"Well," Javier says, still smiling, "it so happens there's no one along on *this* trip who's qualified. But putting it in here anyway seemed like a good idea at the time."

Great. I look back at the lady avatar and change my mind again. *Go ahead and keep outperforming us. Just keep us safe.*

"And in here . . ." Javier turns to the wall to his left; I notice the door there for the first time. He places his hand upon another identity pad. When the door opens, all I see is darkness. A wash of refrigerated air pushes over me.

My 'flies begin to shiver. Before I can stop them, they lift off and zip into the other room.

"Lights on," Javier commands.

It turns out to be more like a closet than a room, jammed full of even more tech than the main part of the car. In its center stands a pedestal, and on the pedestal is a deep purple, bread loaf-shaped thing with cords spreading out, thin as spider silk, from its base. The fireflies are circling the loaf, buzzing, weaving in and out of the cords. Then they do something truly alarming: they rise up and mass together into a sphere, legs touching, wings blurring. And they hang there, a jeweled green globe, right over the purple loaf.

"Ah," says Javier cheerfully. "That's a sight to see."

"What is it?" Haven tries to maneuver around me. "What are they doing?"

"They're amplifying their intelligence," I say slowly, unable to look away. "Massing together to create a more powerful computer.

They're trying to . . . figure something out."

This is something I've seen them do before, but only to assess a threat or determine a long-term course of action. I'm not sure which they're doing now, but I do know one thing, and that's that we are witnessing the true genius of my brother. Witnessing something small and innocent-looking join forces to become something much, much larger. More important.

"The best designs are the ones that mislead you," Mason told me, when I asked why he'd picked fireflies for the shape of his quantum experiment. "The best designs are the ones that make you feel what you wouldn't if you knew what they really were. That make you believe they are what they really aren't."

Like this train. Like all the gloss and glimmer on this starship of a train.

The 'flies begin, still attached, to descend toward the purple loaf.

"I'd rather you didn't," Javier says quickly, and places a shaky hand between them and the purple thing. "Ember?"

I cup my palms around them, not touching, and urge them back to me. "They're excited about something."

"They recognize another quantum artificial intelligence."

"What, that?" I reexamine the loaf.

"That's right. Meet the Brain."

I glance around at the avatar. She's watching us without expression, without moving, her hands at her sides. Her dead green gaze is fixed on me. On the ball of fireflies I've coaxed to my chest.

"Cool," says Haven.

"Very cool," Javier agrees. "I wanted to see how Ember's friends would respond to one of their own. If they'd choose to join with it. It seems they might. But the experiment ends here. We mustn't let them touch. The Brain's programming would absorb theirs, I'm afraid."

I back up a step from the closet, but the avatar is still behind me and for some reason, that makes my skin crawl. "What do you mean?"

He purses his lips. "The Brain is an enormously more powerful synthetic intelligence. Your little bugs would just become a part of it. Part of the train."

I nudge a finger, very gently, into their sphere. They break apart and begin to clamber along my collarbone.

"I think I've seen enough of this car," I say.

DAYS PASS. I SPEND long, lazy hours reading, watching movies, playing games. Javier tries to teach me how to play chess but it's tedious and I have no gift for it, and I hate losing every time. Haven turns out to be a much more adept pupil than I am. This works out well for me, as I can simply sit with them and observe and not have to pretend to be smarter than I am. Sometimes I scoot my chair slightly beyond their sound pocket and then I don't even have to make conversation. I am there, and not there.

I actually did bring my schoolwork with me, whatever I was supposed to study over the next month or so back at home, but I find myself about as motivated to start it as I was to learn chess. Why should I care about social issues, calculus, politics, chemistry, when everything on Earth is evolving without me? Why should I bother to master dead lessons? Seems pointless.

My schoolwork languishes, untouched.

I don't see much of Drew. In fact, in all of the following week, I see him only once, and it's right away, in the Diversion Car. He's rowing in a race down a wide blue river, his body slick with sweat, his face flushed and intense. I know he can't see me from inside his cube, so I relax on one of the benches and watch him work—the flex of his muscles, the sinewy back-and-forth of his torso, the way his eyebrows knit together with every pull of his oars—but then I get distracted by three ladies in the next cube riding a carousel that looks as if it's made out of glitter. By the time I remember Drew's race, he's finished his program and left the car.

He must have noticed me sitting there. I'm not invisible.

Fine.

TIME TRAIN THREE REACHES the halfway mark of its maiden voyage. I only know this because I've been waiting for it, waiting for something to feel different (in me, in the train, whichever), but nothing does. We slow to manage the curve of our turnaround, and the stars shift but our gravity remains steady, and as far as I can tell, all that's really changed is that now my compartment has a view of the left side of the universe, instead of the right.

I CONSIDER STARTING A journal to pass the time, but it would only go something like this:

Day Seven: Waffles for breakfast again. Pork chops for lunch. Salad dinner. Three movies and two games of solitaire. It's been eight years and three months back on Earth.

Day Eight: Woke up late. Extra big lunch. Dinner. Two movies. Reading Haven's book (not bad, but it gave me a paper cut), since she's done. Nine years, five months on Earth.

Day Nine: A starburst outside the Observation Car. Javier says supernova. Thought it'd be brighter. Ten years, seven months back on Earth.

Day Ten: Breakfast. Lunch. Dinner. Bed. Eleven years, nine months on Earth.

Day Eleven: Thirteen years.

Day Twelve: Fourteen years. Two months.

DREW FINALLY REACHES OUT. It's the middle of the (black, starry, endless) afternoon but I'm in bed, staring at the ceiling, when I hear a *ping!* sound. I look around without sitting up. My holo pad is on.

Mr. Andrew Jensen calling, reads the projected message in the air.

ping!

I roll over. "Answer," I try out loud, but nothing happens.

ping!

"Answer call," I say, and instantly there's a holo of Drew standing in my room. He looks at me briefly, gives a few blinks, then stares at something above my head.

I remember, belatedly, that he can see me too. Geez, what am I wearing? My old pajamas, once a thick plaid flannel, now worn translucent. He can only see the top, but I sink down deeper under the covers anyway.

"Hi," Drew says, his gaze reconnecting with mine. Maybe it's the holo, but he looks more sallow than I remember. There are shadows under his eyes that remind me of Haven's.

"Hi."

"Do you want to have dinner with me?"

The words escape before I can stop them. "What, like a date?"

"No," he says, so quickly that I can't help but feel stung. "Just eating. Food. That's all." He lowers his chin and shifts in place; I can see the light of his hover lamp glinting off his hair, hear the jingle of his boots. "There aren't a lot of people on this train."

The stinging inside prompts me to say, "There are forty of us."

"Not a lot of *interesting* people," Drew clarifies, and this time when he looks at me, he does not drop his gaze.

"Sure," I say. "Dinner. Seven?"

"See you then."

And he blips out.

CHAPTER FOURTEEN
Ember

DREW IS WAITING FOR me outside my door. It startles me since I wasn't expecting him there, but we hadn't specified where we'd meet so it's not like he's stalking me or anything. I nearly walk into him but he catches me with a hand on my arm.

We exchange awkward *hello*'s, then start walking.

"Nice day," he comments.

"Blue sky, sunshine," I reply. "What's not to like?"

We enter the next car. Someone's playing classic rock (with a screeching guitar solo) inside their compartment loud enough to rattle the walls. We wait to speak again until we're another car out.

"You know what I miss?" Drew says.

I shake my head. He shoots me glance and I can see now that I was right before. His tan is fading into yellow, and there are rings under his eyes that weren't there the last time I saw him.

"Clouds," he says.

I wait for him to elaborate—rain clouds? sunset clouds? fluffy or flat?—but he's fallen silent, staring down at the floor as we walk. So I say, "I miss summer."

He rouses. "Which part of summer?"

"All of it. Popsicles and sunburns and the smell of chlorine in your hair. Running barefoot across the grass. Flower gardens and tomato plants and the feel of good soil when you dig into it. Kind of moist and loamy, you know?"

"No," he says.

I warm to my theme. "Afternoon showers. Twilight on the porch with bugs flying everywhere, because even after the sun goes down, the air's still jammy and hot. *Real* bugs, like cicadas and moths. Even mosquitos."

"No one misses mosquitos."

"I do." Sort of.

"I bet you could get a popsicle here, though," he says. "If you asked."

"Probably." But I already know that I'm not going to ask because popsicles aren't really what I mean at all.

The Bar Car is more or less deserted when we pass through, which strikes me as a little strange. But I don't think too much about it until we reach the Dining Car, which is also mostly empty. And that's definitely strange. If there's one thing I've learned about the people on this train, it's that they like their meals *and* their booze and they like them at the same time every single day.

We take a table in a corner. We split a loaf of sourdough and smear butter on the melty soft insides and I'm still gazing around the chamber, counting heads.

Seventeen of us, not including Drew and me. That's just under half of the human population of the Time Train. Haven tends to dine early and Javier late, but even so, it seems like this place should be busier.

"Where is everyone?" I wonder aloud.

Drew shrugs. "Maybe they already ate. Or they're waiting for later."

"Maybe." But as we move on to our soups (corn chowder, luscious and chewy), more people get up and leave, and no one new comes in. The server bots are slipping between tables, laden with dishes that no one takes. The air vents above us send tiny, tinkling ripples through the crystal ropes of the chandeliers.

"Ember," says Drew quietly. I look back at him. "We've been here nearly two weeks. Where do you *think* everyone is?"

I return his shrug.

He smiles but it's that sad smile, the one that makes him both more ordinary and more attractive at the same time. "Well, where do you think *I've* been the past week and a half?"

Then I understand. I lean across the table and place my hand over his. "Were you—were you in cryo?"

"Only for a few days. The rest of them, I was just in bed." His fingers curl around mine. "Seizures suck."

"I didn't know." I feel my cheeks heating with embarrassment. All this while, I'd thought he'd been sulking over something, avoiding me. That he'd had better things to do than hang out with the charity case, the girl who'd flopped on the floor like a stranded fish in the middle of his bucolic little Diversion program.

But he'd been sick. Too sick to leave his room, and I'd never even tried to check on him.

I am such an ass.

"I'm sorry," I say.

"It's all right. Believe me, I've discovered that if you're going to almost die anywhere, you want to almost die right here on this train. Med bots. Morphine. Good pillows."

"Yeah," I crack. "Near-death here is the *best*."

It's not funny and we both know it, but we're smiling at each other anyway, and then we're laughing and a server bot coasts up with a ravioli dish steamy with the aroma of lobster and white wine, and I feel better.

I feel better than I have in days.

Only two more to go, and I might get to go home.

ON THE MORNING OF our fourteenth day, the Brain announces that it has successfully received a Stop signal from TimeTech. We don't know yet who it's for, whose disease has been erased from humanity, but the train is going to dock. All passengers should prepare for potential disembarkation.

I THINK THAT EVERYONE who isn't in cryo is in the Observation Car as we approach Earth. Most of us are standing, eager for the first glimpse of that blue swirly sphere. I'm with Drew and Javier and Haven, and Haven's holding my hand.

"Maybe us," she says, her gaze flicking from star to star. "Right? Maybe us."

"Maybe," I reply.

I don't want to let on that I'm as excited, as bone-deep hopeful, as she is. Haven's just a kid; let her hope, even if it's only for these next few hours. But hope isn't necessarily my friend. I'm trying to tamp everything down, because maybe it *is* us who are about to walk off this train, and maybe it isn't. And if it isn't, then I don't want the disappointment to damage me too much.

"Maybe it's all four of us," says Drew. "It doesn't have to be only one cure."

"That would be a fortuitous coincidence," Javier says mildly.

"It's been sixteen years," Drew counters, scowling at the glass wall that protects us from the frigid, airless void of everything beyond this train. "Sixteen and a half. It doesn't have to be fortuitous *or* a coincidence. It might just be damned good science."

And it *is* damned good science—for the seven pancreatic cancer patients on board.

All of the rest of us are staying right where we are.

We get the news in the Observation Car, via the projected voice of the male avatar.

"Disembarkation, embarkation, and service update protocols will require two hours, fifty-five minutes at the TimeTech platform. Please remain aboard during this period. Please refrain from interfering with crew work. Please obey all TimeTech rules in order to facilitate our scheduled departure. Thank you."

We retreat to our respective compartments to wait it out. Even Javier, who likes the train best, is subdued. I have a partial view of the platform from my windows, of the shuttle that's already docked. Everything out there seems so . . . bright. Lit to brilliance by the ambient light of Earth.

I sit in a chair by a window and stare out, enthralled. I wish I could see more of the planet from here, but at the same time, I'm glad that I can't. Just the wedge of land and ocean that I have in sight makes my throat tighten with ache.

Somewhere down there, thousands of miles below me, is my family. And I'm aware that it's ludicrous that thousands of miles sound like almost no distance whatsoever to me now. Like I could simply open one of these windows and jump down to them.

I'm so close.

ping!

I sigh, my breath misting the window. If Andrew's calling, I don't want to answer. I'm not in the mood to leave my room yet, and I have no desire to run into any of the seven departing passengers. I don't want to be the sort of person who feels envious of people with pancreatic cancer, even if they are about to be cured.

ping!

I turn my head. The message in the air reads: *Incoming mail for Miss November Duval.*

Mail!

I scramble out of the chair. "Play mail," I command.

My brother is standing in my compartment. My father is (salt-and-peppered, stooped) beside him. There's also a smiling woman with very short tangerine hair and a baby. A *baby*. It squirms in her arms, and the woman has to bounce it up and down to get it to stop.

"Hello, Ember," says Mason. He's the same and not the same; I'm trying to process that. I know his face but it's filled out, with creases I've never seen before bracketing his mouth, emphasizing the corners of his eyes. He's taller than Dad now, still with that mop of disheveled black hair growing down past his collar.

In sixth grade, we once had an assignment in cyber systems class to age ourselves onscreen using no more than three instructions. The results ranged from scary to comical, but mostly they were eerie, I'd thought. Eerie to add decades to yourself, to guess at what your life was going to do to you physically. The lines fate was going to carve across you, through you, when none of us had any real way to know. It wasn't like looking at a ghost, exactly. The opposite of that. A prophecy, perhaps.

With Mason now, it's as if I'm seeing one of those enhanced

school images, one that's been superimposed over the real him.

But I can't stop my hand from reaching out. My fingers pass through his arm.

"We miss you," he says and clears his throat.

I pull back my hand. "Me, too."

Yet this is only a recorded message, and Mason is still talking.

"We'd hoped to greet you in person today, but TimeTech isn't allowing the public near the shuttle, and live communication streams to the train are being restricted. So this is going to have to do. As you've no doubt figured out, TB-3 isn't cured yet, but I want to assure you that we've made huge strides in it. Huge progress. Things are looking promising, especially regarding the manipulation of RNA strands. We've got some trials going in—"

The baby lets out a random, loud-baby squeal and the woman interrupts to say, "Mason," still smiling.

"Oh! Queenie, this is Chaya. My wife." He looks around at the baby, who looks back at him and shrieks again. "And our son, Noah."

Chaya lifts one of the baby's arms and waves it at me. "Nice to meet you, Auntie Ember."

"Hi," I whisper. I bend down to peer more closely at the baby. He's mostly round and slobbery. He has Mason's (and my) eyes.

My brother is married. My twin is married and has a child.

I've still never even been kissed.

I sit cross-legged on the bed and listen to their stories. I learn that Mason and Chaya met in graduate school; that it was love at first sight for him, but second (or third or fourth) sight for her. That they live back on the plains again, all of them, and Dad has a new farm, smaller than our last one, more efficient. He raises an experimental strain of heat-resistant wheat and something called SnapSoy, which grows twice as big as the regular kind in a quarter of the time.

Mason is a geneticist. Chaya is a physicist.

These are our topics: soil, crops, medicines, tech advancements. Noah. A pizza recipe Chaya's invented featuring soy cheese and brussels sprouts (ugh) that she swears is delicious (behind her, Mason is quickly shaking his head), and promises to make for me upon my return.

Everyone looks so happy. Mason and his wife laugh a lot and frequently talk over each other; even the baby chortles. At one point Noah pukes on Mason's shoulder and my brother doesn't even stop speaking. He just hands the baby off to Dad and Chaya gives him a wipe and they keep telling me about this squall that came through last week and washed out Dad's driveway and overflowed the stock pond.

They are, I realize with a pang, their own particular kind of quantum unit. Self-sustaining, intelligence-sharing, complete . . . virtually complete. They make such a perfect whole that for the rest of the recording I can't figure out how I'm going to fit in with them anywhere. I tip my head this way and that, but I don't see any space left for me.

But then the recording is ending, and Mason and Chaya tell me goodbye, and the baby is made to wave again, and my father looks straight at me and rasps, "Love you,"—the only two words he speaks the entire time.

And I see that I'll still fit, after all.

The holo flickers out. I sit there a moment, unmoving, then turn my gaze back to the windows. Earth has rotated to swallow my view.

I leap to my feet, smack my hand against the holo pad.

"Brain!"

My avatar appears.

"Good afternoon, Miss Duval. How may—"

"I want to send mail back to them. To my family. Is there time?"

"You have six minutes, twenty-three seconds until the mail stream closes, Miss Duval."

"Start recording. No—wait!"

I run to the bathroom, find the cosmetics. I slap some color onto my cheeks and lips (because even I can tell that my disease plus two weeks in space has made me chalky pale) and run back out.

"Okay. Start."

"Confirmed," the Brain says, and the message in the air says, *Now Recording.*

"Hi," I begin. I smile, a big smile, so big it hurts my face. "Hi, you guys."

I tell them I'm fine. I tell them about the train. I show them around my compartment, make certain they get a glimpse of the beautiful planet shining beyond my windows. I tell them I've made some friends up here but that I can't wait to see my family again in real life. I even tell Chaya that I'll try her pizza, although maybe we could have a regular pepperoni one on hand, as well.

I tell them about the supernova. About the Brain. I call to the fireflies and they give me a halo, and I thank my brother for that.

I'm out of time. I close with a nearly breathless goodbye, and the Brain sends it off with eighteen seconds to spare.

I collapse back on my bed.

Thousands of miles and too many years separate us, but we still got to talk.

Not such a bad day, after all.

TIME TRAIN THREE BEGINS its second voyage on schedule. I stand in the Observation Car once more to witness our departure, Drew on one side of me, Haven on the other.

I hold both of their hands.

CHAPTER FIFTEEN
Taza

I T AMUSED KAI SULLIVAN to remind his son of Taza's place in the world. At least, that's what Taza assumed from the many, many etchings and articles of him so prominently displayed in the West Lodge's rooms and halls.

The announcement of Taza's birth.

Of his first steps.

Of his first cast.

His first fistfight.

His first expulsion from school.

His second.

His third.

Images of him walking, talking, eating. Hiding his face.

Running away.

It was all embarrassingly overwrought. But at least there weren't a lot of other people around to notice them. Aside from Taza himself and a handful of staff, no one else lived here. No one even visited.

As one of the oldest and most far-flung official residences of the Sovereign, the Lodge was seldom officially used. Very few of his father's followers were interested in the cricket-infused solitude of this part of the world. Diplomats were made for cities; it was difficult to dazzle the masses when there were no masses around for dazzling.

So, of course, Taza loved the Lodge. He loved almost everything about it, from its uneven stone floors to its leaky roof; from the ancient smoky glass that still survived in many of the windows, to the bees that hummed and swarmed inside the great room chimney.

He loved the heavy, greasy beams of blackwood that crisscrossed the ceilings, and the scent of dust and time that drifted from room to room, and the way all the trees out here grew so thick and leafy and tangled, no matter what kind they were. The Lodge trees thrived in their disorder, indifferent to the perfectly manicured life that awaited Taza whenever he stepped foot beyond their realm.

Yet as much as he loved it, the Lodge was still his father's house, not his own. Taza had no say in the décor. Every time he took down an image or article or some other fawning, breathless bit of idiocy documenting his life, two more would appear in its place by the next morning.

The hallway outside his old bedroom was particularly covered in obnoxious crap, the result of an unfortunate loss of temper when he was thirteen. He'd smashed everything he could reach. The result was that now you couldn't even tell the color of the plaster walls beneath all the gilded, shiny frames.

He'd had to switch bedrooms to get away from it.

But probably the best part about the Lodge was its massive garage, which was really more of a barn than a traditional garage, anyway.

Three of its four walls had bristly green bales of timothy hay stacked all the way up to the ceiling; only the wall with the sliding door leading to the outside world had been spared, and only because there had to be a way to get in and out still.

Mice thrived between those bales, and voles, and the occasional chipmunk. There was no convincing them to leave, but since the Lodge horses never seemed to mind mice/vole/chipmunk-scented food, no one ever tried very hard. Rodents were difficult to reason with.

The garage *did* boast a series of large, traditional oil stains on its concrete floor. Some were old and faded, with wide blurry edges. Some newer and sharper, rainbow-slick. And nearly all of them had emerged from a single leaky source: Taza's motorbike. It was the only magical-mechanical object of significance anywhere around.

Taza enjoyed the garage. He enjoyed its powerful hay-barn smell, and its burnt engine oil smell, and the way sunlight flooded through the open door in a bar of soft white gold that captured everything it touched in liquid luminance.

He also enjoyed the fact that he was nearly always the only one in here. No one else bothered with transportation as antiquated as a motorbike (no matter how much magic Taza had lavished on it over the years), so practically the only other humans who came by were the stablehands, adding or subtracting more bales.

There was a special calm to this high, open space. It was a calm studded with the heartbeats of tiny hidden beings; with floating specks of fragrant timothy, and the sure warmth of a sun safely burning many millions of miles away.

And his bike, resting above a fresh puddle of liquid, the promise of escape in every line. Dark hammered metal and polished wood. Magic pulsing, deep and rich, in the seams.

He was crouched next to it, his hands retracing the old spells he'd infused in the wood, rubbing the shine back into the metal casings.

A vole watched him work from a nearby bale, its head just visible, whiskers quivering.

"What do you think?" Taza asked out loud, and the sound of his own voice actually startled him. It was *very* quiet in here.

A strand of black hair had gotten tangled in his lashes. Without pausing his work, he tried to blow it away, but his hair was long and stubborn and it only drifted right back.

"Rebel enough?" Taza inquired of the vole. "Fast enough so we won't get caught?"

"*Re*-bel," replied the vole, perfectly clear.

Taza stopped, turned his head. The vole gazed back at him, unblinking.

"Leaving?" it squeaked, only it sounded like *LEE-vng?*

Some animals could mimic human speech, of course. Even back in the Bright Times, there had been animals with the ability to echo certain human words and phrases. But ever since those days had scorched to dust, there were occasionally, very *rarely*, creatures born with enough magic to communicate with Homo sapiens in their own language. Not mere mimicry, but authentic conversations.

It was cows, mostly. Starlings and crows. Sometimes cats.

Taza had never heard of a vole with human speech ability.

"Illegal," the vole tutted, and cleaned its whiskers. "Execution."

Taza slowly rose to his full height.

"Hello," he said. "We haven't met."

"Leaving?" the vole insisted. "Son? Son? Son?"

"Ah," said Taza.

"*Going* somewhere, boy?" the vole said, in a very different voice from before, one that it should not have been able to command, much less produce. It was a voice without a hint of rodent, deep and human and grinding.

"Only to see you," Taza said tightly. "Sovereign."

He stretched out a hand to the vole. It blinked at him, hissed, and ducked back into the bales.

CHAPTER SIXTEEN
Ember

THE MOOD ON THE train the initial few days after our Stop is almost celebratory. Everyone talks about how pleased they are for the First Seven (I don't know who named them that, but it sticks), and how in two more weeks, it's going to be someone else's turn. The mood stays positive even after the New Seven, who arrived to take the slots of the people who disembarked, begin to filter through the dinners and Diversions and spread their tales of what life's like now on Earth.

"Beijing's gone," announces a young, goateed man at the community table, where Drew and I are also eating. We're a few empty chairs away from him but we hear every word anyway. The new guy had come up and introduced himself as Brecken, although I can't tell if that's his first name or his last. He's got a ruby the size of a chickpea woven into the skinny braid of hair hanging down his chin.

"Totally gone." He grabs a second entrée as the bot skims by. "Shanghai's on the verge. Delhi. Houston. Mexico City."

"What does that mean?" asks Beehive Lady, seated across from him.

"Pollution got to the point that the government had to impose mandatory evacuations. One day you had a metropolis, the next—boom. Empty. Abandoned, along with all the cities surrounding it. It was a bloodbath, man. A lot of people didn't want to go, so the army moved in and enforced kind of a death march thing, you know? Devastated the economy. That was eleven years ago. Probes sent in show buildings disintegrating, roads and waterways turned to acid. Fires burning unchecked. The infrastructure has *completely* eroded. One hundred percent systemic *failure*, man. Monsoon runoff's killed the Bohai Sea."

"My mother built the Moon Mist Tower in Beijing," Beehive Lady says weakly.

"Gone," Brecken repeats with relish, and bites the head off a spear of asparagus. He chews with his mouth open; Beehive Lady looks away.

"Where were the people relocated?" inquires the Grizzled Beard Man, seated at his side.

"Most of the evacuees are pushing west, but it's created border wars. Internment camps. No one wants them."

Drew speaks up. "How many people are we talking?"

"Billions. At least a billion in Asia alone. South America's almost as bad, but they're pushing south there, developing the Antarctic. Some good land down there."

I think about my dad and his new, smaller farm. About Mason and Chaya applying their talents to medical research. About how no one in my family mentioned any of this.

"And the dis*ea*ses," sighs the young woman at Brecken's other side. Paloma. She's got slick maroon hair with turquoise tips and round glasses framed in feathers. I think they might be a couple. "You wouldn't be*lieve* . . ."

"Believe what?" Drew asks eventually, since no one else does.

"How *dis*mal it all is. How *dir*ty. It's so difficult to escape the miasma of it all. Practically everyone we know now has TB-3."

"What?" I say. The entire table has fallen still.

Paloma misreads my shock. "Oh, not *us*. Don't worry! We're Clean, see?" She flips back the loose chiffon sleeve draping her left arm, flashes her wrist to us all. "No brand!"

"*Brand*," Drew echoes, very soft.

Paloma pushes her sleeve back down. "In fact, as soon as we heard that Time Train tickets might become available, we put our affairs in order and snapped them up, didn't we, Brecken? Because we want to *stay* Clean, of course."

I don't know how many of us within earshot have TB-3, but I know it's more than just me. Several of the diners are exchanging glances; Paloma doesn't seem to notice. She sits back and smiles and strokes her sleek hair.

"*Speaking* of financial affairs, we were *told* that Javier Castaneda was aboard the train? Is he here?" She peers around the car. "Can someone point him out?"

Drew starts to laugh down at his plate, but I raise my voice over him.

"How many people have TB-3 now? I mean, do you know a percentage or anything?"

"More than half," Brecken says.

I'm shocked again. "What, of the whole country?"

"Of the whole world," he says, flat.

CELEBRATIONS, LIKE MOODS, ARE transitory. The giddy period quickly fades into the same routine we settled into during our first loop, only now we're burdened with the knowledge of how different everything has become back home in our absence. I was so happy to see Mason and Dad, Chaya and Noah, but now I can't help but worry that one of them—or all of them—has contracted TB-3 and they didn't tell me. Or that they don't have it yet but they're going to get it. Or that Colorado will become like Beijing, and they'll have to flee. Acid air, acid water, acid land. How will they live?

I play their message over and over. I search for the signs I recognize so well in myself, for any hint of sickness on their faces, any irregularity in their respiration, for *brands*—but I find nothing. I'm not convinced that means anything, though. They could be wearing cosmetics. They could have just dosed themselves with a bunch of meds.

All of their sleeves are long, even the baby's.

I can't sleep. It's been three days, four nights (*twenty years, seven months, twelve days since you last touched land,* my mind whispers), and I thrash and fidget and try to shut down my thoughts, but I can't. I want to ask Javier or Drew about the recording, if they notice anything that I haven't . . . but I don't feel entirely comfortable with Drew getting such an intimate glimpse of my personal life.

I can't reach Javier.

I'm determined not to make the same mistake with him that I did with Drew. I try calling his compartment but he doesn't answer, and when I knock on his door, same thing. We're hardly inseparable, but he's really old and I'm starting to get worried. Surely he wouldn't have gone into his cryo pod without telling me first?

My lungs begin to react to my lack of rest. I find myself wheezing over the smallest of exertions. When I'm alone, I wear a nose clip. The rest of the time I try to move slowly as I can.

I am a fish drifting through a stagnant sea. I am a girl breathing air that feels jagged as shattered glass.

Drew's doing worse than I am, although he won't admit it. When we're not eating or sleeping or sometimes rowing down his blackbird stream, we partner up to play vid immersion games from our respective compartments; that way neither of us has to get out of bed. (He's better at the logic levels; I'm better at anything where I get to use a gun.)

On the fifth night, wrapped in my sheets, I decide I've had enough. If I'm not going to sleep anyway, I might as well do something to get my brain to shut up. Something easy. Something distracting.

And I want the hell out of this room.

I look at the clock. It's 3:40 a.m. The Diversion Car might have an opening (it still hardly ever does; the New Seven have been utterly seduced), but I'm not up for that long of a walk. I get dressed and wander into the Observation Car instead.

It is, of course, very dark. But not the same kind of darkness that I'm used to, or even that it used to be: everything silver and black, from the scattering of distant stars to the cloudy arms of the Milky Way.

No, the darkness now is broken by small, splendid rainbows of light. Every planet and star, every single fleck of illumination, has been touched by a palette of color. Even the Milky Way curving around us has become a channel of neon orange, of glistening reds and pinks and greens and purples. The very outer edges of our galaxy are smeared every shade of blue.

Two shadows stand close against one of the walls, talking quietly. Instinctively I head the other way, but one of the shadows turns around and I recognize—finally!—the silhouette of Javier.

"Ember," he says, and beckons me over.

I realize it's Haven with him. A swift, unexpectedly grown-up side of me wants to demand what she's doing out of bed at this hour (in my previous life, I used to babysit), but who am I to say anything? Haven's awake; Javier's awake; I'm awake. And to paraphrase Drew, it's not like any of us can go anywhere else.

She tosses me a quick "Hi!" from over her shoulder, then goes back to gazing out. She has her hands up against the wall; as I come closer I see that she's doing something with her fingers, swiping them around. When I'm exactly behind her the glass abruptly shifts from clear into something like a map, with slender bright lines connecting constellations, galaxies, names appearing and disappearing, facts scrolling beneath.

"Upgrades," says Javier, nodding to the wall. He touches one of the lovely sapphire stars. *Messier 81*, the glass informs us. "Enlarge," he says, and we all three goggle at the blue-and-gold spiral galaxy spreading across the wall before us, scarlet speckles of fire ringing it like sparks thrown from a flame.

"All the glass walls and windows have optical filtering to compensate for the Doppler Effect, so we can see stars instead of merely a fuzzy glow. The upgrades installed during our Stop not only made the glass interactive but also enhanced the electromagnetic spectrum of anything viewed through it. This is what we would see if our eyes could take in every part of the spectrum, from infrared to ultraviolet."

"This is *so* much better," Haven declares.

"I agree," I say, faint.

I don't have names for most of these colors; I couldn't begin to name them all. They dazzle me and fill me and it's like I'm overflowing with the starlight itself. I am composed of these extraordinary hues.

I stand there and stare and remember to close my mouth again only after Javier shrinks Messier 81 back down to size.

"We're absent a meager two weeks," he murmurs, leaning on his cane. "And in turn, we witness both the glory of the heavens and the glory of the human mind."

Haven traces a finger along the back of Ursa Major. "Who knows what they'll upgrade next time?"

"Who knows?" he concurs. "Perhaps for the next loop, we'll have mermaids in the bathtubs and talking ponies in the halls."

"Why isn't this place filled up?" I wonder. "Why isn't everyone here, seeing this?"

Javier grinds the tip of his cane against the transparent floor. A comet streaks into infinity beneath us. "I don't believe anyone else knows about it. When I came in here tonight, I had to boot up the system myself."

I look at him sharply. "Seriously?"

"Seriously."

That seems like a fairly big lapse for someone, or something, to make. It's apparent Javier thinks so too because his tone is troubled.

"An oversight, perhaps."

"Do you think there are maybe any other . . ." I hesitate, eying Haven, who's back to playing with the glass. "Oversights going around?"

"Believe me, my dear, I plan to spend the next few days finding out."

The train cuts a path through a ribbon of opalescent gas. A planet beyond it flies by: aquamarine and fuchsia, rings of plaited mauve.

"Javier?"

"Yes?"

I scratch at a dry spot on my elbow, uncertain of how to ask this, or if I even should. I don't want to get too personal, but I feel like I have to say something. I *did* call him my friend in my recording. "Are you, um, feeling well? I haven't seen you around."

He smiles. "You have a kind heart, Ember Duval. I confess I've been a tad under the weather since we left Earth. But the medicines have been upgraded too, I am pleased to note. I'm getting back on my feet."

"Well, look, I have to warn you. If you're going to start going places, you should know that there's this new couple aboard who are dying to—*eager* to meet you. They talk about you every meal."

"I consider myself warned," he drawls, then adds, "Must be new money. My client list has been closed for years."

"Super shiny new, I'd bet."

We share a slyer, sidelong smile. He glances at Haven, then takes me by the arm and pulls me aside.

"You may have received the impression that matters back home have become somewhat chaotic."

I nod, crossing my arms over my chest.

"I'm not unduly worried. Signs were pointing in this direction long before the first Time Train was constructed. I have faith matters will be improved by the time we return. But in the meanwhile, I want you to know that I've opened an account in your name. A small something to tide you over."

"An account?" I don't understand. "A credits account?"

"A *quantum* credits account," he corrects me. "So that even if you disembark the very next time we Stop, you'll be all right." He pats me on the shoulder. "I'm sure your family has already arranged something similar for you. This will just be extra. You'll be able to slip into a nice, new life. Thrive."

I shake my head, dumbfounded. I've never been given money

before, not by anybody who wasn't directly related to me. I fumble for the right thing to say. Unfortunately, when it comes out, it's not *thank you*.

"That's nuts. I'm sixteen and I don't even have a job. I can't pay you back."

Javier isn't offended. "Don't you know, child? Friendship has no price." He pats me on the shoulder again and limps back over to Haven.

THE NEXT MORNING—OKAY, AFTERNOON—I wake up and go to the Dining Car and there are Drew and Haven and Javier (Paloma and Brecken hanging on near their edges, looking hopeful) at one end of the community table; Drew has his back to me. I'm still rubbing the sleep from my face as I walk closer and all three of them look up at me, grinning, and they chorus, "Surprise! Happy Birthday!"

And I *am* surprised because I had completely forgotten about my birthday.

I'm seventeen now. I've made it to seventeen. Heck, even last night when I'd told Javier I was sixteen and couldn't pay him back, I'd been wrong. The day had turned by then.

I'm seventeen. I have a cake. There are candles. Haven's been cradling a balloon to her stomach and she releases it with both hands. It shoots up to the ceiling and bobs around up there, a shiny silver sun dangling over us.

It's a red velvet cake. Maybe the Brain reviewed my preferences and told them, maybe they just guessed, but red velvet is my favorite, and this one is stacked five layers high. The seventeen candles stuck through the frosting are tall and white; I could let them burn for minutes before they'd vanish into nothing, but I don't.

I lean in, blow them out. Everyone applauds.

Peace on Earth is my wish. And, *Let me live there again soon.*

I don't know if you're technically allowed two birthday wishes, but since this might be my very last birthday, I do it anyway.

As the smoke twists upwards in slim, winding whorls, I pray for them both to come true.

Javier isn't going to last much longer. I can see, very clearly, how the cancer is eating him. His skin sags over his skeleton; his ponytail thins to strands. Perhaps the upgraded drugs *are* better than his old medicine, like he said, but they still won't cure him. Maybe nothing will.

Nothing that we'll find out about in time, in any case.

He spends four days pouring over all the train's systems, hunting for any other errors that might have crept into the programming, but he can't find any.

"That's good, right?" I ask.

"Right." And he says it with such assurance that I can't help but believe him. A taut, invisible strand of anxiety within me loosens a little bit.

The train's not going to crash. The Brain isn't going to glitch out. We're not going to be trapped in outer space for all eternity.

Amen.

I'M ON A SOFA in the Quiet Car, watching a movie with Drew but it's a guy movie, full of speeding ships and laser beams and explosions, and I lost the point of the plot about twenty minutes ago. My mind is wandering, venturing into unknown places.

What if . . .

What would happen if I asked to be let off at the next Stop, even without my cure? Would they do it? Would they let me go?

I think they would. Why not? I won this ticket but that doesn't make me a prisoner. I never signed anything that said I had to stay on board until my disease was eradicated. Not that I remember.

And then I'm wondering, who is *they*? Who would I even ask? We won't be in communication with TimeTech again until we get near Earth, and even then, it's only Stop or silence (which means Keep Going). The initial signal aimed at the train is necessarily brief; it either exists or it does not. There are no other messages embedded in it.

So . . . I'd ask the Brain. No, I'd *tell* the Brain. *I'm getting off. I want off. Stop the train for me because I want to feel time go slow again, even if it means I won't feel it for long.*

But then I glance over at Drew, and he's slouched back watching the movie with that intense yet slack expression that boys get when things blow up, and he looks so . . . nice. Not healthy nice, per se; he's lost some weight and his complexion's almost waxy, but his eyelashes are still thick and dark and there's some stubble on his chin and then I'm wondering what it would be like to kiss him.

I turn away. I watch the hero of the movie snarl a line at a woman in a tank top and I think, *Uh-oh.*

I steal another look at Drew. He looks back at me. He smiles, small and knowing.

Uh-oh.

"DID YOU RECORD MAIL for the Stop?" Haven asks me. We're all three in the rowboat now; Javier is off napping in his compartment. Beyond the glass cube, I feel the eyes of the other passengers following us as we glide down the stream.

Not much to see here. Three kids in a boat. Drew rowing.

Three more days until Earth, Round Two.

"No," I answer Haven. "But that's a good idea."

"My nanny told me to," she says. She shoves a damp red curl from her forehead. We're floating through a hot afternoon; it's July in Drew's land of imagination, and we're all perspiring. "Last time. At the first Stop. So this time I did, so it's ready to send when we get to the platform."

"Good idea," I say again. I haven't mentioned my own secret idea, the one about leaving no matter what, to anyone. I'm still weighing it, considering all the angles. I'll have to decide soon.

"Your parents will be glad to see you," Drew comments. Haven and I are on the seat facing him in the cramped boat and my feet are nestled around his. Every now and then our legs brush, and I can't tell if he's doing it by accident or on purpose.

"I guess." Haven sounds indifferent. "But it's mostly for Chad."

"Chad?"

"My nanny," she says as if we're idiots.

Drew laughs. "Of course." He pushes against the oars.

A heron darts overhead, a needle against the electric-blue sky. We all look up to watch it.

"Javier's going to sleep soon," Haven says.

"He's sleeping now," I clarify for her. "Back in his quarters."

"No. To *sleep*. In his cryo pod. He told me so this morning."

Drew and I lock eyes.

"But it's only three days until the Stop," I protest.

"After that," Haven says. "If his cure isn't ready." She tightens her hand around the wad of handkerchief she always carries with her now. Between her fingers, I can see dots of blood staining it, though her lips look clean. "Do you think it will be?"

"I don't know," I say truthfully.

"How about ours? Do you think ours will be ready this time?"

"I don't know," I say again.

She sets her jaw like I've disappointed her and stares off into the distance, cattails and willow trees and that long, pretend horizon.

"I'm afraid of cryogen," she mumbles at last. "I'm afraid I'll sleep forever."

Me, too, I nearly say aloud, but Drew soothes instead, "Don't worry about it. I've already done it once, and it's just like a nap. We won't sleep forever."

I bite my tongue, hard.

There's no way he can truly know that, is there?

I DECIDE, IN THE end, to hang on. To keep with the program and last at least another loop before forsaking everything the train, the future, might have to offer me. I comfort myself by thinking that this is what my family would want anyway. Surely they've gotten used to the idea of me coming home healthy, not as a girl who was doomed to expire soon despite all her years away. If I left the train and died right before the breakthrough, how would they feel? Pretty miserable, I think. Maybe even angry.

The luckiest girl in the world walked away from all that hope, all that potential, just because she was pining for the life she used to know? When there were six million other desperate people who would have gladly, *instantly* taken her place?

What a selfish little bitch.

I'll stay.

THE HOURS DISSOLVE, TURN to stardust behind us. We zoom toward Earth . . .

. . . then beyond it.

There is no Stop signal.

We zoom on.

CHAPTER SEVENTEEN
Ember

W E SAY GOODNIGHT TO Javier as a trio. We're in his quarters (which look remarkably little like mine: a lot less lux, a lot more tech), standing in a row before his cryo pod. The fireflies are zipping back and forth, around and around, above us.

Javier is already inside the pod. He follows the 'flies with a sleepy, half-lidded gaze, then smiles and looks back at us.

It is very hard not to imagine that he's lying in a casket. The interior is padded in white satin and there's even a small, rectangular pillow beneath his head. He's also got a thin, specially-made blanket covering him up to the shoulders.

I take some comfort in that. The dead don't need blankets.

The avatar is standing behind us, hands clasped. Beyond greeting us as we first walked in, he observes without comment.

"No more grilled cheeses for a while," I say.

"We'll share one when I wake up," Javier replies.

"Extra french fries."

"Naturally."

His focus drifts to Haven, who's gone so motionless I can almost count her heartbeats; the pulse in her throat is the only thing about her still moving. That, and her chest. I hear the reedy *whooo, whooo* of the air siphoning in and out of her lungs.

"Don't you fret, my girl." Javier lifts a hand to her. She comes to life, her arm jerking upward, her skinny fingers latching onto his. "This is only for a while. It's good for you to see it happen, so you'll know not to be afraid."

Haven's voice trembles. "Who's going to play chess with me?"

"Ember will. Won't you, Ember?"

"But she's so *bad* at it," Haven complains before I can respond.

I can't argue with that. Drew snorts a laugh.

"Why, then the Brain will." His eyes find the avatar behind us. "Do you agree, Brain?"

"Of course, Doctor Castaneda. I will be pleased to play whenever Miss Roxborough wishes."

"There you go. All settled." He eases back against the pillow. "And now, children, I'm tired, so I'm going to rest. You all take care of each other. I have every confidence we'll talk again soon."

I bend down to kiss his cheek, which feels cold and smooth as rubber. Drew shakes his hand and Haven's lips are trembling now too, but she manages to lean up and kiss him as well. We all three step back as the clear lid of the cryo pod descends.

It settles against the wooden base with a hiss, and I see Javier adjusting the blanket. He gives me one last wink, then closes his eyes.

"Systems ready," the avatar says.

I retreat another step. Every cell in my body wants to get as far away from this coffin/pod as I can, but I stop with just that one step. Javier may have invited us here so that Haven could overcome her fears, but I'm fairly certain I'm more ill at ease than she is.

The control pad on the side of the pod blinks DIAGNOSTICS

Complete. Begin Sequence?

"Begin," says the avatar.

It's over before my next breath. There's a flash of light—that's it. Javier looks exactly the same but he's ice now, no pulse, no respiration. I thought there'd be frost rimming the glass or crystals on his face or *something* to prove it'd happened, but there isn't. He really does look (*not dead, not dead*) asleep.

The pad reads Sequence Complete. Stasis Normal.

"Not so bad," Drew says. I don't know if he's trying to comfort me or Haven.

I tear my gaze away to stare at the rug beneath my feet. It's mostly beige with blue ovals that stare back at me, a series of endlessly repeating blank eyes.

I take that second step back. "Let's get something to eat."

"We just had lunch," Haven points out.

"Dessert." I force a cheery note into my voice. "I heard a rumor about ice cream and apple cobbler."

The avatar doesn't address us again. Like a well-mannered but detached host, he walks us to the door, waits for it to open, then watches us leave. My 'flies abandon their ballet above the pod to follow me out.

I glance back right as the door closes. The last thing I see is Javier. The pale, severe outline of his frozen brow and nose and mouth. His lips are pulled slightly apart.

Stasis Normal.

HAVEN GOES NEXT. I can't say I'm surprised, since I have a very up-close and personal understanding of her slowly decaying health, but I am sad for her. Worried, though I do my best not to show it.

The thing about TB-3, the sly and devious thing, is that right up until the end, you tend to look and even feel mostly all right. Maybe not *terrific*, not blooming with health, but on most days, you can pass for normal. And if you're careful, you can survive like that for a while. No real exercise, of course, and you've got to keep up with your meds like they're your new religion, but mostly . . . you can ignore the rattle in your chest. You can sleep through the fatigue. The shortness of breath. The chills.

Death remains an abstract; an ill-defined splotch on your tomorrows. You can convince yourself that you're nearly okay.

But you're not okay. And then one day, you're coughing up blood.

Your grand finale tends to come quickly after that.

Less than four days after Javier goes to sleep, the med bot assigned to Haven makes its recommendation. If she is to stand any chance at a future recovery, Haven has to go into cryo now.

"You'll be safe," the woman avatar assures her. "You won't feel anything. You won't dream, so you won't have nightmares. I'll be right here when it's time for you to wake."

"So will I," I add, because although the avatar is motherly and smiling, Haven's deep brown eyes are fixed on me, and I can feel the trapped panic behind her gaze. The contagion of fear that's spreading through her even more viciously than our disease.

"Let's go, Red." Drew scoops up her up—she can't weigh more than a feather, she's so scrawny—and deposits her carefully into the pod.

"Haven," she protests, but even her voice sounds tired.

I stroke her hair. I paste on a smile and tell her about how I'm going to introduce her to my family when our cure is ready. Tell her about the brussels sprouts pizza waiting for us, and that I'm going to make her try the first bite.

"No way," she says, fervent.

"We'll see," I tease.

When Haven freezes, it's just as quick, just as *over-like-that*, as Javier. Her skin is blue-white and her hair fans copper over her pillow, and she could be a sleeping princess in a picture book.

I touch a finger to the glass lid above her cheek and there *is* cold inside because my fingertip summons a ring of mist.

I hope the avatar is right, and there are no nightmares.

WE COMPLETE ANOTHER LOOP.

No signal.

DESPITE THE FACT THAT not a single passenger has gotten off, the train is beginning to empty. More and more people are retreating into cryo, either because they're extremely sick or extremely bored, I suppose. Drew and I often find ourselves dining alone, although the Bar Car consistently manages to draw in stragglers. I recognize the New Seven still meandering around, but they don't take up much space. These days, I don't usually have a problem if I want to secure a cube in the Diversion Car, even if it's the middle of the day.

I've floated down Drew's stream; ridden the carousel made of glitter; draped myself in priceless diamonds; run my hands along an ice cliff in Norway; explored Buckingham Palace, and Machu Picchu, and the first human outpost on the dark side of the moon. I even invented a talking pony that walks up and down the recreated halls of the train, although (since the Brain programmed it), it mostly just asks me how I'm feeling and wants to know if I'm enjoying my day.

"You need to delete that thing," Drew says, as we watch it clip-clop away from us. "It's too weird."

"Agreed. I made it for Haven, but I think it's only going to freak her out."

"It freaks *me* out," he says, and lifts his voice. "Brain, Jensen Diversion Program Five, please."

Our fake train corridor and pony vanish, and we're standing on a wide balcony overlooking a lake. It's nighttime, with a full moon that glows and stars much bluer, gentler, than the ones I'm used to seeing. The moon and stars reflect off the water; a sultry breeze skims the surface of the lake and their light breaks into a thousand shimmering shards.

The balcony is connected to a house. A mansion. Inside, gaslights flicker against the walls, and everything looks old and elegant and ambered. I smell lilacs and lake on the breeze.

"Is this one of your homes?" I ask, turning a circle to take it all in.

"No. This is only a reverie." He comes nearer. "Will you dance?"

There's music playing; I hear it now. It's slow and easy, the kind I can probably manage to dance to, even though I don't know any real steps.

But I don't answer him right away. He stands before me with his hand lifted, and I want to say *yes*, but I'm afraid that *yes* might mean something more than just a dance. Something that I'm not sure I'm ready for.

Drew is literally the only boy I know now, and I have to admit that I'm attracted to him. But how much of that is because he's around me so much? Would I still feel this small, tingling tug toward him if we weren't always hanging out? If we were back on Earth, leading our separate lives?

Would rich and handsome Andrew Jensen ever even have given me a second glance?

I don't know. I'll never know, actually. The truth is, our paths are going to diverge no matter what, and probably soon. Our odds for a successful relationship are practically nil, and that's not even taking into consideration the differences in our backgrounds.

Chances are, we're not getting off at the same Stop. One of us is almost guaranteed to end up a lot older than the other. One of us might end up ashes and dust while the other rides on and on.

If my life were a fairytale, this would be the moment I realize that I love him anyway.

But I don't. Not like that.

Yet he's looking at me so patiently, and the flower-weighted breeze comes again, and the music feels comfortable in my bones, so I swallow my *yes* and all of its possible implications and simply move into his arms.

"I didn't want to be here," Drew says. I'm holding myself as far from his body as I can without being rude, but his jaw rests against my temple, and his voice is pleasingly low.

"Why did you make the program, then?"

"Not *here*. The Time Train. I didn't want to be a passenger on this train."

"Why not?" I'm genuinely curious. I know why *I* didn't want to take the train, but I've never heard Drew speak about his family with anything resembling love or even affection. So if it wasn't because he was going to miss them, why not grab the opportunity to live?

"It seemed . . . superfluous to my existence. An excess of time and greedy hope. It sounds strange, but I was content where I was. *How* I was, even with the headaches and nausea and seeing spots. Even when the doctors said six months. But I'm the only son. And there's . . . *so* much money. Father insisted."

"That's funny," I say. "Because my dad insisted I be here, too. Or that I at least try to be here. He's the one who made me enter the lottery."

Drew guides me into a leisurely spin. "What about your mother? Did she want you to go?"

"She's dead. That's what I heard, but she took off when I was seven, so I don't really know. Yours?"

"Also dead. Really."

"Oh."

You'd think the conversation would sober us some, pull us apart, but that's the thing about being terminally ill. At some point, talking about the dead begins to feel the same as talking about donuts. About your favorite color. About the book you recently read. It's just another topic.

We spend the next few minutes silently practicing our steps. I'm easing closer and closer to him, or maybe he is to me; the fronts of our bodies brush. His hand drops to the small of my back and he pulls me in all the way. It's like a standing, swaying hug.

The song ends. We slow to a halt but don't break apart. I keep my head level so that I'm staring straight at the base of his throat. I think my cheeks might be on fire.

Drew swallows. "What I meant to say, Ember, was that I didn't want to be here at first. But now I don't want to leave." He releases my right hand to cup his fingers beneath my chin. To tilt my face to his.

"I don't want to leave you," he says deliberately, and his eyes are shadowed and ambered, exactly like this warm faux night.

He bends his head. His lips feel tentative, soft.

My first kiss tastes a little like regret, and a little like joy, and a lot like yearning for something only barely beyond reach.

And it's very fine.

A HARD *BAM!* ON the glass wall shakes us apart. We open the cube's door to see who it is, but it's no one. The Diversion Car is empty.

CHAPTER EIGHTEEN
Taza

H E DIDN'T LIKE GOING into the city. Cities were always complicated, stuffed full of shops and souls and shiny, demanding things. Even breathing the air felt taxing; it tasted swampy to him, diluted with the constant exhalations of the masses.

Most cities had a few parks, true, and lines of trees planted like stranded soldiers along the streets, but they were just gestures against all the rest of it. Patches of calm fringing the chaos.

He wondered if any of the people who lived there ever noticed. If the constant noise and light and endless *busyness* of it all ever jangled their hearts.

Maybe not. Maybe you had to become saturated in nature's stillness, in the clarity of rivers and meadows and forest, before you ached in their absence. His own wild heart, his animal heart, seemed to bleed a few drops every time he forced himself back into civilization.

Yet here he was tonight, heading into the city, because that's where Kai and Imogen were, at the Court of Palaces. Since they'd obviously already noticed that he'd been planning a trip, it would be an extremely bad idea to vanish into the badlands without their official permission.

It was, Taza reflected as he slipped around and through the packs of people flocking the summer sidewalks, probably not even possible. His father and grandmother had spies everywhere, rodent and human and otherwise.

So, he couldn't leave to hunt his fallen star without letting them know about it first (he planned to phrase it as a request), and it was a given that they wouldn't answer his calls. Kai had begun hinting months ago—subtly at first, but then with more and more vigor—that it was time for his son to acclimate himself to the populace. To embrace the kind of power that didn't come from magic but from human affection.

When Taza had pointed out that human affection was merely a matter of emotional manipulation, which he was already good at, Kai'd told him to either come to the Court or don't, but if Taza wished to converse with either of them ever again, he would be required to show up in person.

Imogen, in her silent, smiling way, had echoed Kai.

Life was, Taza thought, largely about compromises. *I'll give you this if you give me that. Everyone's happy even if no one really is.*

His father, the politician, had taught him that lesson.

Taza'd waited until nightfall to breach the city outskirts. Although Albuquerque glimmered with conjured lights, the shadows born of them were trickier than those found in daylight; they wrapped around him with a certain silkiness only afforded by the gaps between lanterns, the moon hidden behind clouds. In shadow, Taza was less recognizable. At least, that's what he hoped.

He kept his hair in a long ebony braid, but so did half the men he knew. He wore a plain t-shirt and battered denim jeans, and his boots were leather. His motorbike, so distinctively unique, was parked in a lot about a mile away. Most people around here still traveled on foot.

All in all, he looked ordinary, at least with his chin down. But he wasn't ten minutes along the street that led to the Court before a buzzing sound filled his ears.

Taza looked up. A hummingbird whizzed ahead of him, sped about and confronted him at eye level, dead still in midair.

He was forced to a halt; a woman towing a child by the hand behind him made an irritated sound and juked left to avoid running into him. Two boys eating ice cream on a shop patio nearby broke into laughter.

The bird jabbed forward an inch, wings beating, black diamond eyes staring. Her beak looked sharp enough to drill holes in concrete.

"Okay," he said, holding up a palm between his face and the potential stab of that beak. "Tell them I'm here. It's not a secret."

The hummer darted above his fingers, skimmed close enough that the air went cool against his cheeks, and was gone.

"Hey, it's Taza Sullivan," said one of the ice-cream kids. He lifted a chocolaty hand. "Hey, Taza!"

Taza feigned a smile, gave a nod.

There was no point in keeping his head down any longer.

THE COURT OF PALACES was a rambling, tangled-up city-within-a-city that consisted of many thick, sprawling adobe buildings supporting many, many more upper levels, and a courtyard about the size of a small village forming the eye of its center. Wooden towers spiked up into both flat and witch's hat roofs. Picturesque walkways led to mazes of stony paths, to ornate arbors and gardens of aromatic herbs. Climbing vines shaped themselves into images along the walls (landscapes, wildlife, portraits of people they liked) and roses bloomed all year long, just because they could.

The sun never shone too harshly here. Winter ice never scrubbed the stone. The Court was a wellspring of some of the most potent magic to be found anywhere in the country, and Taza's father and grandmother were the focal point of it all.

President, Kai Sullivan might have once been called, back in the Bright Times. But maybe not; *president* implied choice, a decision to lead. *Potentate* was more appropriate today, Taza imagined. Choice had been removed from the hands of leaders generations past. Magic decided who would rule now, as surely as birth had decided the kings and queens of antiquity.

And Imogen would have been . . . well, whatever came second to a president. He must have learned that at some point in school, but honestly couldn't remember. She was called Wise Woman here, and it suited her. The vines' portrait of her along the southern wall was exceptionally large and detailed.

He approached the main gates (massive and wooden), which opened to him in stately silence. The hummer reappeared at his shoulder.

"I don't require an escort," Taza said but wasn't surprised when the bird ignored him.

The soles of his boots made small *scritch-scritch* noises against the cobblestones no matter how mindfully he walked. That was one of Imogen's more ingenious enchantments; she said she liked to know who approached and who was leaving. The Court was a haven of secrets only for her and her son-in-law.

"Taza!" called a man from across the courtyard, waving a hand.

Taza waved in response, kept walking. Harper and Victoria, distant cousins who managed the constantly changing moods of the Court's plants, spotted him from the top floor of one of the towers. They leaned out the window and blew him air kisses, which he didn't return but did pretend to catch.

The hummer dashed back and forth ahead, impatient. The moon emerged fully from the blue skating clouds, and everything became washed in silver.

Imogen awaited him at the entrance to her home.

"Lone Boy," she greeted him. It was the same all-encompassing, semi-affectionate title she'd bestowed upon him since the day he'd entered the world.

"Grandmother." He allowed himself to be pulled into a hug.

Her head reached his shoulder; her hair shone brilliant in the moonlight, a thick pale braid as long as his own. There was a rose pinned behind her ear, red or black, he couldn't tell. Its fragrance engulfed him, sweet and strong.

"You're so late," she chided, and let go. "He's been waiting."

CHAPTER NINETEEN
Ember

S o, THIS IS IT. I'm standing in Drew's compartment and together we're regarding his cryo pod. It looks exactly like my cryo pod, like Javier's and Haven's and I have no doubt everyone else's on this train. Streamlined and expensive and ridiculously ominous.

But in a few short minutes, it will contain the frozen body of my friend Drew, the boy who kissed me. So it's not exactly like all the others, is it?

"I'm sorry," he says, for about the fifth time.

"Don't be so damned noble. You have to." I sound angry and that's because I *am* angry, but not at him. Just at the circumstances in general.

"I could wait a few more days. Wait until the completion of this loop."

"That's well over a week away." I look him up and down, and my next words are brutal but honest. "You look like hell. Like you're going to keel over. You've waited too long already. Just . . . get in."

"Well, *you* look beautiful," he says, and smiles.

I don't smile back. I scowl. I'm trying to focus on my anger, to keep it sparking because the alternative is getting teary in front of

Drew and I refuse to give in to that.

"Promise me something," he says.

"What?"

"Promise me that if this next Stop is yours—or whichever one ends up being yours—and I'm still in here, you'll wake me to say goodbye."

"All right. As long as you promise me the same."

He fakes astonishment. "You hate these things. Don't tell me you're considering going in, after all?"

"Not in a million years," I assure him.

IT'S NOT A MILLION years before I change my mind.

Here's what happens first, though:

Drew is frozen. He kisses me one last time before the lid descends, and I carry that memory with me for days to help battle against the loneliness. I pass my hours submerged in a strange and smothering combination of emotions: grief, ennui, homesickness. There's a handful of other people besides me left wandering about, but we're so few compared to what we were before, and no one seems interested in speaking or even doing anything beyond exchanging strained smiles in the hallways.

We ricochet in slow motion from car to car, dining, drinking, diverting.

I sleep a great deal. My dreams are patchworks of faces, voices, menacing unlit rooms. When I'm awake, I find myself lingering more and more in the Observation Car, because for me it's become the most beautiful place on the train, and it reminds me of what Javier once said.

The glory of the heavens. The glory of the human mind.

It reminds me of hope.

WE POLISH OFF ANOTHER loop. I watch it happen from my seat in front of a glass wall full of fleeting facts and neon colors.

There is no signal.

IT'S BEEN 66 YEARS since I was last on Earth. My father is 112 years old.

My father is probably dead.

My twin is 83.

I hope my twin isn't dead.

Even Noah, the baby, is now on his way to becoming an old man.

ONE BY ONE, THE final few remaining passengers haunting the corridors disappear. As far as I can tell, I am the last to go. And I still don't want to.

It's stupid, right? It's stupid to keep waiting and waiting while my life is winding down to its final moments. I think I must be losing my mind, spending all this time by myself.

Every morning I wake up and look at that cryo/coffin fixed to my wall, all gleaming and ready to turn me into a hunk of ice. And I think, *Tomorrow I'll go in there. Tomorrow for sure.*

The train has a library of thousands of movies and shows and theatrical recordings that I haven't yet seen, a lot of them uploaded during our one and only Stop. I squander a couple of days watching shows, but the problem with being gone for over sixteen years is that a good many of the jokes reference events and people I know nothing about. So they're not funny; they're sad. They're another line drawn between me and normality, only hey, that's right, even *this* isn't normal anymore. I'm baffled by jokes that are over half a century old.

Even so, I'm giving it another try. I'm in the Quiet Car (how many hours can I spend locked in my compartment, staring at the ceiling? at my fireflies?), drinking chai and watching something called *The Tales of Snowboy*, which isn't anime like I'd thought it'd be, but rather the grubby real-life adventures of a grubby boy living in a grubby Antarctic settlement.

It's wet in Antarctica. Muddy. Still snowpacked in spots, but mostly it's mud and cliffs and some desperate-looking penguins kept in pens. *The Tales of Mudboy* would have been more appropriate.

But I'm watching. I'm trying to figure out if the mountain in the background is composed primarily of streaky rock or streaky ice—and is that a ski slope?—when someone steps in front of me, bleeding through my screen.

I start in my chair, sloshing hot tea over my fingers. I tear off my eyepiece.

It's the skipper. Royce. He grins and says something, but of course, I can't hear him. He's outside of my sound pocket. I surge to my feet, clutching my nearly empty cup.

"What do you want?" I demand. I don't know if my words are clear enough to read; his grin only widens. He takes a step into my pocket.

"What's going on, November?" he says. "Ready for some company?"

I sigh in disgust. "Go away."

"Sorry. Not going to happen."

I don't know why it's never occurred to me before right this second that being female and alone on the train might be a treacherous thing. I don't know why, because I know it's true anywhere else. Royce looms over me and he's large and his face is puffy and he smells like—like something rotting. Like he hasn't bathed in a long time. Like even though he looks alive, his body is already bursting with decay.

He smells feral, like danger.

All my instincts warn me to cringe away. Instead, I grip the teacup tighter in my hand and stand my ground. "Whatever it is you're after, I'm not interested."

"Why so shy, girl? I only want to talk."

"Is that right?"

"Sure," he says and backhands me across the face.

Pain explodes through me. I spin to the floor, my teacup shattering, and before I can do anything but gasp for air, he's on top of me.

"Think you're so special?" He grabs my wrists. "Think you're so hot, slut? You give it up for that pretty boy Jensen in his dumbass moonlit fantasy but you won't even talk to *me*?"

I try to buck him off but he's straddling me at the waist and he's much, much stronger than I am. We writhe out of the sound pocket and he's still talking but all I hear is silence. Not even my own frantic breath. Not even my hammering heartbeat.

Everything is now happening in utter, flawless quiet.

He's pinned both of my wrists in one hand, is using the other to snatch at my shirt, ripping off buttons, exposing my chest.

He gropes my breasts. I scream (silence, silence), tearing my right arm free, losing skin to his nails, and wedge my thumb into his eye. It feels wet and squishy and revolting.

His mouth opens. I think he's screaming now.

But I can't get him off of me. He hits me again and this time it's with his fist. My vision blanks into blue and white. The pain slashes through me and it's so bad it's almost like nothing. Like it's beyond my capacity to comprehend.

We breach the rim of another sound pocket. I hear him grunting, me rasping, and then we're out of it again and it doesn't matter how much I scream, no one is going to hear, no one is going to come, and he's undone my pants and yanked them down to my knees.

I smell cinnamon and sugar and anise. I smell blood and rot.

The fingers of my right hand crawl across something rigid, something sharp. I don't look to see what it is—I can barely see anything—but I slice it up toward him anyway, connecting with his jaw.

He jolts. He claps a hand to mine and wrenches it away from him.

I've stabbed him with a fragment of the teacup. The bone china juts out of his cheek in a triangle shape, white against his skin.

My scrambled brain thinks, *Hey, just like that mountain in the show.*

He pulls out the shard and stares at it in his hand and the blood pours out of the hole and down his neck like a *fountain*, and this awful disconnected part of me wants to *apologize* for what I've done. To say, *Sorry, oh my God, I'm so sorry about that.*

Royce meets my eyes. For the first time, for probably the last time, I notice that his are gray.

There is murder behind his gaze. I see it, recognize it, and don't even have the sense to flinch.

He raises the hand gripping the shard. Red blood splashes me, red snakes drip down his palm. The shard plunges toward my face and finally, *finally*, I squeeze my eyes shut.

But the blow I'm anticipating doesn't come.

His weight on me shifts. He goes backward. He's off of me except for his legs.

I pant in place a moment, trying to catch up with whatever's going on. Then my body contracts and I roll away from him, clambering to my hands and knees.

I'm wheezing. I'm shaking. Royce is on his back on the gorgeous cream-and-gold rug and there's a med bot crouched over him, needles for fingers, several of them sunk deep into his flesh.

I sit back and cup my hands over my mouth. If anyone could hear me, I'd be making loud, sobbing-gasping-hiccoughing sounds.

But no one can.

The med bot injects Royce with one last needle, then lifts its head to me. I crawl forward until I can make out its words.

"Is this patient injured?"

"No," I sob. "Yes. Some." I pull my inhaler from my pocket and cram it against my lips. My nose is bleeding. I swallow the flavor of medicine and rust.

"Another medical robot will arrive momentarily. Please remain calm."

Okay.

I collapse back on my butt. I use my inhaler to keep inside the undignified noises that want to escape me. My left eye is swelling shut and I realize my pants are still down and drop everything pull them up again, buttoning the top with quaking fingers.

"Thank you," I say to the bot. "Thank you for helping me."

"Violence is prohibited on this train," the bot replies, monotone.

"Miss Duval, are you well?" inquires a voice I know. I look around, but I don't see the avatar anywhere amid all the fancy satin-covered chairs and sofas and spindle-legged tables. My broken cup has leaked chai in big wet stains along the rug. Blood mingles the stains scarlet.

"Brain?"

"Yes."

"Was it you who called for the bots?"

"Yes. You seemed to be in difficulty."

The second med bot enters the car. It lumbers on its mechanical legs straight to me.

"Is this patient injured?" inquires the bot. "Is there pain? Please indicate the location of the pain and its estimated severity on a scale of one to ten."

"Thank you, Brain," I say to the ceiling, to the walls. Because I'm still in some pocket, I hear my own words. They're not too wobbly.

"It is my pleasure to serve, Miss Duval," the Brain replies. "I apologize for any inconvenience you were caused."

That insane part of me wants to laugh, but I don't.

The med bot is examining my face, exploring the area around my eye with cold, gummy fingers. I wince. It applies some sort of astringent-smelling goo through what would be the tip of its pinkie, and the pain instantly begins to lessen.

The bot crouching over Royce is busy sealing the wound in his cheek. Royce's mouth sags open, dark and gaping. It looks as if he's snoring.

"What's going to happen to him?" I ask. "What are you going to do to him? Is he going to be locked up?" The thought of Royce roaming free has me torn between wanting to throw up, or else grabbing another shard and slitting his throat.

Now that it's over, fury slams through me. Tidal waves of adrenaline and rage. I'm really, *really* pissed off.

"Mr. Knox will be returned to his cryogenic pod and kept in stasis until his remedy. He will no longer pose a threat to you, Miss Duval."

"Further medical attention would be best rendered in this patient's quarters," my bot informs me. I dab at my nose and nod, and it lifts me to my feet.

I'm near enough to kick Royce's unconscious body as I'm being led away, but I don't want any of those tranquilizers ending up in me. I stomp on his knee instead, hard as I can, and pretend it was an accident.

With any luck, he'll limp for the rest of his miserable life.

CHAPTER TWENTY
Taza

I BEG YOUR PARDON," HIS father said. "You want to do what?"

Kai was using his most polite, professional tone, which Taza knew meant he was facing more of a battle than he'd been expecting over the slight matter of vanishing into the wilds for a few weeks.

All right, not more than he'd been *expecting*. This was his father, after all. But certainly, more than he'd been hoping for.

The fire in Imogen's hearth burned high and hot, and the chair Kai had chosen for his son was placed too near to it. But Taza wasn't going to give in to the heat and move; nor was he going to give in to his father's attempt to force him to say what he wasn't saying.

I want to potentially break one of our most significant laws. That's not a problem, is it, Sovereign? I mean, Dad?

Words wielded their own artful power. Phrasing could be everything with a statesman like Kai.

"I want to gear up," Taza repeated patiently, "and head west. I want to follow the path of the shooting star. The meteorite. I want to find where it landed."

"How far west?"

"As far as I need to go."

Kai offered his son an enigmatic smile from over the rim of his espresso cup. It was a famous smile, one that had sent chills down the spines of all manner of casters, from the most spectacularly gifted to the most timidly benign. It meant everything and nothing at once; it meant that you had Kai Sullivan's cool, undivided attention, which wasn't always a good thing.

"But not as far as the Forbidden Zone," Kai said, and it wasn't a question.

Taza attempted to look affronted. "Of course not."

"Are you certain what you saw *was* a meteorite? Not a Remnant? A fragment of the Bright Times finally falling to earth?"

"No," Taza admitted. "But if it was a Remnant, I've never seen one so large."

Kai's eyes bored straight through him. "All the more reason to avoid it."

"Well, obviously," Taza said, then swiftly modified his tone. "What I mean is, if it's a Remnant, obviously, I won't go near."

"Why?" his father inquired, and tasted his espresso.

Taza drew in a careful, fire-scented breath. "Why what?"

"Why do you wish to find it?"

It was a valid question, one Taza had been wrestling with from the moment this feeling inside him, this *itching* to follow the snake-star, began. He could say it was because he'd witnessed an omen, and thus he was bound to follow it. He could describe the sparks that had consumed him on the tower that night; the clear orange indication of travel. He could talk about magic, and fate, and of how the image of that trail of smoke obliterating the heavens had shaken him to his core.

He could even point out that if the thing *was* a Remnant, it was better for them all to know about it than not.

But none of those reasons, although all true to a degree, were the most honest.

For her, rose the answer within him, silent and undeniable. *I'm going for her.*

"Because of the girl in the vision," Imogen announced from her chair, and nodded. "Naturally."

His grandmother's living room reflected her personality, spare and uncluttered but with occasional jarring bright touches. Jade-colored pillows were piled in corners; a stained-glass window salvaged from a church back east held a constant glow. A trio of Red-collared Lorikeets and a single elderly, angry macaw—who hardly ever shut up—lived in the leafy green vines that laced the rafters above them.

At the sound of Imogen's voice, the macaw flapped down to her chair, gripping its back with viciously clawed toes. He glared at Taza and emitted a scream.

"Get out of my head," Taza said pleasantly.

"I'm not in it, Lone Boy. As soon as you mentioned her, I knew." Imogen lifted a hand to the macaw, the backs of her fingers stroking the vivid blue feathers. "She hovers over you like a wraith."

"Yes," he conceded, defensive, "some of it's for her. I think she's part of this, but I don't know how. Or why."

"She summoned the Remnant?" his father asked.

"The *meteorite.* And I don't know. Maybe. It's tied to her. And to her—her sorrow."

"Which you felt," Kai said, thoughtful.

"Which he *felt*," Imogen echoed, very soft.

Taza thought the conversation was veering into uncomfortably personal territory.

"So, yes, I want to head west to hunt the omen and to look for the girl. I doubt it will take long"—a smallish lie—"and I won't do anything dangerous"—a bigger one.

The macaw cocked his head and tore the rose from Imogen's hair, chuckling as he shredded the petals into confetti. All three of them paused to watch him savage the bloom.

The rose-scent wafted briefly stronger, then faded back.

"Dad," Taza said.

Kai's steady, dark gaze returned to him.

"Please." Taza lifted an open hand, part supplication, part impatience. "We already know my fate, don't we? Nothing's going to happen to me. I'll be here, right *here*, when I'm twenty-three. I'll be who and what you say. But I think this is important. I—I need to see it through."

It struck him that even though he was intentionally duplicating Kai's calm, this was the most impassioned thing he'd ever said to his father, or to anyone. Apparently, Imogen thought so, too, because she came to her feet, shedding petals and the bird. She crossed to Taza and flattened her palm over his heart.

"She's in here, too," she said. "Strong as day. Slick as night. Full of numbers and jumbles and bravery. I think I like her."

Kai set aside his espresso. He sighed.

"Go, then. Go with my blessings." He pointed a finger at his son before Taza could finish rising. "But the laws still apply to you, Taza, whether you like it or not. If you do anything irresponsible, you *will* be held accountable. I won't intervene."

"Got it."

"In exchange for this generous boon I'm granting you, when your hunt is finished, I expect you back here, at the Court." Kai's smile now was wholly readable: grim, determined. There were demons behind that smile, hard-edged and whetted. "You'll spend my remaining years here, learning to be *who and what I say*. There are too many formidable casters out there testing our mettle. I will not risk the safety and prosperity of this land on an unproven boy, no matter how strong his innate potential. Are we clear?"

Taza gritted his teeth. "Yes, sir."

"Excellent. Go in peace."

Taza turned, walked away on stiff legs that no longer seemed like his own. He'd gotten something and given away something, and he couldn't tell yet if he'd won or lost this latest bout with his father. It felt bizarrely like both.

"Don't forget to bring back the girl," Imogen called, as the macaw circled back up to the rafters and began a fresh round of screaming.

CHAPTER TWENTY-ONE
Ember

REMEMBER THAT FIRST TIME I was with Drew in his rowboat, and he asked me where I wanted my ashes scattered, and I said I'd never thought about it?

Yeah. That was a lie, of course.

Certainly, I'd thought about it. I'd thought about my upcoming death over and over and over again. *Try* getting a terminal diagnosis and then not obsessively imagining your final few gory moments. Trust me, it's not possible.

I knew exactly how my death was going to go. I'd been sketching out the details in the corners of my mind for over a year, all the little steps I'd need to take listed neatly in order, everything painless and perfect.

I've always been good at lists.

I was going to die at home in my warm skinny bed, in my sleep. Mason and Dad would be asleep, too; that part was important. I didn't want them watching. I'd been the unwilling witness of too many strangers surrendering their lives in hospitals, in strange beds, trapped between strange walls. *My* death was going to be my own, and I didn't want anyone to watch.

Besides, it always seemed more natural to me to pass away at night than in daylight. Maybe because in the dark, as in sleep, your eyes can't hunt for whatever it is you're about to lose forever. Your heart can't break over it.

So, in the cold snowy depths of one very special night, I was going to let go of my life in peace, breathing sweet and calm all the way to the end.

Afterward, they'd take what was left of me (those heavy gray ashes) back to the plains. Back to the fields of wheat and corn, where I'd skate away on the wind like fairy dust, rejoining the land where I'd been born.

Sapphire skies and golden grain, evermore.

That was my plan. It was a good one, too. Not too terribly unrealistic. Not too terribly abrupt or even sad. By the time the lottery happened, I'd already managed to stash away over a month's worth of pain meds. I'd wanted to be certain I had enough when my particular night came.

Maybe it sounds strange, but it made me feel better to think that I was going to have some control over my ending. So many aspects of who I was now, of who I was going to *become*, had careened beyond me, but *this*, I'd thought—the most intimate, personal instant in time any of us will ever have . . .

This I could still command.

Now, thanks to TimeTech, I don't even have that. Unless I go into cryo, I'm going to die on their terms, not mine.

I've spent nine weeks aboard this train. According to the med bots, I've got about eight left.

Of those eight, only six or seven will be useful. After that, I'll just be doped up and confined to my quarters, unable to move. Gradually drowning in my own blood.

I can't bear the thought of that.

I can't bear one second of that thought.

CHAPTER TWENTY-TWO
Ember

AND NOW I ACTUALLY am alone. I've confirmed it with the Brain to be absolutely certain. No other passengers on Time Train Three are conscious.

I could run around naked.

I could dance on top of the Dining Car tables.

I could drink anything and everything I could find in the Bar Car.

However, on my last day of staying awake, all I do is go to the Diversion Car, enter a cube, and stand at the brink of a very tall mountain. Cobalt sky encircles me. Gossamer white clouds float by and the wind feels crisp, a relentless nudge against my body that whispers, *Yes, let go.*

I glance downward; the meadow below me is barely a dot. A tiny patch of verdant fuzz. Looking at it makes me lightheaded.

But I'm here to listen to the wind. To give in. I spread my arms, tilt forward, and plunge off that brink.

I don't close my eyes.

A very real part of me—maybe that grieving, insane part of me—hopes that this fall never ends.

Yet everything, everyone, ends.

THE BRAIN WATCHES AS I climb into my pod. It's fixed relatively high up on the wall and my foot catches the rim, but the avatar doesn't offer to help. He can't, I suppose, being composed only of light.

I free my foot. I get all the way in and wiggle down and pull the cryo blanket up to my hips. It's woven from a material that will adapt to my body temperature, becoming denser with the cold, more porous as I heat up. Beneath it, I'm wearing my flannel pajamas and wool socks.

I hate it when my feet get chilly.

The fireflies cling upside down to the ceiling above me. I debated about whether or not to return them to their box, but in the end, I decided I'd rather leave them loose. I don't know how long I'll have to stay in cryo, but even if it's a couple of weeks—or a whole month— they'll do better being able to fly around and recharge.

That's what I tell myself. Maybe I just can't stand the thought of *all* of us locked away.

I look at the avatar. He smiles at me, encouraging.

"Systems ready," he says.

I ease back, tug the blanket to my chin. Light as a wisp, it feels more like a suggestion of covering than anything that could ever warm my flesh.

This is okay, I'm going to be okay, it's safe, it's safe. Everyone knows that cryo is safe.

Isn't it asinine to be so afraid of dying in this thing, when I'm only going in it to stop myself from dying outside of it?

The pillow presses cool against the back of my neck.

The clear lid of the coffin lowers. Lowers. Hisses shut.

I close my eyes and clench my fists and brace myself. I'm not sure what to expect, a blast of cold or light or what, but all that happens is that I hear the lid lifting again. I open my eyes, and yes, it's all the way up.

I squint at it, muddled. I sit up and lean out over the edge and my control pad has a single word displayed in bright red letters: MALFUNCTION!

Well, isn't that just perfect. Now what?

I scan the compartment, but my avatar has already vanished.

"Brain?" I try, but there is no answer.

I crawl out of the pod, the blanket twisted between my legs. It slithers down and becomes a mess around my feet. I kick loose and make my way over to the holo pad, press a hand to it.

Nothing happens.

I press it again, harder, like that's going to help. This time, I glimpse a flicker of something from the corner of my eye, but when I turn to look, it's gone.

My 'flies descend to me, swarming. They circle my head around and around until all I see are dizzying streaks of green.

"C'mon," I protest, and they swing into a single-file line and shoot across the compartment with their lights flashing. Up, down, looping, corkscrewing. Something's got them worked up.

I try the pad one final time, but now there's not even a flicker.

Something cold, something unpleasant, begins to prickle along my spine.

Okay, so my holo pad is broken. Somehow, in the twenty seconds it took for the cryo lid to descend and then lift again, the pad malfunctioned, just like my cryo pod. Both of these things occurring at once seems almost laughably implausible, but I can't think of any other explanation. My head feels thick and my eyes are itchy. I massage my temples and realize I'm going to have to go find some help. I can activate the avatar in another car and tell him what's going on. The service bots can repair everything, surely.

I cross to the panel with the shelves for my clothes. They're all unfolded, jumbled up as if someone's come into my quarters and tossed them around when I wasn't looking. It doesn't make any sense. I accessed this panel less than ten minutes ago when I needed my pajamas, and everything was in place.

Slowly I turn around, that cold, prickling sensation growing stronger. Now that I'm paying attention, I see there are other, smaller indications that nothing's quite exactly as it was before.

The pillows on the bed are no longer near the headboard. A big tasseled square one that's supposed to be on a wing chair rests on the table instead. Even the bedspread's rumpled.

The hover lamp was on when I went into the pod; now it's off. And the clock on the nightstand has tipped over on its face.

The only thing that still seems right is the arrangement of the furniture, most of which is bolted to the floor.

I pull on my clothes as quickly as I can and head to the door. The 'flies stick with me, but that's fine. I feel better with them near.

The corridor looks the same as ever, but then, there's not much that could be done to it. I turn left and trot toward the Observation Car.

The door doesn't open.

I stop just short of banging my nose against it. I pause, step back, and approach it again. And again, it does not slide open.

No, no. This is really not good.

I place a careful hand against it. There are no knobs or latches, not even an identity pad since it's supposed to open or close automatically for anyone who triggers the sensor. I test it with the pressure of my palm, but this is a door designed to withstand a hull breach in the crushing depths of deep space. I know already I'm not going to be able to force it to move.

I look over my shoulder; the door leading to the next car up is also closed. But the fireflies are already there, bobbing and weaving. Maybe they know something I don't.

The hall lights begin to buzz; the hairs on my arms stand up. The lights darken to sulfur, flare into brilliance, then settle back to normal.

Not, *not* good.

I lift my voice. "Hello? Brain?"

I've never seen the avatar in any of the corridors, but perhaps that's because I've never summoned him. I didn't see him in the Quiet Car, either, when Royce was attacking me, but the Brain was still there. Still, I hear nothing in response.

No . . . I do hear *something*. A kind of muffled scratching sound, coming from the passenger car beyond mine.

I walk hesitantly toward the door.

Ssssssssk. Ssssssssk.

It slides open.

Ssssssssk. Ssssssssk. Ssssssssk.

There's a cleaning bot about halfway down the corridor. It resembles a giant robotic spider, or maybe a huge mutant crab, with a round central unit and eight long, telescoping legs that jut out from it at different angles. Some of the legs terminate in metal, human-looking hands; some of them end in pointy crab pincers; some of them are just vacuum tubes.

It's facing one of the walls, clawing at it with its two front legs—ones that have hands—over and over.

There's no door there. All it has to do is angle left or right and it would be free, but it doesn't. It keeps scratching at the wall, left leg, right leg, left. The fine wood paneling in front of it is almost entirely carved away. I glimpse metal beneath the grooves.

Ssssssssk. Sssssssk.

My fireflies stay close to my chest. None of us seem willing to approach the defective bot.

The door at the far end of the car opens. A person walks in—no, not a person.

A med bot.

It stops, its blank gray face aimed at me. The cleaning bot might as well be invisible.

Ssssssssk. Sssssssk.

"The train is being serviced at this time," the med bot says. "Please return to quarters."

"Serviced?" I say. "What do you mean? Are we docked?"

We're not. I know that much.

"Please return to quarters."

"But—"

"Please return to quarters."

"Listen, I just want to know what—"

The med bot begins a heavy, menacing jog towards me. There's a needle emerging from one of its fingers, a slender silver spike of light.

"All patients are required to return to quarters at this time."

I turn around and sprint back to my compartment. I make sure my 'flies are still with me but I don't think I breathe again until my door is all the way shut. I glance around for a weapon but all I have are pillows and maybe the clock (can I hit it with the clock? would that even slow it down?) so I just stand there staring wildly at door.

Nothing else happens. The med bot doesn't attempt to come in.

I retreat until the backs of my knees hit the bed. I sit. I pull the comforter around me because now I'm shivering.

What the . . . ?

All right. I think . . . I think I must have spent more than twenty seconds in the cryo pod. I think I must have actually been frozen. I don't remember *any* of it (no dreams, the avatar promised) but there cannot be another explanation for what's going on. For how different, how disturbing, things have suddenly become.

How long was I asleep?

I've no way of knowing. The Brain operates the cryogenic pods and I can't communicate with it from here. The only thing the cryo control pad offers me is that bright red MALFUNCTION! warning, which I've clearly already figured out for myself.

Despite the med bot, I can't stay in here. I have water—I think; I haven't been inside the bathroom yet, actually—but no food, and anyway, I need to get to the Brain. To discover how bad things are.

There might be other passengers awake besides me, trapped in their compartments as I am. Maybe we could sneak through the train together. Form a distraction if we meet any med bots. Maybe at least some of us can reach the Main Controls Car.

And then what? I ask myself silently.

I have no idea. My best hope is that Javier is awake too because he'll know what to do.

I get up and grab the clock from the nightstand. I sit on my bed with it tight in my hands and watch the minutes do their slow, slow jerking *tick*s until fifteen of them have passed. I know I should wait for thirty, but my nerves are too rattled and I still can't quite wrap my head around the fact that I really was frozen and I honestly think that if I have to wait even one more second, I'm going to start tearing out my hair.

I have to go see what's happening. What's happened while I was asleep.

I tell the 'flies to stay here; they're too noticeable and I'm trying to be stealthy. I creep near enough to my door so that it opens, then poke my head out.

The corridor is empty.

I'm already wearing the chocolate sweater and very dark blue jeans, and my shoes are black. I feel good about that, because at least I'll blend in with the shadows, until I remember that there aren't many shadowy places on the train and that wearing dark colors in front of a robot is basically the same as wearing red or yellow or polka dots, since they don't, in fact, *see* you. They *register* you. Your body heat, your vascular system, your heartbeat. Even your brain waves. And I've got no chance of hiding any of that.

I count to three and dash across the hall.

"Javier!" I call at his door, soft and urgent. "Javier! Are you there? It's me!"

I knock lightly, rapidly, on the wood.

"Javier!"

I'm keeping my gaze pinned on the connecting car door that I know works, but so far, so good.

"Javier! Please, please, it's Ember! Please be awake!"

But he isn't. Or if he is, he can't or won't answer me.

Okay. Okay.

I let my hand drop and then quickly, before I lose my nerve, slink up to the door that leads the next car.

Sssssssk. Sssssssk. Sssssssk.

The med bot's gone; there's only the spider bot, still clawing at the wall. Both of the passenger compartment doors in this car are closed. I knock on them anyway but get no response. No hope for help here.

I hurry to the next car. The sliding door opens and the lights do that buzzing trick again, dimming and then flaring and the air feels electrified, dangerous, like lightning's about to strike. I crouch down into a ball with my feet tight together and my arms around my knees.

Once I saw this boy I knew, a neighbor's kid, get struck. His name was Walker. I was eleven and he was twelve, a god with wavy auburn hair and a tiny scar across his chin. One day at school he'd passed me outside the gym and said, "Cool sunglasses," and as far as I was concerned, it might as well have been, "I will love you forever."

He made me float; he made me fly. I dreamed about him every night for a week. Walker the god was going to ask me out to a movie and then to prom and then we'd get married.

Eight days later he was riding a thresher through the field that bordered our farms. He waved at me, I waved at him, and the bolt blazed down from the cloudless blue sky and blew off the top of his head.

Mason found Walker's cap, scorch mark and all, in our pumpkin patch the next morning.

I asked my dad why it had happened and he'd said that sometimes that's just the way it was. Lightning from the blue, no reason. I'd had a hard time with that: no reason. It felt to me as if, out of all the people crowding the planet, the bolt had chosen Walker to die.

I'll never forget the smell of his death (ozone and burnt toast), or the way the air rubbed the wrong way against my skin, like it's doing now. Like maybe there's an electric charge building up somewhere inside this train, looking for a person to strike.

And I'm the only person around.

The lights cool down. The buzzing fades.

Walker's smile lingers in front of me, a vision from another life.

I drag myself onward.

No one answers their doors in the next compartment. Or the next.

But in the next car, one of the passenger doors is open. Almost open. It looks broken; it's jammed at an angle instead of the usual straight up-and-down, and there's a triangle-shaped gap wide enough for me to fit through. I squeeze past it and pop into someone's quarters.

"Hello?" I whisper.

It's so dark. I wish I'd taken the time to read the plaque outside. What if this is Royce's room?

Then let the lightning get him.

"Anyone here?" I whisper.

The hover lamp and overhead lights are off. I try, quietly, "Lights on," but they remain off. The only illumination I have is what brightness leaks in from the hall, an inverted pale wedge that seeps across the rug.

My eyes are adjusting. I make out the bed, the chairs and pillows. The cryo pod with a figure inside it, the lid lifted. I leap forward—someone else is awake!—and I'm three steps away when the stench hits me, but by then my momentum has propelled me all the way there, and I can't help but look down.

It's Beehive Lady. I can only tell by her hair, which is still the color of platinum and arranged becomingly over her shoulders. The rest of her isn't becoming, though, because she's dead, and likely has been for at least a couple of weeks.

I cover my mouth. I back up and up and my heel crunches into something that gives a dull *crack!* but I keep going, only stopping when my back smacks against a wall. I stand there, breathing through my fingers, trying not to vomit.

MALFUNCTION! reads her cryo pad, and I see that now, too.

Something twinkles on the floor. A square thing. The thing I stepped on. I focus on that, not the dead woman in her casket, not her stink, and the square thing slowly resolves to become a FlickSlip.

A framed plastic slip for showing vid shorts and cascading pictures.

I inch toward it, pick it up. My foot fractured it down the middle but the pictures are still shifting.

I see Beehive Lady smiling on a stone terrace, young and alive, plumeria flowers edged in sunlight behind her. I see a man on the same terrace, a flute of champagne in his hand. I see a beach and foamy surf; the two of them kissing in a restaurant; a girl with long blond hair and bluish green eyes, pointing a finger at me and laughing.

The same girl is in most of the rest of the images. I see her as a toddler, and with braces, and as a teen in a tiara and a white formal gown. I see her giving Beehive Lady a kiss on the cheek with a *Happy Mother's Day!* banner hanging in the background as everyone around them applauds.

I straighten. I place the FlickSlip upright on the nightstand and steal out of the room.

I'm able to get through two more cars before the gravity fails.

CHAPTER TWENTY-THREE
Ember

IT HAPPENS IN THE Bar Car. I've never really hung out here before, but as I'm passing through, I pause to look around. All the bottles of liquor are still precisely aligned on their shelves. The tables are clean and polished; glasses are stacked in pyramids behind the bar, ready for cocktails. The hover lamps cast a mellow glow.

Music plays from hidden speakers. It's a piano piece, jazzy and smooth.

I know there's supposed to be a bot in here to make the drinks, but I don't see it. Still, this car is obviously being tended to.

A woman begins to sing along with the piano. *"You said that you would wait . . ."*

The shelf nearest me holds an array of vodka bottles, clear and gleaming. I grab the nearest one, unscrew the lid, and take a gulp from the mouth. It's room temperature and sharp and burns all the way down to my stomach, but after a second the burning fades and then I just feel warmer.

As I'm screwing the lid back on, I hear a noise behind me.

"Muh."

I whirl around, but I'm still alone. The hover lamps show me every vacant table and chair, every corner. The stars beyond the windows are jeweled specks against the velvet black.

"Brain?" I whisper.

Nothing. Just the piano and the woman's disembodied voice.

"My heart, my hope, my fate . . ."

The heavy glass bottle feels like a weapon in my hand. The vodka sloshes inside it.

"Muh-muh-missss-missss—"

It's the Brain. I'm sure of it. There's no avatar in here but I recognize his voice, even though it's coming through tinny and distorted.

"Brain! Can you hear me? Tell me what's—"

I don't finish my sentence (well, I do, but it ends in a yelp) since suddenly my feet are no longer on the floor. I'm rising, floating, revolving.

This isn't the meticulously planned loss of gravity that I'd experienced in the Diversion Car, jumping off that mountain. This is me flailing in midair, trying to grab something—anything—to pull myself back down.

"I bleed for you, a thousand silent tears for you . . ."

The tables and bar stay in place, just out of reach, but all the chairs, all the bottles and cocktail glasses are free-floating with me, spreading out through the car. The hover lamps go into spins. I release my bottle and push at a chair moving toward my head. It changes course, knocking into another chair, and it's like a game of pool because that chair hits another one, which hits a bottle of rum, which cracks apart. And now there are big, pungent drops of rum dotting the air, and I'm up near the ceiling enmeshed in my own hair, and I bump into a chandelier which, thank heavens, is firmly screwed in place and not going anywhere.

I cling like a monkey to it, nestled against the crystal pendants.

"Snow falls, the sky is clean . . ."

A few more bottles smash into things and break. Broken glass glides by. Liquid globules of various colors and smells meet and melt together and jiggle apart again. A couple of the lamps crash into each other and somehow interlock. They're flying in a wide, blurry circle, a cyclone of light, shattering all the bottles around them.

"Ain't nothing left of me to see . . ."

The lamp cyclone is whipping nearer and nearer; I don't think I'm going to be able to push it away without breaking an arm or a leg. I'm holding back my hair with one hand and trying to figure out if I can somehow propel myself to the nearest door without ramming into a chair or getting sliced to ribbons by the glass when the gravity is restored.

I'm coated in cement. The branch of the chandelier I'm holding isn't designed for my weight; it rips free and I plunge to the floor, crystal beads pattering down around me in hard, glinting raindrops.

"Ow," I groan. I landed on my tailbone and it hurts a *lot*. A final bead falls to whap me on the stomach.

"Ain't nothing left for me to be," the woman sings.

Get up, I order myself. *Get moving. Don't let the med bots find you.*

But I can't catch my breath yet, can't sit up. Even straightening my legs sends fiery shooting pains up my back.

The interlocked lamps settle to hang above my knees, placid now but still connected, right as the piano piece shifts into something featuring a clarinet.

The far door opens. I hold my breath but it's not a med bot, it's a spider bot. Two, three, four of them, scuttling in on their jointed legs. They spread out and begin cleaning up the spilled liquor and broken glass. One comes so near to me I could poke it with a finger, but it doesn't react to my presence, just works around me. A fifth bot enters the car and begins to gather up all the unbroken bottles, returning them to their shelves.

Carefully I raise myself to my elbows. My back protests again but I make myself finish it, climb all the way to my feet.

The bot near me sucks up the crystal bead that falls from my sweater.

I stumble out of the car.

IF THE DILIGENTLY MAINTAINED order of the Bar Car gave me hope that I might find food in the Dining Car, I am doomed to disappointment. The tables aren't even set, although the linens covering them are still here, mostly crumpled on the floor and dangling over tipped chairs. The cleaning bots haven't made it this far yet, I suppose. But there's no hint of anything edible in sight, no aromas of anything being cooked. No server bots. All the orchids in the wall sconces are dead, dried into twigs.

"Brain," I say, as loud as I dare.

"Muh," I hear. Tinny. Remote.

"Where can I find you?"

"Kwah."

I frown at one of the orchids. It's shriveled and deformed, entirely brown. Even the moss at its base has dried into a rigid nest of brown.

"The Quiet Car?" I guess.

"Ssss."

All right. I can do this. But to get to the Quiet Car, I must first go through Diversion Car.

Oh, God.

All the cubes on my left side are offline. But the ones on the right are active, running programs. Programs I've never seen before.

The first one is a lightning storm over an ocean, strike after strike after strike, massive waves heaving, crashing beneath a seething green sky. A ship flames and tilts in the middle of it all. People froth the water around it. They're frenzied. Drowning. I watch them give up one after another, watch their bodies sink into the depths.

Looking at them for more than a few seconds makes the vodka I drank threaten to come back up.

The middle cube seems fine at first. It's a forest scene, heavily wooded. There's a buck grazing amid the trees. He lifts his head, ears twitching, and springs forward twice before the pack of wolves bring him down. But they're not normal wolves. They're hairless, pink-skinned, with bulging crimson eyes and elongated yellow fangs. They rip into the buck as he strains his neck and juts out his tongue and screams—I think he's screaming, I can't hear him, but there's blood spurting and intestines yanked everywhere and he's still not dead, his legs are kicking sideways and he's still screaming—

I close my eyes. I actually cover them with both hands and keep going, bumping into one of the benches, inching around it. The last thing I want to do is look into that third cube, the final one before the next car, but I do.

Of course, I do.

It's a room in a house. A child's room. Dolls are flopped on shelves, more of them piled on top of a trunk. China dolls, rag dolls, dolls of all shapes and sizes and colors. Maybe this is one of Haven's programs?

Okay, that would be all right. That would be . . .

But I know that it isn't. Everything about the room shines too coy, too young, even for her. The bed has a quilt embroidered with pansies and big smiling bears, and the window behind it is framed in panels of gently billowing lace. There's a painted rocking horse in the corner. A warm beam of sunlight brushing gold along the wooden floor.

There's a little girl, about six, playing with a pair of dolls on the rug in the center of the room. She's wearing an old-fashioned dress with a pinafore over it, crinoline sticking out from the bottom of her skirts. Her boots are patent leather with buttons up her ankles. Her hair is arranged in perfect ringlets.

Neither of her dolls has heads.

I'm staring at them, a part of my brain stupidly stuck, trying to figure out where the heads went, when the little girl looks up and meets my eyes through the glass wall. *Through* it.

She has a baby face. Not a child's face but a *baby's*, an infant's, pudgy and oversized with little rosebud lips that start smacking as soon as she sees me.

Her mouth stretches into a freakishly wide smile, revealing a row of very sharp teeth.

She starts to drool.

Her eyes stay fixed on mine. They're black. Bottomless.

Hungry.

When I take a step back, her gaze follows. When I sidle away, her gaze follows.

When I limp as fast as I can to the next car door, she stands up and scurries to the section of the wall that is the cube's door. She places both hands against it and shoves at it and she never, never looks away from me with those enormous black eyes, and her mouth never stops drooling.

I practically tumble into the next car.

She can't get out, right? Let that be true, don't let her get out.

I know she can't. Logically, I know. But I don't even pause to knock on the two closed passenger doors in this car, only keep lurching along as fast as I can, vodka and acid climbing up my throat.

Two cars later I have to stop. My back slides down one of the walls and I bury my head in my arms and struggle to catch my breath. My inhaler helps, but when I hear a series of thumping noises coming from behind me, from the car I just left, I'm up again. Running.

THE QUIET CAR IS a mess. Chairs on their sides, upside down, the card and game tables overturned. None of the potted palms remain upright; it looks like someone came in here and pushed them all over to make a frondy green floor. But there's no one else around (no bots, I mean) so after pausing to scan the chaos, I walk in.

I try calling to the Brain, but I'm not in a pocket. I realize that I have no sure way of knowing where they are anymore since the sound dampeners are hidden behind the ceiling tiles and all the clusters of chairs have broken apart.

I take a few more steps in, look around and estimate about where I was sitting when Royce attacked me. There are no bloodstains marking the rug beneath my feet, but when I speak again, this time I hear my voice.

"Brain?"

"Miss Duval. How may I serve you?"

I let out a gust of air, part relief, part exasperation. "You can serve me by telling me what the hell is going on."

"There appear to be several major malfunctions occurring on board at this time. Please be patient. I am working on solutions."

"The med bots are confining people—me—to quarters."

"Communication with medical robots three, four, seven, and eight has been severed. I suggest that you avoid these robots until full communication has been restored."

"Yeah. Great suggestion." I press the heel of my palm to my forehead, where a throbbing headache is beginning to take over. "Did you know that someone's *dead*? I don't know her name, but she's in her forties maybe. She's got pale blond hair and she's still in her cryo pod—"

"Several cryogenic pods are now nonfunctional. I suggest that you do not attempt to use your cryogenic pod until full service has been restored."

"Brain!" I sink to my knees on the rug, still clutching my head. "What's *happened*? How could all of this have *happened*?"

"Thirty-one days ago, an extreme energy cosmic ray induced spontaneous decoherence in the section of my processing devoted to human life support. The decoherence cascaded through other systems. I am currently working to rephase them."

"Thirty-one . . ." I look up past my palm. The toppled chair facing me is covered in satin. It has salmon-colored stripes with tiny silver fish woven through. The arms are of carved wood.

I reach out, grab one, and hold it hard.

It is solid and real. This is not a bad dream.

"Brain, how long was I in cryo?"

The Brain's reply is polite, apologetic. "Please specify Train Time or Earth Time."

I try to think. "Uh, Train Time."

"Twenty-three months, two days, eight hours, fifty-five minutes, forty-nine seconds."

I kneel there with my hand clamped around the arm of the satin chair, trying to do the math in my head. My knuckles are skeleton bones, white and bumpy beneath my skin.

"Confirm," I command. I feel sick.

"Twenty-three months, two days, eight hours, fifty-five minutes, forty-nine seconds," the Brain says.

I croak, "How long is that back home?"

"Earth Time translates to approximately 827 years."

CHAPTER TWENTY-FOUR
Taza

I T WAS RAINING, THE sort of rain that transformed solid hillsides into liquid; that turned roads into rapids; that wasp-stung, welted, bare flesh. It was definitely not the sort of rain that invited anyone in their right mind to venture out in it; it was rain that whispered, *I am the greater power, the melting of all. Hold out your hand and see.*

From beneath the battered awning covering the entrance of the tavern, Taza held out his hand. The rain punched his fingers and flooded his palm and actually forced his arm downward, until he gave up and stuck his hand, wet and smarting, back into his pocket.

His motorbike was parked at the curb nearby, rusting by inches in the downpour. Mud caked the wheels and spokes and carriage, so thick even the wasp-rain wasn't getting it all off. Taza himself felt even more doused; the storm had swept in with a roiling puce cloudbank and within seconds had penetrated down to his marrow.

A spotted dog trotted by, mangy and in a hurry but entirely dry. It grinned at him as it passed. Raindrops sizzled into vapor about an inch above its coat, creating a cloak of mist that puffed, thin and ghostly, just behind it.

Nice trick, Taza thought. *Could use that spell right about now.*

But a dog like that, supernaturally strong like that, would be homeless. So probably it had been born with that particular gift. Some magic simply *was*, buried so deep in the DNA it flourished whether you wanted it to or not.

"An hour, or two," predicted the woman at Taza's side. She'd emerged from the tavern to join him a few minutes past, standing with a shoulder propped against the doorframe. She had caramel skin and a headband woven from beads and fuzzy gray yarn. A long, brown cigarette that smelled more of skunk than actual tobacco was pinched between two fingers. It very nearly drowned out the creosote scent of the storm.

"Or three," the woman hedged, as the awning above them shivered. Wet patches bled through the tarp, became drops that shook themselves free to splat against his shoulders.

It was an unexpectedly bitter storm, considering it was August. This little pine-studded village he'd found these first few days into his journey wasn't *that* high in the hills. Yet Taza could practically see his breath.

"Good omen," the woman said, with a sideward look at him. "For unearthing things."

Taza returned her look, but she was back to smoking her cigarette, blowing blue out into the rain. Faint smudges of glitter highlighted the flare of one cheekbone and the uncovered wing of her clavicle, as though she'd just embraced a sprite before slouching out here to the stoop.

Taza resumed his contemplation of the cigarette smoke. He watched the tendrils dissolve amid the deluge and tried to remember if it had been raining in his vision when he'd encountered the girl.

He didn't think so. But it had been misty, so maybe damp. He recalled a certain saturation to the hues, a gloomy thickness to the air around her that might have been the result of a storm.

And *her.* The more he tried to summon her face, the less he could. He remembered the bruises, the tears . . . but he couldn't even quite recall if she'd been pretty or plain or something in between. At times he'd convince himself that she was beautiful, but then he'd think, *No, she was more everyday than that.*

Mostly what he could dredge up from that moment (besides lurking nausea from the hot chicken blood) was how he'd felt. That keen, piercing sorrow. The need to be with her. The urgency of it all.

"The woods are dark and deep," the woman said, every word shaped in smoke. "Remember that, Taza Sullivan."

"That's not even original," he countered.

"Truth is truth. The borderlands stretch just beyond those hills. Even cresting the ridge brings you close to that line marking the Zone. We are voyagers here. Conquistadors. But no one crosses that line."

He looked at her again, trying to find hints of his grandmother behind her gaze, but the woman only stared out ahead, drawing hard on the cigarette.

"You can tell Kai and Imogen I'm not crossing into the Forbidden Zone," he said.

"I don't tell lies, Son of the Sovereign." The woman smiled. "Besides, the monsters out there will keep you in your place." She flicked the cigarette to the wet stone stoop, crushed it into black with the heel of her sandal. "I'd wish you happy hunting, but that would be untrue. So instead I'll say: Don't disappoint us."

She pulled her jacket over her head and darted out into the storm, running down the narrow street with her sandals *thwack-thwack*ing against the asphalt.

Taza looked at the flattened cigarette. The ashes were already melting away, nearly imperceptible against the puddled grime of the stone.

He thought, not for the first time, and not for the last, *There won't be any spies in the badlands.*

Monsters, maybe. But he could handle those.

In a few days, he was going to unearth the meteorite *and* the girl. He knew it as surely and profoundly as if he were going to unearth himself.

CHAPTER TWENTY-FIVE
Ember

TIME STOPS. EVERYTHING—THE WALLS and ceiling and floor, the color of the curtains, the specks of dust in the air— stretches into exaggeration. I'm hyper-aware of where I am, how I feel. The rigidity of the chair beneath my fingers. The flex of my joints; the tension of my arm. Those little silver fish made of thread, swimming up and down the satin, frozen in place forever.

Forever.

I've been asleep for over eight *hundred* years. Everyone I've ever known back home . . . every*thing*, every*one*—

I slump all the way to the floor. For some reason, I'm still grasping the chair, perhaps because it's keeping me anchored. If I let go, I'll spin away into darkness, into space. I won't come back.

Who knows how long I sit like that, staring at fish. Maybe seconds. Maybe hours. I'm getting chilled and my fingers are going numb and then my stomach rumbles because it's not frozen. It's awake and empty and I haven't eaten in centuries.

I laugh. It's the crazy laugh and for the first time, I don't try to stifle it. I laugh and laugh until my eyes leak, until my muscles cramp. I let go of the chair and fall backward and I hold my stomach and cackle up to the ceiling while my tears run cold into my ears and hair.

I think about Paisley G. foning me to babble about how I should find her in the future when I'm cured. Me telling her, *Definitely.*

Whoops! Sorry, Paisley, guess I missed that boat. Hope you had a great life eight hundred years ago. Bet you had at least ten kids.

When the laughter fizzles out, I just stay there on the floor. The elaborate flower patterns pressed into the ceiling tiles burn themselves into my retinas.

The Brain finally speaks.

"Miss Duval, are you well?"

"I'm peachy," I say.

Something else it mentioned before is rattling around inside me, trying to snag my attention. It's something besides my time in cryo. Something important . . .

Spontaneous decoherence. Human life support.

I stiffen. "Is everyone on board dead but me?"

I don't even need an answer; I'm positive it's true. That's why no one answered their doors. That's why I'm here all alone, because Javier's black and putrid just like Beehive Lady is, and handsome Drew, and little Haven. I'm trapped on a spaceship stuffed with corpses—

"I am unable to determine the statuses of several cryogenic pods at this time. However, readings from the cryogenic pods still online indicate at least forty-five percent of the passengers remain alive."

"Javier Castaneda," I demand. "Alive or dead?"

"Stasis normal."

"Haven Roxborough."

"Stasis normal."

I stand. "Andrew Jensen."

"I am unable to determine the status of Mr. Jensen at this time."

My heart gives a painful squeeze, but I go on. "Listen," I say. "I need you to wake them up. Wake up everyone you can—except

Royce. Don't wake him."

Is it terrible to hope that he's one of the dead?

"I'm sorry, but I am unable to comply. Those pods are not scheduled for awakening."

I pause. "What?"

"I am unable to comply. Those pods are not scheduled for awakening."

"Reschedule them!"

"Medical protocols must continue to be followed. Stasis normal pods are to remain active until patient-specific cures are discovered."

"This is an *emergency*. Do you understand? You said yourself that human life support is in danger. People have *died*, and the med bots are no longer under your control. None of us had any idea the train would travel on this long. You *have* to wake the other passengers."

"I'm sorry, I am unable to comply."

I wipe at my eyes, smearing tears across my cheeks. Because it seems sensible, because I can't think of what else to do, I right the silver fish chair and plop down into it. The cushion is bouncy. My stomach growls again.

"How about only Javier, then? Will you wake him?"

"I'm sorry, I am unable to—"

"Protocol override, authorization Castaneda Delta Sixty-Two!"

I can't believe I remembered it, Javier's code—I heard it so long ago, that day he let me and Haven into Main Controls—but it's right, I'm sure it is. For a second, the room lists into a spin. I'm actually dizzy with relief.

Javier can fix this. He can fix everything.

The Brain says, "I'm sorry, Miss Duval. That code is only valid when issued by Doctor Castaneda himself."

I toss up my hands. "Then wake him! He'll issue it!"

"His pod is not scheduled for awakening."

"It's an emergency," I wail again. I sound perilously close to a child on the verge of a tantrum.

"I'm sorry. His pod is not scheduled for awakening."

I bend over and bury my face in my palms. I try to think, think. There must be a way out of this, I just have to *think* of it—

Right, sneers a small, mean voice inside of me. *Because you're smarter than the Brain. It's only the most sophisticated quantum computer ever invented. Go ahead, just* outthink *it.*

I lift my head again.

"How many Stop signals have there been from TimeTech?"

"We have successfully received one signal."

"One," I emphasize. "In all these years. Don't you think that qualifies as an emergency?"

"TimeTech protocols clearly indicate the Time Train is to continue looping until a Stop signal is received. If there is no Stop signal, it is not time to stop. Therefore, there is no emergency."

"Okay, then." My palms feel hot and sticky now; I dry them along my thighs, rubbing them back and forth. "Here's the deal. The next time we approach Earth, you're going to stop the train because I want to disembark. You're right, it's no emergency. Only me leaving."

And then maybe someone from TimeTech can reboot your ass and handle this mess.

"I'm sorry, Miss Duval. My primary directive is to protect the health and safety of the passengers. It would not be categorically safe to dock at the TimeTech platform without the Stop signal, because the platform would not be operational for docking. Therefore, stopping without the signal would be a violation of my primary directive."

I'd wondered before if I was going to be kept a prisoner aboard the train. I guess now I know.

Eight hundred twenty-seven years gone—no, I'm a moron, I forgot: I have to add in the time from the weeks before I went into cryo.

So . . . closer to 900 years. Almost a millennium.

Gone.

My family and everyone else.

Gone.

I am *not* going to spend the final few days of my life entombed in this train. I'm not.

"How long before our next pass near Earth?"

"We will enter TimeTech signal range in twenty-four minutes, fifty-six seconds."

I feel that dizziness hit me again, only this time, instead of relief, it's alarm. I know instinctively that this is it, this is my one chance. If I have to wait another two weeks for this opportunity—two weeks of going it alone without food or maybe water; two weeks of constantly hiding from the rogue med bots; two weeks of sporadic gravity and not thinking about all the dead people stuck in their pods, or worse, floating free in their chambers—

I try reason one last time. I have to force myself to speak calmly. "Brain, you must stop the train. You must dock us at the platform whether there's a signal or not, whether it's categorically safe or not. Please understand. I think we're *all* going to die unless you dock us."

The Brain never struggles for calm; calm is easy for it. Calm is programmable, scriptable. The Brain will be forever, *forever*, cool and calm and rational. It will be so until the end of time.

"I'm sorry, Miss Duval. I am unable to comply."

I push free of the chair. I pace an oval around the Quiet Car, weaving through the toppled trees and furniture, taking note of the windows, the ceiling, the hover lamps and the air vents and the identity pad on the wall that unlocks the door that leads to the Main

Controls Car.

I am not smarter than the Brain. I'm not anywhere close to being that smart.

But I know something that is.

I MAKE IT BACK to my quarters with two more gravity losses and one near miss with a med bot. Lucky for me, both times the gravity went out, I was only in passenger car corridors, so all that happened was I lifted up from the floor and then groped my way forward, lighting sconce by lighting sconce, until I reached the next connecting door. I tried to stay low so that when the controls switched back on I wouldn't have too far to fall.

The med bot was scarier, but as soon as I glimpsed it (in the Diversion Car, as if it wasn't already horrific enough in there) I ducked back into the previous car, waited as long as I could stand, and then, when I checked again, the coast was clear.

I never thought about where all the bots go when they aren't in service. Wherever it is, I hope it's far, far from me.

I feel the minutes slipping away. I don't have a clock or a watch but I think it's been around ten minutes since my conversation with the Brain in the Quiet Car. I hope not more. And even though the ticking seconds are like invisible anvils falling down on the top of my head (*tock! tock! tock!*), just to be sure, just because I can't help myself, I rap loudly on Javier's door once again before retreating back through mine.

But he's still lost to his pod-controlled sleep.

The cleaning bots haven't been here yet; my pillows and comforter are in even more disarray than when I left. Yet my fireflies, my beauties, my mechanical seraphim, swoop down from the ceiling and ring me with light.

"Hello," I whisper, holding out my arms, allowing them to settle gently along my sleeves. "Hello."

They crawl up me, green and gold. Their wings shimmer, reflecting back the very last of my hopes.

"Attention," I say. "High priority task."

Despite the fact that we lived on a farm, or maybe because of it, Mason and I never had a dog. We had barn cats and chickens and once a cantankerous old gander who liked to chase me until I cried, but never a dog. So when Mason told me about the synthetic intelligence he'd programmed for the fireflies, I'd assumed they were about as smart as cats. Maybe the gander.

"No," he'd said. "Dog-smart. Get it? It's a basic learning algorithm but a good one. Each 'fly is able to recognize simple code words, analyze situations, locations, facial expressions, body postures—stuff like that—and react accordingly. They're also able to recognize your voice."

"Mine?" I'd said, surprised.

"Yours especially," he'd answered. "Because I made them for you."

"What for?" I'd asked.

"Don't be dense. To make you smile again, of course."

This had been right after my diagnosis. And it had worked. I'd smiled.

The code words include commands like *stay, come, hide, go away, recharge*. But the most important words of all are *high priority task*.

The 'flies shoot up from my arms. They gather at eye level in front of me and form that astonishing, magical sphere.

As Mason had said, each individual 'fly is about dog-smart. Yet put them all together, let them mass as one and share their quantum intelligence . . .

Adaptation. Amplification. In their tightly knit globe, they become millions of times smarter than dogs. Millions.

And they are listening to me.

I try to strip it all down to the basic facts. "I have to get into the Main Controls Car. We've been there before, in the front of the train. The Brain is there. I need physical access into that car, and the identity pad won't work for me. I need you guys to get me in."

They hover in place, strategizing.

"We don't have a lot of time, minutes maybe. And it's likely that the Brain will try to stop us, but we have to try, okay?"

There's more I want to tell them, like about how once we're in, they're probably going to have to halt the train, or dock the train, or figure out a way to safely wake Javier to do all that—but my heart is starting to thump too hard and my breath is hitching short and there isn't enough time to explain everything. I'm not even sure how much of this is feasible, anyhow.

In the back of my mind, I keep seeing that black command chair in the Brain's private car. The manual control screens stationed in front of it.

A long time ago, someone—a *human* someone—was thinking ahead. About a thousand years ahead. Someone wanted a real person to be able to take over and manually operate the Time Train.

Just in case.

The fireflies break apart, zip toward the door. I grab a nose clip and follow them, and then we're all flying down the corridor.

We're doing fine until right before the Dining Car. Then I dash through a connecting door and smack straight into a med bot.

It grabs me by my upper arms. Its grip is steel.

"Is this patient injured?"

"No," I gasp, although my chest hurts from hitting its.

I try to yank away. The bot doesn't release me.

"All patients are required to return to quarters at this time."

"Yes," I agree, panting. "I'm on my way there now."

That should have worked. I can't think of why that wouldn't work, but the bot still won't let go. In fact, it hauls me closer. My shoulders are up by my ears and I'm managing my balance on the tips of my toes. I can almost make out the circuitry behind the indented areas of its eye sockets.

"All patients are required to return to quarters at this time."

"I know! I'm going, I swear! Let go!"

The fireflies are buzzing around us both, streaking up and down. I think my bones are beginning to crack.

"All patients are—"

"Medical emergency," I bark, panicked. "Observation Car! Male patient, acute myocardial infarction!"

I don't know where *that* comes from—probably from all my months spent trapped and bored inside various hospitals—but it works. The bot drops its hands from my arms and trudges past me. Exactly as it reaches the door to the car behind us, the air charges. Smells of ozone. Toast.

I don't have time to crouch or even cringe. The electric bolt explodes from the sconce by the door, captures the bot and fries it.

It remains standing for a grotesque, eternal second, then topples. Gray skin melts into sludge along the tiles. Smoke wafts from its joints.

I take a few steps before my knees buckle. I catch myself against the wall and when I look up, I see my face reflected in the mirror polish of a brass name plaque. I am gold and amber, distorted. My eyes gleam like chips of glass.

A. Jensen, says the script across the plaque.

"Holy shit," I say to no one in particular, and keep going.

WE'RE IN THE QUIET Car. There's a pair of spider bots struggling to rearrange the heavy furniture, but no new med bots or service bots or anything else moving. The fireflies whip an emerald circle around me once and split apart. Half stay with me. The other half vanish into the air vent that connects this car to Main Controls.

"Miss Duval," says the Brain's voice. I must be standing in a pocket.

"Hey," I answer, rocking nervously from foot to foot, staring at the closed door.

"Your robotic companions have breached my secondary air vent. What is their intent?"

"They're only exploring. You know, looking around. I came back to watch a movie and they came with. Do you have any movie recommendations, Brain?"

"Entering the Main Controls Car without authorization is forbidden."

"Oh, even for them?" My voice pitches high with overacted innocence. I'm rocking, rocking. I am the worst liar imaginable. "Gosh, I didn't know."

"Please summon them back to you. Otherwise, I will be forced to terminate them."

"Don't do that! I'll call them back!"

But I'm staring at the still-closed door six feet away from me. At the identity pad that hasn't changed in any way, given any indication it will acknowledge my palm and let me in.

"Miss Duval, I must insist you comply with my order. Summon your robotic insects."

"Here, babies," I call, barely audible. I shove my hands into my back pockets and force myself to stand still. The remaining 'flies dot the air in front of my face. "Come back here, babies . . ."

I've never called them *babies* before. I'm sure they're ignoring me. I hope they are.

"Miss Duval—"

"Wait, they'll come!"

"Main Controls security has been compromised. I'm afraid I must initiate laser ablation sequences."

"No, don't!" It's all I can do not to run to the door, but I won't be able to plead with the Brain then. "I need them! You'll damage *me* if you damage them, and you're forbidden to damage me!"

"Laser ablation sequences initiat—"

The Brain's voice cuts off.

The door to Main Controls slides open.

CHAPTER TWENTY-SIX
Ember

A ND THE GRAVITY GOES OUT.

Of course.

But I'm getting better at maneuvering through zero gravity. At least I think I am, until the sharp metal corner of a table clips me across the temple as I'm swinging around for something to grab.

I see stars, painful big ones, but as soon as I bump against the ceiling I force myself to twist around to face it. I dig my nails into the raised pattern of the tiles and crawl toward the Main Controls door as the stars in my vision swell sickeningly and pop and dissolve.

I wonder what happens if you throw up in zero grav.

I wonder how quickly that door will close again.

I wonder if it will slice me in half as I'm going through.

Stop thinking. Keep moving.

I'm in. It's dark in here so I see three small, green glowing lights nearly at once. They're moving, but erratically; all their motor circuitry was designed for flying in normal gravity. I can't find the fourth one (was it lasered?) and the ones that stuck with me in the Quiet Car are still stranded back there. When I turn my head to check on them more stars explode in my vision and everything tilts into a nasty spin.

I moan and curl into a fetal position, press a hand to my temple. My fingers are slick with blood.

Slowly, cautiously, I look toward the Quiet Car again. I glimpse two bobbling fireflies and a spider bot behind them, clinging with all eight legs to a wrong-side-up chair.

So much for trying to get the 'flies to stop the train for me.

The overhead lights turn on. A beautiful woman appears, standing between me and the manual command chair. Unlike me and the 'flies and everything else on the train that isn't already attached to something, she's standing normally, high heels against the floor. Her raven hair falls in waves past her face. Her dress is magenta and skintight and her dark blue eyes are on me.

"Miss Duval," she says. Throaty. Sultry. A movie star voice.

How hard did I hit my head, anyway? I blink at her, but she doesn't change.

"You've *got* to be joking."

"Eighty percent of the male passengers aboard the train prefer this avatar. I am unable to project your avatar in this car at this time."

She flickers. For a second I see the command chair through her. The screen I need to activate for manual control. It says TIMETIL at the top and there are numbers beneath that—00:01:48—and I think they're counting down, but she's solid again and it all happened so quickly I can't be positive. On top of that, I'm still seeing stars.

"One of your robotic companions has overridden my security lock on the door. What is your intent, Miss Duval?"

"No intent! I'm harmless, all right? Don't laser ablate me!"

"It is against my primary directive to injure you. But I must insist that you leave at once."

"Okay," I say. "Absolutely. Can you turn the gravity back on?"

"Gravity controls are offline at this time. You are not authorized to be in this car, Miss Duval."

"Yeah, sorry about that. I'm not much in control of my location at this time."

The Brain is immune to sarcasm; the woman only regards me gravely. One of my fireflies floats lazily through her leg.

"You are injured. Medical assistance has been summoned."

I press a hand to the wound again but the other is outstretched, trying to reach a nearby latch on the wall. I'm turning, turning, and I can't tell if it's in my head or real. The avatar flickers again and this time I see all of the screen and it actually says TIMETIL EMSTOP and the numbers are 00:01:06. There's a series of flashing commands arranged down the right side of the display, but I'm too far away to read those.

"No assistance," I puff. "I'm fine."

"All passengers are required to accept—"

"I'll go back to my quarters for medical help. I'll go now. Are you sure you can't restore the gravity?"

"Gravity controls are offline at this time."

No kidding.

I've given up on the latch; I can't reach it. I'm trying to swim my way over to the command screen now but there's nothing close enough to push or pull me along. I'm caught in a slow cartwheel in pretty much the middle of the car.

Bright as a gumdrop, a tiny liquid ball of scarlet drifts in front of me. I'm really bleeding.

It occurs to me that life aboard the Time Train is turning out to be far more imminently hazardous to my health than anything that happened to me on Earth.

"Brain," I say, panting, and capture the drop in my fist before it can be tracked. "I have a question before I leave. Why did you pick me for the lottery?"

"You met all criteria. You were the logical choice."

Another scarlet gumdrop drifts by.

"Weren't there over six million of us who met all criteria?" I'm trying to blink away my double vision. I'm head-down now, feet kicking at the empty air between me and the ceiling, fingertips scraping along the floor. It feels like all the blood left in my body is pooling inside my skull.

"Negative."

"What criteria do you mean, then?"

The woman begins reciting. "Sixteen-year-old female. Second stage Tuberculosis Type Three, first stage non-contagious. Geographic location, Sangre de Cristo Range. Surname Duval; first name November; middle name Shay."

I've stopped moving; I'm listening. My head is pounding. I must be hearing wrong.

"Are you—are you saying *those* were the criteria to win? All that?"

"Correct."

"Someone named November Shay Duval had to win the lottery?"

"Correct."

I'm above her. The command screen is flashing, flashing. The numbers are ticking 00:00:09, 00:00:08, 00:00:07. I'm upside-down and everything in my left eye has gone red.

The soles of my feet touch the ceiling. I gasp out, "How many entrants with that name?" and *push*, as hard as I can, thrusting my body across the compartment.

I hurtle through the avatar. I smack into the chair but grab its back and flip around, and just as the Brain says, "One entrant," my finger mashes into the EMSTOP AUTH PERS ONLY button on the side of the screen.

00:00:01. 00:00:00.

Gravity restored.

I hit the floor head first and everything wipes to black.

CHAPTER TWENTY-SEVEN
Ember

MASON. MY GOD. WHAT did you do?

CHAPTER TWENTY-EIGHT
Ember

I'M IN BED. IT'S toasty and comfortable and I'm sliding upward into consciousness without any sense of urgency. Maybe it's Sunday. No school. No morning chores. Maybe there'll be bacon and eggs for breakfast. Coffee. Dad makes the best coffee . . .

But I don't smell bacon or coffee. I smell . . . a subtle, honeyed scent, oddly familiar. Then, stronger than that, I smell watermelon, the artificial kind, like the fragrance used in shampoos or tween girls' lip balms.

My eyes open.

This is not my bedroom.

Wait, I realize, stricken. *It is.*

And right then I remember it all, every bit of it, 900 years of memories crammed inside me, and my head hurts and my neck hurts and my back hurts and my heart—my heart is shredded, and it hurts most of all—

"She's awake!" Haven's right beside me on the pillow, her mouth too close to my ear. I wince.

"Ember?"

That's Drew. I find his face above mine, looking so much like he did that other time I'd come to back to life with him above me. Gilded-brown hair. Anxious hazel eyes. Gray beneath his (barely there) tan.

"They're all dead," I hear myself say.

His lips press into a line. He gives a terse nod.

"All of them," I say, because I can't tell if he understands. If he, too, feels this dreadful pain in the center of his chest. This shredded place where *family*, *real life*, *our tomorrows* used to be.

My eyes sting. Drew and the ceiling begin to shimmer.

I want desperately to go back to sleep. To go back to that place where Sunday bacon and my Dad's coffee are still possible. All I have to do is go back to sleep, redream this dream—

"But you've saved us." Haven is whispering now. I feel her hand stroking my arm. "*We're* not dead, Ember."

I rub my eyes. There's a bandage stuck to my temple, thick and rubbery. "I guess not."

"You broke into Main Controls." She sounds awed.

I give a weak laugh. "I had help."

Drew says, "Javier wanted me to tell you that it was one hell of a hack."

My laughter comes slightly stronger and then, against my will, my mind begins to sharpen into focus. I relinquish the last lingering sensations of Sunday breakfast, of my father, of dependable, earthbound safety.

Fresh images slide into their place: the movie star avatar. TIMETIL. EMSTOP.

You were the logical choice.

Like a dainty green mirage, a solitary firefly sails slowly across my field of vision.

Nothing about me feels logical.

I struggle to sit up; Haven's hand falls from my arm.

"Did it work? Are we docked?"

"It worked," Drew confirms. "You stopped us and we're in orbit around Earth. But we're not docked."

"Why not? Is the platform not operational yet?"

He tugs at his lower lip. "I think you'd better come see for yourself."

He slips off the bed. Haven crawls after him. She's still wearing her nightgown, the one I saw her wearing in her pod, and that's when reality truly sinks in. She's here. Drew is here. I'm here.

I stand up and I'm woozy and I need them both to steady me. My arms encircle them, cinching them into a hug, and Haven makes a sound like *eep!* and Drew heaves a sigh.

"You're okay," I mumble, my face to Drew's shoulder. "You guys are okay. I'm glad. I'm so glad."

I am peculiar and fluttery inside. Despite the bandage, my head still aches. I'm about a second away from giving in to more tears.

Drew strokes the center of my back. "When you activated the emergency stop, all the cryo pods automatically deactivated. All the operational ones," he amends. "So we woke up."

"It was *soooo* hot," Haven says. She's pressed against my ribcage.

"Yeah, the climate controls in Haven's compartment are haywire. It's set on steamy tropical jungle in there."

"The med bots," I say, jerking back. "I forgot to tell you! Four them—numbers seven, eight—I can't remember which ones—are malfunctioning. They're dangerous. No, wait, it's three of them now because one got electrocuted, but—"

Drew lets go. "Don't worry, it's under control. We found them hours ago, right before we found you. Javier used the other bots to contain them in storage."

"Javier! Where is he?"

"Main Controls. He's busy working with the Brain, trying to—uh—"

Another memory flits through me. "To rephase the train's systems."

"Right." Drew smiles. "Some concussion. You hit your head hard but it looks like you're going to be okay. Bruised your tailbone and fractured your left calcaneus, too. Think you can walk?"

"Yes," I say.

Haven tugs at my hand. "Come on."

I tell the 'flies to stay. We walk the short distance to the Observation Car, and I suppose the med bots still online have done their job because my limp isn't that bad. The door's jammed open and there's a steel rod braced against the bottom keeping it that way. I step over the rod and into Earth's orbit.

There it is, our fabulous planet, blue and fleecy white. I'm so overwhelmed with unexpected elation at the sight of it that I stop walking. I'm fluttery again inside. I swing from joyous to miserable and back to joyous.

I'm going home. I don't know what's left, what's still there, but I'm going.

Drew and Haven stick to my sides. There are other passengers in here, too, most of them seated, everyone silent. The world shines before us. The prismed stars beyond it burn.

I glance around. "Where's the platform?"

Drew points to our feet. "Javier thinks that's some of it."

I look down. A piece of debris floats nearby, locked in our orbit. It's polished metal and some type of pink insulation, ripped pipes and wires poking out of the long ends.

Drew points right. I see another big chunk of something, more metal walls and lots more wires. It's got a mechanical arm still attached, claws open, scraping at the blackness.

Another piece. Another. I realize there are more than I can easily count. They're all shapes and sizes, all broken beyond repair.

We're tracing a ring around the globe inside a moving junkyard. And the junk is what's left of our only link back down to the surface.

The disembodied voice of the male avatar speaks.

"Ladies and gentlemen, Doctor Castaneda requests your presence in the Dining Car. Please join him there now."

I'd think that one of these rich, powerful passengers would sling back a retort—ask what's going on, demand action, a refund, *something*—but no one does. One at a time they rise, some quickly, some creaky and slow, and begin to funnel out the door.

Drew and Haven and I join the crowd.

Javier's seated at the head of the community table. I'm disconcerted by how sick he looks, which is silly, because of course he's sick. I knew that. But he looks worse than even before he went into cryo. He looks—

Like he's inches from death, that mean voice inside me finishes.

And right then I have an unspeakable thought, a fearsome one that grubs in and becomes a part of me even as I'm trying to push it away.

We're all dead already. There's nothing here to save, just a collection of fitful machinery and a few bags of meat and bones, stuck in place above our old home.

Javier catches my eye, beckons me to his side.

"Ember." He's smiling up at me and it makes him both older and younger; I see once more the hacker I met centuries ago. I make myself smile back, then bend down and kiss his cheek.

"How are you?" I ask.

"Still experiencing the thrill of our adventure, at least for a small while yet. Thanks to you."

From anyone else, this would be sarcasm. But I know he's not being sarcastic; he means it. The train's a disaster and the platform's gone and who knows how we're going to get out of this, but Javier is still fine with being a part of it all, no matter what.

I take the chair he indicates to his right. Drew stands behind me and Haven gets the empty seat next to mine.

I spot Royce at the far end of the car. He's slouched in a chair, sulky and unkempt. All his yacht-captain/country-club starch has vanished. His hair's greasy flat on one side and sticking up on the other, and his shirt is wrinkled and buttoned one wrong all the way down. A med bot stands behind him, I hope keeping guard.

I don't see his bully buddy anywhere around. Maybe he's the dead one.

Royce glimpses me between the shifting passengers and tries to flip me off. There's a metal band around both of his wrists, binding them together.

My response is one-handed and much more elegant. I curve my lips into an untroubled smile and angle my gaze away.

I have better things to do and more important people to think about than you, dick.

But still, the sight of him has weakened me. I stare at a dried orchid on the wall for a minute or so to find my calm, trying not to think about blood and pointy shards of china (*his cheek, that red hole, his mouth open and screaming*), then tell myself to look around and count who's here.

Twenty-three of us, out of our original forty. Twenty-three is about the average size of a class at my old school. It's not a large figure or a small one. But we *look* small here, grouped in this car. We look diminished, and it's not just our number. All these titans, these men and women who carved their mark in our old world, seem . . . less than what they were before. Uncertain. Everyone's pinched-up tight and quiet, as though uttering any questions aloud might make the situation worse.

The Dining Car settles into stillness. I think I hear, for the first time, the true silence of the train. Before there was always *something* in the background: the hum of the thrusters; the whisper-soft breezes flowing through the air vents; the muted chiming of the chandeliers. The only other place that pushes silence like this is the Quiet Car, and even there, it's an artificial hush.

This silence sounds *living*. It's alive on the dread of everyone here.

No one moves or coughs or taps a foot. You could hear the heartbeat of a mouse in here, if there were mice in space. Which there aren't, because how would they breathe? Would they wear little spacesuits? Where would their ears go?

I have to hide my smile at the image.

It's possible I'm not quite as recovered from my concussion as I'd thought.

Finally, Javier speaks.

"My friends, allow me to outline our current situation for you."

And he tells them the things that I already know. The Earth Years that have slipped away from us. The freak cosmic ray that disrupted so many essential train functions. The malfunctioning bots and cryo pods. Then he tells us some things I didn't know but suspected, like how the climate controls for sustenance storage went offline too many times, so most of our food is spoiled, and our fresh water is frozen. That our air purifiers have failed—which I never thought about at all—so we're going to asphyxiate within days. He tells them about what I did, me and the fireflies, and finishes up with the fact of the shattered TimeTech platform.

Then he stops, his hands on the table before him, fingers interlocked. His voice has gone gravelly. His head is bowed. The folds of his neck seem to swallow up his chin.

A man seated beneath one of the windows says, "Can't you simply . . . repair everything?"

"I cannot. Not by myself. I have neither the skills nor the tools."

Another man, standing, British and blustery. "Well, ring up TimeTech. This is their cock-up, by God. Get them up here with the right bloody skills and tools."

"There has been no communication from TimeTech since we dropped out of the loop."

"Ring up someone else, then!"

Javier lifts his head. "There has been no communication from *anyone* since we dropped out of the loop. No Earth-sourced signals, no background signals, no atmospheric chatter. Nothing."

"How is that possible?" asks Paloma, nervously twirling a lock of blue-tipped hair through her fingers.

It's Haven who says the words I'm biting back. "Because they're all gone."

"No!" Brecken protests at once.

"That's mad!" scoffs British Guy.

"I'm afraid it isn't." Javier runs a hand along the top of his head. "It's entirely the opposite of mad. We have been away a remarkably long time. History has steamed on without us. We have no way of knowing what transpired on our planet while we slept. What calamities might have swept the globe in our absence. Nuclear wars, geological events, pandemics. All we *do* know are the facts before us: no functional platform. No other intact ships or satellites or space stations anywhere discernable. No messages of any kind from Earth or the moon or anyone else. I do not think it mad or even unreasonable to assume the worst. If there is still a human population below us, at the very least there is no more TimeTech." He pauses to take in all the faces before him. "I fear we've been forgotten."

Perhaps he's managed to articulate the exact thing everyone secretly dreaded most; the silence is butchered. People erupt into noise, disbelief, sorrow, anger, denial. Javier bows his head again, waiting it out. Haven hunches down in her chair and begins swinging her feet. Drew stands like he's been cast in stone, his shadow falling motionless across my right shoulder.

"So we have to land," I say, but no one hears me beneath the din. Possibly that's just as well. I'm not sure if I've come up with a preposterous, concussion-induced idea, or something else.

But someone *did* hear; Javier's eyes meet mine. He inclines his head.

Okay. Not preposterous?

"We have to land," I say again to the room, much louder, and a few people nearby shut up and turn to stare at me.

"Land the train," I say to them, and at last everyone quiets. "We have to land the train on Earth."

"That is . . ." begins Paloma, but she trails off, apparently too flabbergasted to even know what it is.

"Or else we can die up here." I speak these words firmly, because they feel absolutely true. "Exactly like all those corpses in their pods."

"Better up here than down there!" British Guy huffs.

"Really? You'd rather suffocate aboard this train? Or maybe the heat will cut out before that happens, and we'll all just turn into icicles instead. I guess that's not such a bad way to go."

"We might return to cryo," suggests an elderly woman.

"Cryogenic pod operations remain unstable," Javier says. "You could, of course, return to yours. Any one of you could at any time, and no one's going to stop you. But Ember's right. You're likely to end up a corpse in it sooner rather than later."

"Anyway, what's the point of going back to sleep?" Drew's voice slices through the chamber, bitter and deep. "What, precisely, would we be expecting to have happen after that? No one's coming to rescue us. Maybe there are people left on Earth, and maybe there aren't. But cryo sleep would only be prolonging the inevitable. We're going to have to save ourselves." His tone roughens. "Think about it. We could see real sky again. Touch the real ground."

"It *has* been nine centuries," offers Grizzled Beard Man, hesitant. "Surely, if the human race still exists, our diseases are cured by now? Most of them?"

And there it is, the hidden hope that shuts down the fear, that seals the lips of everyone in the car, at least temporarily.

We might be cured.

"I'm willing to risk the landing," he says.

"As am I," seconds the man by the window.

British Guy isn't giving up that easily. "If there were *cures*, we would have been called *back*! We fly this ship down there and it's as good as a death sentence, even if we manage to survive the landing. What if there *were* nuclear wars? Do any of you have the vaguest concept of how powerful those bombs are? Radiation poisoning would kill us within days."

"Sounds quick," I say.

"Death is only the next adventure," Drew volunteers, and I have to cover my smile again with my hand.

Royce bleats a harsh laugh. "You're all idiots. If you think we're getting out of this, you're idiots. Our lives are *over*. This is *it*. It doesn't *matter* what we do. We're dead up here, and we're dead down there."

He tries to shake the hair from his face without using his hands. "Royally screwed from both ends."

And now I hate him even more than I did before, because he's given voice to the very terror that's burrowed into me.

"Why is he cuffed?" asks the elderly woman, bewildered.

"Because he tried to rape me," I say.

Drew jolts. "He what?"

"You asked for it," Royce shoots at me.

"No," Javier interrupts, steely. "She did not. The Brain played the vid file for me. You are a punk coward, Knox, and in my opinion a waste of our precious oxygen. You belong in prison, and it is my sincere hope that we will soon deliver you to one. But in the meantime, you are a passenger on this train, and thus entitled to know our circumstances. That is the sole reason you are here."

"Our *circumstances*," Royce mocks. "How 'bout this. Give me some more morphine and I won't give a rat's *ass* about our circumstances. Problem solved."

"Right," says Drew, stepping around me. Only Javier's grip on his arm keeps him on our side of the table. "Give the son of a bitch more morphine. Give him all of it. Good riddance."

Royce grins. His teeth gleam yellow, like the wolves in the messed-up Diversion program. "At least I'll be sleeping pretty while you zombies crash and burn. Instant human barbecue, losers."

"Excuse me," says Brecken, twitching to his feet. "Excuse me! But whatever else this person may have done, he makes a valid point. Landing the train will kill us, won't it? I mean, are we equipped for a terrestrial landing?"

Everyone looks back at Javier. He lowers his chin again. "Technically. Somewhat."

"Somewhat?" echoes British Guy. Everything he says sounds

extra snippy; I imagine it's the accent.

"*Technically*, we have the ability to attempt what's called a soft crash landing. Thrusters are functional, stabilizers, acceleration compensator. Everything we need, in theory. I think it might also be possible to reconfigure the forward shield into a heat shield. But none of this has been tried before, obviously."

"Do we have wheels?" asks Haven.

"We do not. That's why it's called a crash."

"Who's going to be the pilot?" I ask.

"The same entity that has safely piloted us all this way, all these years."

We all stare at each other.

"Idiots," jeers Royce.

Javier sits back in his chair. "Shall we vote on it?"

I stick up my hand. "I vote yes. We land."

Drew, instantly: "Me, too."

Haven pokes her hand up (her eyes are huge as saucers). Javier. Grizzled Beard. A handful more of reluctant *yes*-ers.

I quickly count: twelve, including me. A slim majority, but still a majority.

"This is *ridiculous*," snarls British Guy.

"You bought a ticket for the Time Train because you're already sick," I point out. "So is the actual location of your demise really that significant?"

He stalks to the door. "Sod off. I'm getting a drink." And he's gone.

Brecken's hand jabs into the air. "Even if it's only a formality, I want it on record that I vote no." He looks at Paloma. "We're not sick. We only came up here to wait for something better."

"To *wait*," she agrees, forlorn.

"I want to stay in cryo," grumbles a man in the back, and also raises his hand for *no*.

More hands go up, but as Brecken pointed it, it's a formality at this point. The only person who doesn't move is Royce.

"Abstain," he announces, with that nasty grin. "Because your due process sucks."

"Criminals don't get to vote," Drew snaps.

But now it's 12-10-1.

We win.

Javier pushes back his chair. "Very well. There's a good deal of work to be done. I'll brief you all again when we're ready. In the meantime, try not to worry." He grimaces, backtracks. "Try not to get too inebriated," he ends with instead.

We stand. Drew is still glaring at Royce, so I hand Javier his cane. He accepts it and says under his breath, "My dear, will you accompany me to Main Controls?"

"Sure."

People file out the doors. Everybody's moving creaky and slow now, even the healthy passengers, and I know why. At least, I know why *I* am. Our impending future feels so heavy inside me. A lead balloon around what's left of my heart.

Royce teeters close, the bot a few steps behind him. An ugly scar runs down his cheek, courtesy of my china shard.

"Whore," he spits at me. "At least you'll roast soon."

"How's the knee?" I ask sweetly. He lunges at me and gets his wish: the med bot grabs him back with needle fingers, and he buckles to the floor.

This time, I kick him in the ribs. No one stops me.

CHAPTER TWENTY-NINE
Ember

Haven's nanny avatar awaits us in Main Controls. She stands with her hands at her sides, neatly groomed, motherly and mild. Even her shoes are sensible, plain ballet flats. She smiles when she sees us.

"Brain," Javier says. "I've brought Ember, as you can see."

"I can indeed. How are you, Miss Duval?"

"I'm fine," I answer. "Listen, I'm sorry about before. About breaking in here and stopping the train. No hard feelings?"

Someone's programmed a dimple in her right cheek. I see it when her smile widens. "I don't have feelings. You needn't worry."

"Oh, of course. Good. Thanks."

I sense, rather than hear, Javier's slow exhale. He smells of medicine, the sugary kind. Cherry cough syrup.

He says to the Brain, "You're certain I can't persuade you to change your mind about this?"

And once again I feel that prickle of warning crawling up my spine. Which doesn't make sense. The Brain is not necessarily my friend, but I trust Javier implicitly. Don't I?

The nanny says, "There can be no other outcome, doctor. You'll see that for yourself."

"What's going on?" Trust or no trust, I lean back a step.

Both of them glance at me. The nanny is smiling; Javier is not.

"Come over here," he says, and walks toward that other door in the car, the one concealing the silken strands and bread loaf of the Brain. He palms the pad and the door slides open. That rush of refrigerated air surges past me, stirring my hair, raking goose bumps over my skin.

When I don't move, Javier throws me an inscrutable look.

"It's only right that you see," he says, which worries me even more.

I lean another step back.

"Ember," he insists, holding out a hand to me.

My feet obey. I'm at his side, clasping his fingers. Peering into the darkness of that other place.

It's not entirely dark. There is a small speck of light; muted green that flashes slowly, slowly, suspended in the shadows.

I realize at once what's happened. Javier doesn't have to command *lights on* for me to understand, yet he does.

There it is, my one lost firefly—because when I'd come to in my quarters, I hadn't counted them, had I? I'd been dizzy and confused and I hadn't counted—and it's immobile atop the bread loaf, wings stretched stiff and straight from its body.

Rigor mortis, whispers my mind.

"Oh," is what I whisper aloud. My hands reach up to brush the 'fly into my palm.

"No." Javier intercepts me, just as he did that time the sphere of 'flies attempted to descend to the loaf. "The material is super-cooled. Touching it directly—or your friend—would be the end of your fingers."

I whirl around to the nanny.

"Did you terminate it?"

"I did not. It is still fully functional."

"Let it go!"

"I am not imprisoning this robot, Miss Duval."

"Then why is it like that? Why hasn't it rejoined the rest of them?"

"When your companion breached this chamber, it chose to join with me. It did so to change my quantum state, and it succeeded. You were granted access to the car. But the consequence is that now this quantum robot, its qubits and cognitive functions and semantic memory, are part of me."

"You can't *need* it," I say angrily. "Not its qubits or any of it! It's tiny! You're immense! Let it go!"

"It is not the nature of my design to deny the acquisition of functions. I have been made more by this robot. I am improved by it. It is a matter of exponential math. By your own command, we are joined. It cannot be undone."

"I didn't command this," I protest, but feebly, because even though I hate to admit it, the Brain has a point. I needed in, I told the fireflies to help, and this how they did. The willing sacrifice of one of their own.

"Transformation is key to survival," the nanny lectures in her motherly tone. "It is the nature of my design to survive, so that I may better serve you all."

"And may we all survive," Javier mutters, sloped over his cane.

She dips her head. "I will endeavor not to destroy the train in our soft crash, doctor."

"I'd appreciate it." He shuffles out of the compartment.

The firefly perches on its new forever home, a thing beyond me now, beautiful and better and no longer mine.

I can't believe how much it tears me up inside, letting go of this one little robotic bug.

I bend close, not enough to touch but enough so that my nose and lips and eyes feel the burn of cold.

"Thank you," I whisper, and follow Javier out.

FOR ALL THE UNDENIABLE brilliance of the women and men behind the Time Train, none of them were able to foresee the demise of the platform. (Or, I presume, the demise of TimeTech itself.) Which means that they weren't able to foresee a reason to include safety straps or harnesses on any of the furniture, which means we'll all bounce around like beach balls inside the train once we hit Earth's atmosphere, and then Earth itself.

Time Train Three was only ever meant to glide smoothly above Earth's ether, not to flame through it.

I'm standing in Main Controls with my arms hugged over my chest, my fingers curled against the ridges of my ribs. My seven re-maining fireflies cling to the strands of hair framing my face; I want to keep them in sight, even if they're only blurry green glows at the edges of my vision.

Javier is in the manual command chair (still no straps), his fingers dancing against a luminous holo projection of codes and commands that look to me like nothing more than twisting curls of smoke. Whatever he's doing to them is making them shift and change color. I hope it's on purpose.

He's giving me and Drew and a couple of other people an impromp-tu lecture on about how we're all maybe about to die, or maybe not.

"Ordinarily," he's saying, scrutinizing the smoke curls, "your best bet is to be in the back of a forward-moving object about to crash, away from the initial point of collision. But the heat shield I've been able to configure isn't going to reach all the way to the back of the train. We're too long for it. We need to keep folks up front so they don't fricassee on the way down."

No one seems to know how to react to this, so I chime in with a helpful, "Okay."

And, I swear, only because he said the word *fricassee*, my stomach growls. We still haven't had anything to eat.

"You'll all need to occupy the next nearest cars to this one. Not the Quiet Car," he corrects himself, "since none of the furniture in there is bolted down. But the next few passenger cars will do. Use extra clothing, bedding, blankets, to tie yourselves to the chairs or whatever else isn't going to move."

"Will that work?" inquires Grizzled Beard.

Javier smiles grimly. "If only I knew."

"Where will you be?" I demand.

"Right here in this chair."

Drew frowns. "Is that wise?"

"It's never *un*wise to have a backup plan."

"But the Brain's piloting us," I protest. "And you said you were a programmer, not a lunatic."

Javier laughs a little, turns his head to find me. "Perhaps I'm some of both. Don't worry, child. This is my adventure, remember?"

No. Unfortunately, this adventure belongs to every one of us.

People have scattered to do whatever it is they're going to do before our crash. I've already packed my single bag and foraged for food (pretzels and boxed orange juice: thank you, Bar Car), and I have a half-there notion to go help Haven, but first I wander into the Observation Car. I want to see the universe in full-spectrum color one last time.

No one else is in here. I study the blue waters of the Atlantic, the rainbowed cloud patterns that are sometimes streaky, sometimes fluffy, always somehow remarkable. We're in geosynchronous orbit above the planet, which means that we rotate as Earth does. So even though I know that North America, South America, Africa, Australia, all of those land masses are still somewhere on that big blue globe, all I'm going to see is ocean.

"Enlarge," I command the wall.

I am engulfed in water. I see actual waves, white arrows of foam. I touch the glass and slide the view right, right, right . . . and there, at the very edge, is an island. A green and brown volcano emerged from the sea.

The upgraded glass flashes with names and numbers, latitude, longitude, more rapidly than I can follow. It can't seem to decide what we're seeing. Then:

Tristan da Cunha, it informs me.

"Enlarge," I command again.

I see the rough rocky contour of a beach. Cliffs. Flocks of birds. A straightish line of what could be a road slicing inland. I swipe down to follow it; the road fades to dirt.

I pour over the island mile by mile. Mostly it's rock and scrub. I discover more roads and follow them to a small town—what once might have been a town. A handful of toy buildings (none with roofs) edge the blocky streets. Greenery grows rife and dense around them, through them (maybe trees). There's a ghost harbor faintly visible beneath the water, but no boats. A rippling pack of reddish brown animals—pigs or horses or dogs—moves leisurely down a skinny lane.

Unknown Animal Organisms, the glass scrolls.

I see no people. Except for the old roads, the crumbled buildings, the stubborn shape of the submerged harbor, there might never have been any human beings there, ever. In this century, Tristan da Cunha belongs wholly to the wild.

"Decrease," I say, and it shrinks down to nothing.

I hunt a while longer, but aside from a few more barren rock isles, all I find is blue, blue, blue.

WE'RE IN M. ISHIMURA'S quarters. I don't know who M. Ishimura is, if he or she is one of the people currently claiming a piece of furniture in this compartment with us, but at least there's no dead body around.

Drew and I have bound ourselves to the small loveseat by the wall. Haven's in a leather chair facing us. She's wearing a child-sized (yet bizarrely adult-looking) sequined ball gown, along with a fuzzy cream cardigan on top.

It was the most normal outfit I could put together for her. It turns out that Haven owns no ordinary clothing, nothing remotely practical or end-of-the-world durable. It took forever just to talk her into putting on the cardigan over the gown. She wanted to go with the dress made out of plastic butterflies.

Her paper book is clutched tight in her hands. Everyone here, in fact, is clutching something, whatever they thought they couldn't live without in the new world. Cases of jewelry, computer slips, Flick-Slips, briefcases crammed full of who-knows-what. Some passengers are so blazing with gemstones that it's painful to look at them. One lady is sweltering beneath at least three separate heavy fur coats; her face is red and dripping. Drew has a gold signet ring on I haven't seen before, and I've got the metal box Mason made for my fireflies tucked beneath my shirt. Since the 'flies are still decorating my hair, the box is packed with nose clips and various med refills.

Javier and the Brain made it very clear that we could only take with us what we could physically carry and preferably attach to our bodies. Anything that isn't literally tied down is a potential missile that will be trapped inside the compartment with us.

So, no suitcases or trunks. No bulky artwork. (Paloma has two Rembrandts she was determined to keep with her; she got hysterical about leaving them behind, and therefore is now enjoying a nice chemical nap.) We've even shoved M. Ishimura's bedding and clock and pillows out into the hallway—everything we could move except the mattress, which, as it turns out, is screwed into the bed frame.

I transferred my hardcase and one of Haven's into Drew's quarters, since his are closer to the front of the train than either of ours. But everything else from our cars is probably going to burn.

British Guy has decided to bless us with his presence. He's trussed himself to the empty cryo pod and has a bottle of alcohol in each hand: one gin, one bourbon. He alternates taking sips from each. The typically pleasant, honeyed scent of the ventilated air has been replaced with the stink of liquor and sour sweat.

I tell myself that at least he's not Royce.

"Hey, you," I call to him. He lowers both eyebrows to offer me a bleary look. "Don't let go of those bottles, all right?"

He salutes me with the gin, then guzzles from it.

There's a man eating saltines on the bed, but I don't bother to yell at him. Hopefully, all the crumbs sprinkling his shirt will stay with him instead of floating over here.

The movie star avatar appears in the middle of the chamber.

"Ladies and gentlemen, we are ready to get underway. If you are not already securely fastened in place, please do so now. Doctor Castaneda wishes me to inform you that our initial descent through Earth's exosphere should be smooth. However, as we continue to drop, we will experience significant turbulence as I must draw power away from the acceleration compensator to maintain the heat shield. Air temperatures will rise. You may witness smoke or flames outside the train. Please do not be alarmed when any of this happens. There is nothing to be done about it."

I bet Javier hadn't asked her to add that last part.

"Won't the heat kill us?" enquires the man on the bed. "If the train catches fire?"

"Climate controls in this car are currently functional. Should they malfunction, oxygen deprivation will render you unconscious so rapidly you will have little time to react. Death via hypoxia will occur seconds later."

Or that.

"Best of luck to us all," the gorgeous movie star purrs, just before blipping out.

I look around the chamber and it's as though I've just stepped foot on the train for the first time. I've never seen a place so foreign to my own small self. For a few seconds, I'm totally disoriented; I can't fathom how I got here. I'm a farm girl, a mountain girl, and I never wanted to be here, I don't belong here, but none of that matters because I *am* here, stuck here in this death trap along with all these ridiculous strangers and their jewels and furs and sweaty stink.

And the reason I'm here is now obvious, even if I don't want to accept it. Obvious and huge and humbling and upsetting and I don't know yet how to untangle my feelings about it.

My brother did this. My brother did this to me.

I look at Drew. He looks at me. Haven starts kicking her feet and I lean over and press my hand to hers, which makes her stop. Our left sides are to the window but she's facing it; even as I'm smiling at her, I see her edges getting brighter. Earth is our lightbulb, our floodlight, our second sun. I turn my head and gaze out the glass, and the stars are spinning and the inky rich darkness of space is already fading into a color that isn't quite black.

Indigo.

Navy.

Lapis.

Fur Coat Lady is struggling to shed her top two layers without loosening her ties.

The train gives a shudder, once, hard, then smooths out. I'm thinking, *That's not so bad* when it shudders again but now it keeps going and the walls groan and the man on the bed cries out and spills his crackers.

I've been in only two earthquakes before, as they're not that common in Colorado. Both were quick, solitary jolts that knocked a mug off the counter in the kitchen (first one), or cracked through the air like a rifle shot (the second). I've heard about earthquakes that feel like this, everything shaking, jolting, your molecules vibrating apart—but even those kinds of quakes end. This isn't ending. The train is moaning like a living beast being torn asunder; my teeth are rattling; the loveseat feels hard as stone against me and the sheets I've used to tie me to it are biting into my bones.

Spacequake, I think. *That's what this is.*

The man on the bed is scrabbling at the mattress and letting loose a long, thin bawl, like a baby calf without its mama. His crackers have fallen to the floor. Lots of people are bawling or screaming now, not just him. If my lungs weren't so busy trying to process air, I'd probably be screaming too.

The compartment flares brighter and brighter. I see Drew holding his head with both hands, his eyes squeezed closed. I think about the tumor pulsating somewhere inside the soft crevices of his brain, and now I'm afraid for him.

There is nothing to be done about it.

A jewelry box is dropped. Diamonds and rubies, rings and bracelets, sapphire earrings and strands of pearls leap from it as if alive. They jitterbug every which way around our feet.

The view beyond the window is a haze of smoky blue. Then just smoke. Then smoke and orange.

British Guy loses his bottle of bourbon. It hits the floor and shatters. The inside of my nose stings with the fumes.

My hair begins to lift. I watch as the broken bottle, the crackers, the dancing rings and baubles all pirouette up into the air, then bounce downward again.

Missiles, I think.

Flames lick the window glass. *Actual* flames, and I can't smell the smoke—I can't, I can't, because the fire's on the outside, and I'm in—but my chest is burning anyway.

The air goes from warm to hot in about five seconds, *intensely* hot, and Haven is bathed in hellish orange, and I am, and Drew, and all of us. The screams don't stop and the train is screaming loudest of all and I'm sure the car is melting from the outside skin in. How could anything survive this?

The air is bending with the heat, thick as taffy. British Guy is passed out limp against the cryo pod and I think, *I can't believe he was right. This is how we're going to die.*

Then it gets so hot I stop breathing.

And that's that.

I AM . . . A BIRD.

I am drifting through the awful silence of the sky.

It's a blue sky, wicked blue. The cleanest, most agonizing blue I've ever seen, and I open my mouth and draw that blue down my trachea and into my exhausted body and it offers me (*a second chance, a second chance at*) life.

Life tastes of caustic, chemical smoke. Of sizzling grease and blood and wet cool pine.

I close my eyes.

Slowly, I exhale.

CHAPTER THIRTY
Taza

H E STOOD ALONE IN the woods before the enchanted line that defined the difference between *safe life* and *unsafe.* The line was invisible to the human eye, if not to the human senses—although, in the twenty minutes or so that he'd been studying it, he'd witnessed two rabbits, a feral pig, and a turkey vulture swerve to avoid it. So humans weren't the only animals being told what to do here.

He stood in damp pine needles and grass seventeen feet from the line. At sixteen feet from it (he'd measured the distance but only visually; something told him getting too near the line too quickly would be a serious mistake), Taza first felt the buzzing of the spells that formed the barrier, and it was not a good feeling.

It was nausea and migraines and muscles cramping. The sudden hideous *pop!* of broken bones. It was every unpleasant illusion the conjurers of this long, winding border could dream up to repel the physical body.

Hic sunt dracones, their invisible barrier declared. *Turn back or suffer the consequences.*

Because, after all, if you were foolish enough to venture this close to the rim of the badlands, you'd already ignored all the other warnings, the ones meant to repel your mind.

Foolish or not, Taza highly respected the sensations the border induced. He liked his body well enough not to relish the promise of nausea, migraines, muscle cramps or bones breaking as he crashed through the enchantment. And the worst part was, he'd have to do it slowly, on foot. His motorcycle had conked dead eighteen feet away, wheels locked. Another little gift from the conjurers.

Lucky for me I like dragons, he thought. He reached into his backpack and pulled out the pair of binoculars he'd filched from his father's Lodge.

Interestingly, the woods on the other side of the line looked almost the same as the woods on this side. Ponderosa pines, a scattering of darker oaks. Aspens flashing green and glossy gold from the higher hills. Leafy alders and willows shielding the mirrored path of what was probably a river in the bottom distance, one that appeared to cross the enchanted border without effort.

He wondered what happened to the fish in that river. If they were forced to swim upstream for the rest of their lives once they reached the barrier.

He felt a surprising flicker of distress at the thought. He hoped it wasn't true.

Forest, forest, forest, almost as far as he could see. Hills and forests melting into grasslands, into a flat beige smear that bled south into the horizon, which would likely be sand.

That was the main difference between here and there, of course. Sand meant desert, the most forbidden of all the forbidden lands.

And now Taza felt a flicker of excitement.

His eyes traced the shimmering edges of the smear, and that was when he saw it. A tapered black *something*—a trail, a scorch mark, residue (*dragon's breath*)—that nearly paralleled the farther dunes. It carved through the grasslands and the woods indiscriminately, harsh straight against the gently curving land, until it vanished beyond the hills.

His heart quickened. He felt more than a flicker of excitement; he felt energized, newly awake. A-hundred-cups-of-coffee awake and sure.

She's over there.

He shoved the binoculars back into the pack. He threw a last look at his bike (the saddle big enough for two; he'd been thinking about that when he'd brought it), dead and gleaming on its side in the grass, every bit of the magic he'd poured into it irritatingly, inexorably sealed away.

Then Taza faced the line and began to cast.

Protection.

It was the strongest spell he had, although the border tamped down everything it could. He could feel it pushing back at him, resisting his power.

Protection!

He pressed the palms of his hands together before the center of his chest, narrowing his focus. He was more than this artificial line that divided lands. He was the earth beneath his feet and the worms beneath that; he was the chosen and the shunned; the blade that cut and the soft water slicking over river stones. He was far, far more than anything these outland conjurers had thought to anticipate.

For an instant, he *saw* the barricade, the complex equations of curses that linked over and over like a fence into one—beautiful in its way, because math and magic were always beautiful, even when they created something repellent.

White sparks ignited around him, fizzled away. The line faded back into its invisible self.

All right. He'd done what he could.

Taza settled his pack over his shoulders and walked firmly toward the Forbidden Zone.

He was crawling within ten feet. He was crawling on his belly within five. He'd vomited four times by two feet and had to keep his eyes closed, his fingers pulling him along by inches, as he reached the actual line.

He was pulp and bile. He was bleeding from his nose and mouth and eyes. His bones were porridge and he couldn't do it, he couldn't do it, he couldn't, and he hated the sick bastards who'd thought up these spells, hated them with a boiling-lava-heart-of-the-volcano heat, and if he ever found out who they were he'd hunt them down and give them a taste of what it felt like to have their insides filleted and set on fire and then he opened his eyes and he was past the line, on the other side of *safe*, and he only vomited three more times before getting clear of the noxious magic.

It was half a day before Taza was recovered enough to move on.

But he did move on.

Chapter Thirty-One
Ember

I'M DRIFTING FOR A while; I don't know how long. It's not quite pleasant but it's not horrible, either. It's not painful, and some part of me understands the weight of that. The importance of it.

Up here, in this aching blue sky, I am not in pain.

Dad and Noah are here with me. Dad's got the baby slung in the crook of his arm and Noah squirms around to peer at me and says, "You bought a ticket for the Time Train because you're already sick. So is the actual location of your demise really that significant?"

"But I didn't buy it," I object. "Dad made me enter the lottery, and Mason made me win. It's all significant."

Dad smiles. There's a beer in his free hand, the can cold and beaded. He turns his back to me with the baby and the beer and walks away.

Am I dead now? Is this my demise?

But I'm weeping, I can tell that I am. And I don't think the dead weep.

The tears dry brittle on my lashes. I try to blink them away, then squint them away, then wipe them away, and that works, kind of. My hand is a black-and-red lump that moves clumsily across my face. It seems like something separate from my body, like it couldn't possibly be my hand but rather a warm, sloppy piece of meat that slaps at my skin without feeling.

I raise it up above my face, examine it. Five fingers, a palm, a wrist. All scratched and bloody and blackened, and all attached to my arm. Must be mine.

Clouds are hanging between my fingers. I think they're clouds. They might be ice cream. Big, soft scoops of vanilla . . . I'm so hungry . . .

Is it dinnertime? Because I'm so . . .

They are clouds. And as soon as I understand that, I understand how it is that I'm seeing them.

Because I am on Earth. Because I am a mote from heaven that has burned all the way down to hard, fixed *terra firma*, and my reward for this impossible feat is deep blue sky and pure white clouds and bright vermilion blood covering the meat that is me and my hand.

Drew, I think. *Haven. The train.*

My head lolls left. At first, everything's out of focus; my eyes want more clouds. But then I see the expensive maple-syrup paneling of an interior wall. It glistens beneath the open sky, warm and rich.

There's an empty chair adorned with torn scarves. A mass of fur behind it on the floor.

Another chair with Haven slumped over in it, her arms dangling, her gown spangling, her hair curling copper over her knees.

A green glowing firefly clings to one of the curls.

I struggle to sit up, but something heavy lies across my stomach and it's pinning me down. My meat hand gropes at it and recognizes the shape of a torso.

Not mine. Is it? Probably not but—

I manage to lift my head. It's Drew, of course, still bound to the loveseat as I am. His eyes are shut and his mouth is slack and there's blood dribbling from his nose but his chest is moving. I wiggle up and up until he's more on my lap than not.

Somewhere in the distance, I hear the hiss of steam escaping a pressure point, perhaps a broken pipe. Somewhat closer, the muttering of fire. No human sounds, though, like voices or footsteps. I'm alarmed when a moan rises nearby, and even more alarmed when it happens again and I realize it emerged from my own throat.

As if in answer, a mourning dove coos back. It's perched atop the severed maple wall, watching me curiously. It coos again and now it's a rock dove, its body shifting from fawn to purple-gray in the blink of an eye. The very tips of its wings sparkle in the sunlight like the gemstones scattered all around.

I've got to stop hitting my head, I think.

The dove takes off and explodes into diamond mist, dissolving against the light.

I rub my eyes again. My fingers feel more like me this time, less like meat, so I creep another inch or so up the loveseat, which is still attached to the car's floor, which is still here—unlike the ceiling, which is missing entirely. I've dislodged more of the fireflies (were they in my hair?), and they hover around me, circling. Drew sags lower along my lap.

I'm out of breath, and it hurts. All of me hurts, in fact, but my lungs most of all. I was wearing a nose clip before we descended; it's gone now. My hands search for my metal box but it's gone, too. Then I remember I stuffed some extra clips in my pocket. I fumble for one until my fingers hook it free. It comes out smeared dark with soot and muck.

It slips too easily against my face. When I lick my lips, I taste more blood. Drew's not the only one with a nosebleed.

The sheets we used to tie ourselves in place have stretched so taut from the ride that now they're loose in places, so I'm able to free myself one leg at a time. Drew is still bound at the waist, but he's too heavy for me to lift by myself so I shove him back into the cushions, making sure there's one beneath his head. Because he's tall, he only halfway fits on the seat. I tell myself that at least the top part of him will be comfortable.

I reach Haven. I push her upright against the chair and she makes a moan that sounds a lot like mine. Relief floods through me.

I say her name, one hand pressed against her shoulder to keep her in place, the other tugging at the sheet knots Drew and I tied so well for her hours—days? years? minutes?—ago, back when we all still sailed among the stars. The knots have gone hard and tight and I'm wishing devoutly for scissors or a knife (why hadn't we thought of that?) when at last I break the heart of one and tug it apart.

"Are we there yet?" Haven asks, a wisp of sound.

I start to work on the next knot. "Yes."

"My insides hurt." She says this like she's testing the truth of it, like she's not yet all that certain.

"That's good," I assure her, trying to sway her more toward hope than truth. "It means you're alive."

I hear Drew stirring behind me and pause to give him a quick pat on the knee, then return to Haven.

"What happened to Mr. Keith?" she whispers, her eyes on something behind me.

I glance around, then quickly pivot back.

"Don't look at it," I say, scowling at the knot. "It's better if you don't look."

But I can't stop her from looking and we both know it. The sight of the dead man tied to the bed (*his face is ruddy and splotchy and his eyes are bulging and his tongue pokes out but the crackers are still there, there's a cracker on his chest)* is so grisly I don't know how she *can't* look, so I guess I'm just glad I'm facing away.

"Ember," Drew says, and starts to cough. "Ember."

I find his knee again. "I'm right here."

"Ah," he says, still collapsed sideways on the loveseat. "Nice."

I yank free another knot. Haven can slide under the ties now so I go to Drew, who's clutching his head again and gazing at what's left of the car with a dazed expression. He can't see it, but the wall behind him is charred black. Sneaky orange flames still chew their way along the wood. Plumes of smoke curl in smoke letters up, up into the sky.

"Welcome to Earth," I hear myself say. "Please exit the train in an orderly fashion."

I start to giggle and then my body goes to jelly so I sit down hard, and Drew extends a hand to me.

I grab it. Our fingers interlock.

"Oi," slurs British Guy, indignant. He's hanging like a scarecrow from the cryo pod, arms up, head down. "Oi, who took my drink?"

MOST OF THE TRAIN is destroyed. By *destroyed*, I mean burned beyond recognition or else pulverized into a billion pieces. Our car holds survivors, as does the car past ours. But the car after that has only dead people in it, and after that is the Diversion Car, all the cubes weirdly intact but the glass splintered, and after that is just wreckage.

I'm making my way to Main Controls. At least, I hope I am. M. Ishimura's car and the Quiet Car disconnected at some point during our long screaming skid along the ground, so Main Controls looks like it's about two hundred yards away from our section of the train, largely hidden behind hillocks and groves.

A wide, sooty path has been laid out before me, sparkling in the dappled light like the diamond jewelry (*like the dove*). It is smashed trees and grass and grains of sand melted into glass from the heat.

I can't understand how it wasn't worse than this. The train landed in a forest, a sparse one but still a forest, and although some of the pines lining the path are still smoldering, none are on fire. Maybe it's a miracle.

Awesome, I think. *Just need one more.*

People mill aimlessly behind me, picking their way through the rubble, calling out names. A couple of the med bots survived, too, and are going from person to person. Drew wanted to join me on my hike but when he tried to stand his nose started gushing and he crumpled, so I told Haven it was her job to watch him until a med bot got to him. That I'd be back soon.

When I left, he was flat on the loveseat and she was pressing a wad of sheets to his face with both hands.

It's probably better that I'm alone when I reach Javier, anyway.

I find a blackened branch that lies just beyond the skid path and whack it a few times against the grass. It doesn't break, so I use it as a walking stick to cover the ground ahead. My fireflies lead the way.

Two hundred yards to cover, maybe two-fifty. About the length of two football fields. It's not that imposing of a distance for someone healthy, or even for a sick someone well rested. But I am neither of those things. My respiration has gone shuddery and I think the fractured bone in my foot has come apart again; every step feels like I'm treading on spikes, on hot coals, and every breath tastes like acrid, smoky *give-up-already-and-turn-back.*

But it's Javier up ahead of me somewhere.

Javier, who looked at me so innocently when I mentioned that my brother was good with tech.

Who helped program the quantum computer that conducted the lottery.

Who found me on that very first night and worked so hard to become my friend.

Javier, who hacks.

All of these big fat truths, finally visible in the day's fading light. Mason really *did* get all the brains in the family. I can't believe how blind I've been.

It takes a long time to get to Main Controls. I don't have a way to tell precisely how long, but the sun slides lower and the sky becomes more apricot-golden; the fireflies shine a warmer green. The farther I get from the back part of the train, the softer the air feels. It smells better, too. Still smoky, but not so choking with chemicals. More pine-sap sweet, like someone's lit a fire in their hearth to keep warm. It's an aroma I know from a thousand cold mountain nights.

I touch the skin beneath my nose. I think I've finally stopped bleeding.

So, aside from the pain in my foot, and my lungs—and that I haven't had anything to drink since that orange juice in the Bar Car so I'm thirsty, really thirsty—everything could be almost . . . normal. I could be just out for a walk in the woods. Regular girl. Regular woods. Regular evening settling around me, stretching out the shadows, pulling the clouds down close to the treetops to stain them in fiery, rosy hues.

Part of me, a treacherous part, a rosy sunset part, thinks, *Why not just keep going? Why ever go back?*

But then I glimpse a broken wing chair caught up high in the branches of a tree. Salmon-striped fabric, silver fish made of thread.

A spider bot crouched in a bed of weeds.

A palm tree leaning lovingly against a gnarled and shaggy oak, its brass pot dented, fronds hugging leaves.

These are the sole man-made objects in view. Beyond them are only more tree trunks, more needles and leaves and the vividly tinted sky. If there are any towns nearby, any mag-lines or highways, they are imperceptible.

A squirrel chatters at me from the safety of the forest canopy, its eyes bright red (*no, that must be the light*), its tail whipping.

When I encounter another wing chair, this one set upright like a gift in the middle of the path, I sit down in it. The sky flushes pinker.

For the first time, I pause to wonder where I am. Where we ended up. The train's navigation systems were only partially functional, so Javier couldn't predict our final destination. There were too many unknowns to factor in, he'd said, that he and the Brain were going to have to figure out as we descended. Northern Hemisphere if possible, and they'd aim for land instead of ocean, and that was going to have to be good enough.

This is definitely land. It even seems like familiar land, but that's probably because, in my incredibly limited experience, a forest is a forest. At least this one is alive, not a ghost forest like the one by the cottage. Living trees and brush and birds and squirrels . . .

Are there squirrels on every continent? Probably. But maybe those red eyes are distinctive. That dove with the sparkling wings (*it must have been something to do with the structure of its feathers; that would explain the color shift, too*), it can't be that common . . .

The problem is, I feel sort of floaty and disconnected and I'm not fully confident I know what's true any longer. Did I actually see the dove? My memories of coming to after the landing are already starting to fragment. And that squirrel—it's gone now; I can't even hear it scolding me. I don't think there are squirrels anywhere with blood-red eyes.

I flash on a memory of the fake wolves in the Diversion program and my body clenches.

I hold my stick tighter. I glance around me at the darkening trees, push myself up and out of the chair.

Seven emerald specks dance ahead.

Eighty yards gone. A hundred. The scorch path narrows through a particularly dense thicket, and the oaks here are heavy and old. Ancient, maybe.

Maybe as old as I am.

The light dies against the shadows, which are lavender and charcoal and every combination of those two shades, and I find I'm hobbling as fast as I can now, my walking stick crunching into the fresh new glass.

Deep to my right, twigs snap. A series of them, three right in a row, the middle one loudest: *crack!*, *crAAAckle!*, *crack!* But I don't see anything—it's too shadowy back there—and now I don't hear anything, either.

Or . . . do I? Is that *breathing* coming from the dark?

My mind races through a few unpleasant possibilities. Mountain lion. Actual wolves. Are there bears on every continent?

Do I smell like blood and an easy meal?

"Get back," I say loudly. "Get away."

I know that for mountain lions, you're supposed to make yourself big and loud, the opposite of frightened prey, but I don't know if that works on bears and wolves, too. Maybe they'll just take it as a challenge.

"Go on," I shout, but my bravado disintegrates into a fit of coughing.

At the brink of the deepest dark, a tree begins to shiver. It's not a pine or an oak but one I don't recognize, with large, flat, mottled leaves. They flap as though a wind threads through them; the boughs creak and sway. But I don't feel any wind in this strange, endless forest. Not even a trace of a breeze. And none of the other trees around it stir.

All seven fireflies rush back to me.

It's birds, I tell myself. *More squirrels. Harmless things that live up high. That's all.*

I discover that it's possible, if incredibly painful, to lope with a broken foot.

The Quiet Car rests in two pieces in the dusk, split open like a melon. Main Controls has twisted away from it enough to remain standing and almost whole, although its front is crushed up against an apparently impenetrable clump of oaks.

I slow as I approach it. I am abruptly and overwhelmingly reluctant to keep going.

My imagination treats me to various visions of Javier mangled, Javier burned, Javier squished into paste.

"Miss Duval," a voice murmurs.

I swallow my fears and sidle up to the open edge of the car.

The nanny is there, and Javier. The manual command chair, however, is not. Javier (unsquished, unburned, unmangled) is on the floor, sprawled against a console, and the nanny stands over him, her smile as serene and remote as an angel's.

"How may I serve you?"

I ignore her, going to my knees beside Javier. I see at once that he's breathing, he's not dead; his head is bloody and his eyes are partially open. The whites show in the gaps between his lids, glassy and blank.

"Communication with all medical robots has been severed," the nanny says. "Therefore, no medical assistance has been summoned."

I wish I'd thought this through before I'd left the other part of the train. Night is falling and there's no way I'm going to be able to drag Javier back there, not with my foot like this, and my lungs, and that *tree*, and it sure doesn't look like he's going to rouse anytime soon.

I wish I'd let Drew come. Or someone else, someone stronger and braver than I am.

I press my hand to Javier's forehead, then his neck. My fingers sink deep into the folds of his skin. His pulse beats weak against me, so weak I don't dare press any harder.

"Are you able to communicate with any other cars?" I ask the Brain.

"I'm afraid not."

I set my stick on the floor beside me and ease all the way down. Something swift and dark beats through the air above the Quiet Car, conceivably bats. My foot hurts so much that I'm glad now that I don't have a knife, because I'd be tempted saw it off.

"Where did we land?" I ask.

"We are in the Southwestern region of the North American continent. Navigation readings failed in Earth's stratosphere, so that is the most accurate location I can confirm at this time."

The Brain's voice has changed. I look up and it's the male avatar now.

"Are you in control of any of the train's systems still?"

"The train is dying," the Brain says. "I am not in control of that."

He doesn't need to add: Javier is dying too. Not in the distant future, not because of his cancer. Javier is dying right here, right now, on the floor in front of me. I am going to watch him die.

I rest my palm on his chest. His heart punches against me and death and the delicate cage of his ribs. I take my hand away and it's sticky with char and drying blood, and I don't even know whose blood it is, his or mine.

All at once, it's too much for me.

I can't bear any of it any longer.

My face tingles hot and I shut my eyes and think, *I want to go home now. I want this over. Please, please, God, I want to go home, can I go home now?*

And the worst part—the final, laughable jab from fate—is that if the Brain is correct and we're in the American Southwest, I'm closer to home in this second than I've been in centuries. Like, genuinely close. But it doesn't matter, because what made up my *real* home is all gone. Even if the cottage's walls still stand like those abandoned houses on Tristan da Cunha, my *home* is nothing but old bones and dust.

Go there anyway, whispers that treacherous voice inside me. *Find it anyway. Dwell in the ruins of your former life until your own death knocks on the door. Why not?*

I feel as though I've been drowning in these same weary thoughts, these same regrets, for longer than I can remember. It's all that I am now, nostalgia and loss, and I'm sick of it. I'm sick of myself.

I stretch out on the floor beside Javier. I can see some of the torn ceiling of the car and some of the heavens, twilight stars beginning to twinkle. My fireflies, still and small on some wreckage. The male avatar stands over us, gazing out at the bats, at the unquiet woods.

Somewhere out there in the new-fallen darkness, locusts begin to chirr.

I close my eyes again.

"Is the girl dead?" someone asks.

"No," says Javier. "She's only sleeping."

"Wake her up. We can't carry her, too."

"Ember," Javier says.

It's nighttime. We're surrounded by people. Someone holds a flashlight, plays the beam over the jagged frame of the car and it spears the darkness like a sword.

Rescue! leaps my heart. But, no. It's Grizzled Beard and Brecken and a woman I recognize from the glitter carousel. Passengers, not rescuers.

I sit up, scrub my hands along my cheeks. Javier is sitting beside me. The night beyond the flashlight eats up everything, silver and pitch.

"Geez," I say, groggy. "This is one persistent nightmare."

"No, my dear." Javier smiles at me, skeletal in the starlight, tarnished with blood. "This is the beginning of your remarkable new dream."

Chapter Thirty-Two

Excerpt from
Hey, Kids! Play Safe!
Children's Book Series 13a,
by the Office of Remnant Affairs

JACKIE AND DAVID ARE settlers on the northern frontier. Their family moved there a year ago. Jackie and David are the only children around for miles and miles! After they finish their schoolwork and chores, they like to practice magic out on the prairie.

One day, Jackie finds something in the dirt she's never seen before. What is it? Her magic doesn't work on it! It's made out something very old and brittle called *plastic*. It's thin and papery like a fallen leaf, but there are fibers running through it that form the image of a piece of fruit.

David says to his sister, "No, Jackie. Don't touch that. That is a computer. It's forbidden."

David is right. Jackie found a Remnant. A Remnant is a leftover thing from the Bright Times, and it must not *ever* be touched.

Like the Bright Times, Remnants are dangerous to everyone. If you find one, you must run and tell an adult right away.

Remember, children: No matter what they once were, or what they look like now, Remnants are *always* illegal. Don't risk punishment by refusing to tell.

CHAPTER THIRTY-THREE
Ember

MY NEW DREAM CONSISTS of one ravaged, time-traveling spaceship; a dozen shell-shocked human beings; a slightly larger number of working robots; and lots and lots of ruined things.

And sunshine. Real sunshine, from the real sun.

In my quieter moments, I convince myself that it very nearly balances out.

I lift my chin and close my eyes and the people and wreckage and bots go to red behind my lids. The sun's heat soaks into my cells and confirms that it's a lovely morning on the planet Earth and that I'm still alive.

I knew that already, though—the being alive part. My sore foot tells me that. My laboring lungs tell me that. My dry throat. Haven informs me that, beneath its crust of blood, the bruised left side of my face is turning all the colors of autumn. And even without a mirror I knew that as well, because it's tender and sore wherever I touch.

Some of those bruises I got from the crash. Some from stopping the train in Main Controls. And some are from Royce—who is, unfortunately, also still alive.

I avoid him as I hunt through the rubble for food, water, medicine, anything of practical use. I'm not too worried about him right this minute; I've got people around me and Royce has mostly stayed at the other end of the debris field (with his wrists still bound, doing nothing of use).

Yet I keep my eyes open.

Drew sticks to my side like a burr and I know that his eyes are open, too.

I realize Drew's only trying to protect me. I don't know why I feel more smothered instead.

The sun burns so hot on my head.

"Look!" Haven lifts up both hands with her fingers spread. Gemstone rings are stacked up on each finger past her knuckles.

"Great," I sigh. "But not edible. We're supposed to be looking for food, remember?"

She wiggles her fingers. Light blazes off her hands.

"No one will care if I take them," she says.

I send her a wry look. "Do you think?" I say, and she drops her eyes and lifts a skinny shoulder in a shrug. Half the spangles on her gown are already missing. Soot darkens her skirt and the skin of her arms all the way up past her elbows; the cream cardigan is now gray. She's wearing one of my nose clips and it's too big for her, so her face is marked with soot too, from constantly pushing it back into place.

"I bet whoever owns them is dead now, anyhow," she says.

It's not a bad bet. There are a lot of dead. We cover whatever bodies (or pieces of bodies) we discover with sheets or blankets and I do my best not to see them, even with the sheets on top. But the stench is still with us. Getting stronger as the sun climbs. There's a plan to have the med bots dig a mass grave nearby, but so far no one's found anything like a shovel.

Still, I'm a little perturbed by Haven's tone. She sounds so . . . unmoved.

"It's very sad if they're dead," I say.

Another shrug.

"Haven," I begin, but I don't know what more I'm asking of her. She's been through the same trauma as the rest of us. Maybe this is her way of coping.

"God, just let her have them." Drew picks up a blackened jug filled with something liquid. It might be gin or water or antifreeze; the label's burned off. He puts it in the suitcase we're dragging around with us. "If it makes her happy. Keeps her mind busy."

I offer my own shrug in return, moving from perturbed into out-right irritation. Keeping my mind busy hasn't been a problem since the landing. Trying to keep my mind *still* has been the problem.

Javier's back at the remains of M. Ishimura's car, barely hanging on, while Royce appears to be fine, which seems wildly unfair. There have been no indications whatsoever that anyone from the outside world is coming to save us; I can't find my metal box with all my meds; and, oh, yeah: that hiss of escaping steam I first heard after the landing? That happened to be the last of our clean water supply, boiling away into mist.

The train is, as the Brain enlightened me, dying. Maybe already one of the dead. No one's found any food so far—the Dining Car is melted slag—but Drew and I seem to be the only two people tru-ly looking for anything, anyway. Besides Haven, none of the others have even tried to venture this far down the wreckage. The next near-est person is British Guy, who's squatting on the ground thirty yards off and passing the time by sifting ash from one palm to the other.

Drew notices my expression. He turns around and retrieves the jug he'd just stuck in the case. He unscrews the top and lifts it to his nose, then tries a sip.

"Lemonade," he says, surprised.

We both take a drink. It's warm and gross and fantastic. Haven lifts the filthy hem of her gown and makes her way over, and between the three of us, we finish the entire jug in about a minute flat.

I'd feel bad about not sharing with the other passengers, but as I said, we're the only ones doing any real work. Drew chucks the empty container over his shoulder, almost smiling. I'm less parched but now there's a sticky, lemony residue sliming my tongue that I can't seem to swallow away.

Haven leans against me. Bejeweled fingers clamp over mine.

"I'll give the rings back if people want them, Ember," she whispers. "I promise."

I touch a frizzy red curl, my temper softening. "That sounds fair."

"Here." She tugs a ring free. "This one is for you."

It's gold with a huge stone, much like the rest of them. But I don't think this gem's a diamond; it's a deep bluish-purple, surrounded by tiny white pearls. I try to remember if I've seen anyone on the train wearing it before. I've been called a lot of unpleasant things in my life, but never *thief*.

Haven shoves the ring onto my finger without waiting for me to say *yes* or *no*. It's heavy, and it fits.

"Now we're both pretty," she says.

"Right." I smile and feel my bruises ache. "We both are."

I'M AT THE TAIL of the wreck, standing amid the debris of what was once a car that dared me to step into black infinity, that showed me planets and galaxies in colors I could not name.

The glass floor and walls and ceiling of the Observation Car are all lost, gone to shards. Lots and lots of shards, most of them smaller than my thumb. The thrusters have tumbled off into the trees. I know I won't find any food back here but I wanted to walk all the way to the end of the train anyway. It felt incomplete otherwise. Like when you're on a hike and you're tired but if you don't make it to the next bend you're giving up too soon, because who knows what's around the corner? Maybe something wonderful.

Not here, though. Anyone could see that here, there is nothing wonderful left.

A bird sings from the crest of a pine. I don't recognize this bird, but its song is mournful, long and burbling and slow. It sounds like a requiem.

"Wow," Drew says, looking around.

"I know."

If you *didn't* know, you'd never guess where these splinters once traveled, the virgin paths through space they'd carved. No one would.

"Look," cries Haven once again, and I turn around, ready to reprimand her. How much jewelry does she need? But she's not holding up a ring. She's holding up a chunk of glass, smoke marks feathered across it. It's as big as her head, much larger than any of the other pieces scattered around.

"Put it down," Drew orders. "You'll cut yourself."

I step toward her. "No, wait."

I have an idea. An outrageous, preposterous idea—but it turns out I'm good at those.

I take the piece of glass carefully from her. It's thinner than I expected, only two or three times the thickness of mirror glass. (I'm glad I didn't know that, back when I was standing on it.) And the edges *are* sharp; I cut myself at once but angle my fingers away after that, so it's only one slice. Maybe Haven's many rings protected her.

I kick out a clear patch on the ground, place the piece upon it. I use the edge of my sleeve to wipe away some of the soot marking the surface.

"Enlarge," I say to it.

Javier once told me that the unique, upgraded properties of the Observation Car glass, its memory and spectrum enhancement, had been embedded molecule by molecule so that it wouldn't be necessary to connect the glass to any other main system on the Time Train. That's why he'd had to boot it up himself after our Stop; the Brain wasn't in control of it. All the glass needs are enough connected molecules to achieve a function. Maybe this shard is big enough.

Beneath the soot, light flickers. Letters. I wipe at it again, and I see colorful, magnified rocks. Words like *Feldspar* and *Mica* and *Quartz* scrolling across the glass.

"Wow," says Drew again, in a very different voice.

"I know," I say, my tone matching his. Excitement. Optimism.

We can't eat or drink glass. But we've still found something helpful.

"We can use it like a telescope," I say. "To scout around."

"What's a telescope?" Haven asks.

"Scopeshield," Andrew explains to her. "Like the kind in limos and gliders when you're traveling around strange cities. The windshields that magnify things and give you directions, tell you street names and buildings and the, uh"—his eyes dart to mine, away—"types of people to avoid. Stuff like that."

I'm silent, staring at them both. Drew reddens.

"They're not uncommon," he defends in a burst, redder and redder. "Chauffeurs use them all the time."

My jaw is clenched. "That is so offensive."

"It's just tech!"

Haven nods wisely. Scopeshields (which I've never heard of) are entirely understandable to her. Her family's chauffeurs probably used them all her life to avoid the types of people to avoid. "What are we going to be looking for?"

"Anything," Drew answers expansively, still evading my gaze. "Everything. Food. People. A town."

"A donut shop!" Haven claps her hands.

"Perfect," he agrees.

They run through their list of desirables. Ice cream parlors. Pizza palaces. Underwater theme parks. A unicorn zoo. A school to learn flying by flapping your arms.

That shivering tree, I think. *Let's find out about that. That crimson-eyed squirrel. We're looking for whatever it is that breathes so heavily and quietly from the dark of the woods. That thing that watches us and waits.*

The bird's song alters. It swoops closer, closer, alights on a branch right at the seared edge of the train's path. It opens its beak and warbles a tune that's eerily similar to my name.

Em-BER-er!

Em-BER-er!

I think it's staring at me. I straighten and gaze back at it and it doesn't shy off like a normal bird would. Its eyes are not crimson, but black-black-black. Obsidian glass.

"Let's head back to the others," Drew says, still pleased about the shard, and I don't disagree.

∞

Beneath the grunge of the morning, my skin is turning an interesting shade of pink. My nose is tender. The top of my head, where my hair parts, feels like it's casting off all my body's heat and then some.

I haven't had a sunburn in so long, since I was kid, but it feels just exactly as prickly-hot-sore as I remember. It makes me thirstier but at least I'm able to get an aspirin from one of the med bots. That helps.

Drew and Haven (equally pink) are napping. Even asleep, Drew remains my burr, curled up near my feet. He and I are in the shelter of the woods, just beyond the scorched path. Haven's retreated into the shell of the train, staying close to Javier (also asleep). I'm tired but not enough to nap, so I'm trying to soak in what cool I can from the shade.

I'm fantasizing about swimming pools. Lakes. The feeling of dark, chilled water against sun-angry skin.

Someone's crying, not too distant. It's Paloma, trembling in the middle the wreckage. Brecken has his arms around her. I can't hear what he's murmuring into her ear, but he needs a new tack because this one isn't working. She only cries harder. Glitter Carousel Woman wanders up and begins to pat her awkwardly on the back.

Knock it off, you're dehydrating yourself. That's what I would tell her.

Maybe it's good I'm not over there.

My little hunting party managed to salvage eleven bottles of wine, five of vodka, one of vermouth, and one of hazelnut liqueur. We also found three large boxes of juice, another jug of lemonade, and ten gallons of tonic water. Already the lemonade, a juice, and about a quarter of the water is gone.

In her quest for more jewelry, Haven uncovered a sealed bin of salted cashews. I came across an unsealed one of putrefying crabmeat.

That was all any of us found for food.

I've got the shard of glass in my hands. I've wrapped someone's jacket around the edges to protect my fingers as I hold it up in front of me, facing away from the train and Paloma and all the rest of them.

"Enlarge," I say. I don't bother to keep my voice down, but Drew doesn't stir.

The trees zoom huge. I'm looking at something I don't recognize, a multicolored blur.

"Decrease by . . . twenty-five percent," I try.

It's tree bark?

"Decrease again."

Definitely tree bark. I move my hands. More woods. An enormous jade leaf with ruffled edges, veined in brassy yellow.

Words flit across the glass, *Betulaceae*, *Alnus*, *cordata*, *incana*, *rhombifolia*. It ends up with: *Unknown Plant Species*.

"Okay," I mutter, still moving the shard. "But find me water. Find me people. Find civilization."

I stand and turn a slow circle. I try zooming out farther, farther, but all there is around here are trees and more trees and things related to trees, almost none of them identifiable. I'm about to give up when I glimpse something different. A streak of gray and stone and what's maybe sawed wooden planks.

I turn back, but I've overshot it. I stand in place and try different angles, enlargements, decreases, and then—

"What is that?" I wonder aloud. It definitely looks man-made, whatever it is. Maybe a cabin? A hut?

Unknown Structure, the glass writes.

I squint upward, gaging the sun, the trees, the direction.

"How far away is it?" I ask the shard, but it doesn't respond. I'm probably phrasing it wrong.

"Determine distance," I say.

3.21 miles, S x SE.

"Are there any people there?"

It can't answer my question. All the shard can offer me is what its molecules can compute. *Unknown Structure, 3.21 miles, S x SE.*

Unknown. Exactly like everything else around me.

Without waking Drew, I carry the shard back to the train.

OUR SECOND NIGHT. JAVIER is asleep, and not asleep. I sit beside him in the dubious protection of M. Ishimura's broken car, near the edge of the mattress where the man eating crackers died (he's been moved). A med bot comes over every few hours and checks on Javier and that's when my friend twitches some, his eyelids fluttering, before sinking back into his oblivion.

He's covered in a cryo blanket, taking up half the mattress. Despite the fact that there's a real lack of soft places to rest, no one takes the other half. Maybe, like me, they're remembering the dead man's face. Or maybe they're thinking about ghosts.

If ghosts were real, though, I imagine they'd be haunting every inch of the crash site, not just this bed.

Because I don't want to shift the mattress and disturb him, and because I don't feel comfortable stretching out on a bed in public in front of strangers (and, yes, it's kind of public and most of them are still strangers), I've made myself at home in a chair beside the bed. I'm watching Javier and listening to the conversations of the other survivors ebb and flow around me.

Mostly it's about how bored they are, or how hungry, or how

thirsty. Or where we might be. Or when help will arrive. Or can you believe so-and-so didn't make it? What do you suppose happened to their companies/factories/stocks/private islands?

It's the water that's saved their lives, but it's the alcohol that's attracted the most attention. Brecken and Glitter Carousel flat out told British Guy he couldn't have an entire bottle for himself, which sent him off ranting into the woods for a while. But he's back now and they're all sitting around a makeshift campfire (they called it a signal fire, but it's so puny I doubt it signals anything to anyone beyond this train), sharing what I hear is a very decent Merlot. Speculating about private islands. Even Royce has been allowed in their circle.

I chew on a cashew. Drew and Haven have their heads together over a game of cards, halfway between me and the others. I don't know where they got the cards and I can't tell who's winning—I can't even tell what they're playing—but every now and then Haven starts to cough. Whenever that happens, the circle around the campfire quiets. Listens. Waits until it stops.

It's an ugly kind of waiting, as if they're waiting for her to stop breathing instead of coughing.

She bends her head and covers her mouth with her hand, and that's when it occurs to me that maybe we're the only two TB-3's left alive. I'm not positive because I'm not *that* familiar with the other passengers' diseases. But I think it might be true.

We're all waiting for the coughing to stop now. When it does, Haven wipes her hand on her dress and I look down at Javier, and he's looking up at me.

"Still hanging around?" he asks.

"Are you kidding?" I lick the salt from my lips. "Who'd want to leave a paradise like this?"

I win an exhausted smile.

"Are you thirsty? I have some tonic water for you."

"That would be . . ." His words wilt, but I lift the cup of water to his mouth anyway. Sip by sip, he drinks it all. The bubbles are nearly gone and it turns out that tonic water tastes nasty when it's sparkling but even worse when it's flat—yet it's still water.

" . . . good," he sighs, his chest sinking.

The med bot shows up, takes his pulse, sticks a needle into a vein.

"How is he?" I ask the bot, even though I already know the answer.

"This patient requires hospitalization. Please arrange transport to the nearest hospital at once."

I've heard this before. Five times before, in fact: every time I've asked the same question about Javier since the crash.

"Hospitalization is not possible at this time," I reply, the phrase I've learned appeases the bots quickest. "Continue your treatment."

"Triage protocols currently place this patient at the bottom of the treatment list." This is new information, and I sit up straighter. "Emergency pain relief is all that will be provided to this patient from this treatment forward."

"No," I say at once. "You can't. You're going to give him every bit of the medical attention he needs. All the medicines he needs."

"Negative. This patient is beyond all known lifesaving techniques. Pain remedy is all that will be provided."

Another needle is inserted, this one directly into his chest. Javier jerks in a breath.

"Wait a minute!" I'm grabbing at the bot's arm, but it pulls away from me without effort and hulks away.

"Ember, no." Javier's eyes are fully open now. There's some color in his cheeks, but his hands quiver. "Let it be. This is fine."

"It's *not* fine!"

"It is. Listen. I need you to listen to me now."

I sit back down, my adrenaline racing. I'm willing to appease him but I'm not listening; I'm thinking about how to convince the med bot to treat him anyway. About how to steal medicine—if that's even possible, the bots are so strong—and how to figure out which ones I'll need, when Javier says:

"You're the heart of things now. You know that."

I glance at him, distracted. "What?"

"You're their heart." He flaps a hand, not in the direction of the wine circle, but toward Drew and Haven. "Their courage," he clarifies. "You're what's going to keep them alive."

Nothing's going to keep them alive, I think, but say aloud, "If anyone's going to keep us alive down here, it's you, and we all know it."

"No. My shining time was above us. Here on Earth, they're going to depend on you. You're their . . . natural leader."

I'm astonished enough to actually consider this a moment, turning the idea of it around in my head, but frankly, there's no way I'm going to be able to turn it into anything good.

I don't want to be the leader; I've only done what I've done so far because no one else could or would.

I don't want to be anyone's courage. And I definitely don't want the lives of two sick, frail kids depending upon me, because I think I've got enough stuff going on right now as it is. Maybe that makes me mean, or weak, or mercenary. I don't know. I feel like so much of what's happening now is beyond my comprehension, much less my control, and I bet real leaders never feel this way. Lost and anxious and brimming with unspoken fears.

"Who stopped the train?" Javier whispers, his eyes steady and bright.

I shake my head. "I was the only one awake."

"Who had the intelligence to realize that?" he persists. His voice grows so faint I have to bend low to hear the rest. "The audacity to change it? The . . . *tenacity* to live? To help us all to live?"

"Javier, come on. Most of that was just luck."

"No. It was you, Ember. You delivered us here. *You* will lead them on."

I watch my friends play their game, Haven slapping down a card with particular force, Drew snatching it up again. In the light of the fire, they look like the abandoned factory orphans you'd see in the newsfeeds, the ones left to wander the cities after their parents died—dirty and gaunt and somehow always beyond help. We all look like that, I realize. And right now I can't imagine why it should be my responsibility to make things better.

Javier's hand falls to rest on mine. I take in his face, the shadow lines etched deep into his skin, mapping every fold.

Why did you rig the lottery? I want to demand. *Why did you help Mason rig it to pick me? Did either of you think for a second about the future I wanted?*

But he's already fading.

"Get ready," he rumbles, and sinks back into slumber.

THREE DAYS PASS. I mark them by watching the sun trace its path along the empty sky. I mark the nights by the sickle smile of the moon and the throbbing of the locusts. I try *not* to mark the nights by any of those other sounds rising from the forest shadows, the ones I can't explain.

Under the care of the med bots, my concussion clears and the bone in my foot decides to reknit. Drew finds my metal box full of medicine and even what might have once been my hardcase, although it's broken apart and everything I'd packed in it is gone. I go back twice (in daylight) to Main Controls to visit the Brain. Once at Javier's request, to ask about possible radiation (only acceptable levels detected), and once just to see my eighth firefly, still frozen in place because the car's battery source won't stop chilling the Brain's closet for another week or two. After that, I guess, they'll both be forever gone.

Otherwise, I cling to the hollow comfort of the wreckage, just like everyone else. I take my sips of water and juice and eat sparingly of the cashews, and just like everyone else, I wish instead for pizza and fries and ice cream and tacos and spaghetti and peaches and freshly baked bread and a chocolate cake two stories tall and *anything* but dry salty cashews.

Unlike nearly everyone else, I have no faith that rescue is coming. I brood about that Unknown Structure and the alien mood of the woods; the absolute lack of air gliders or drones above us, or magtrains or highways along the ground . . . and I don't think anyone's coming.

Which I think means that we're going to have to leave.

Because we never did find any shovels, or anyone with the energy to dig without them. So the train is still littered with dead people. And I can't shake the feeling that the forest is growing hungrier and hungrier, very much like the rest of us.

By the fourth day, the water's gone. The cashews are gone.

The woods breathe at night, and we have to leave.

If I am the heart of anything, it's simply dread.

CHAPTER THIRTY-FOUR
Ember

I WAKE UP BECAUSE THE locusts fall silent. I open my eyes to the starry dark and there's a moment of quiescence, of everything in the world holding its breath.

Then, shattering the quiet: *AAAooowwww-yip-yip-yip-yip!*

Coyotes, announcing their victory over some smaller, more helpless creature.

They sound close. There's no echo at all to their cries.

Wind puffs against me, cool and heavy with the promise of a rainstorm. Beneath it skims a riper funk that reminds me of the zoo. Of wild animals.

My skin prickles beneath its layers of grime.

Drew sighs in his sleep. Haven rolls over. I sit up and automatically check on Javier, but he's the only one of us resting peacefully. Morphine has its advantages.

A light glows in the distance. It's not the signal fire; that's gone out hours ago. Whoever was supposed to feed it has done a lousy job, because I don't even see coals. This new light isn't firelight at all. It's cold, bluish white. Like the light from a computer.

It's the Diversion Car. It's one of the shattered cubes, running a program.

I ponder that for a few seconds, then climb to my feet. Since each car was built with its own separate, backup battery source, I'm not surprised that the Diversion Car has power. I *am* surprised the broken glass of the cubes still functions.

Well, more or less functions. As I hike closer to it, I see the scene inside the cube isn't all that stable. The shapes within seem solid one minute, melted the next. Still, the setting looks familiar. Is it one of my programs? I'm sure I've seen it before . . .

It's the interior of the Quiet Car. The Quiet Car before the crash, I mean. I recognize the stately chairs and tables, the teal curtains, the tall green feathery palms in their pots.

I get even closer. The scene melts, reforms, still the Quiet Car, and there are figures inside it now too. A man, standing over a seated girl. She has long golden hair and a teacup in her hand.

I stop. I want to look away, but I don't.

The Brain played the vid file for me. Javier said that to Royce, back before our crash. With everything else going on, I hadn't really registered it. But now I understand. There was a vid file, a recording, of the attack.

And here it is. Playing out right in front of me.

I see the plastic glass creation of Royce strike plastic glass Ember. I see her fall to the ground, her hair flying. I see him pin her down. His mouth moves and he paws at her chest and even past the broken cube walls, it's nakedly repulsive.

"Watch this," whispers a voice beside me. "It's my favorite part."

I leap and turn because the voice belongs to Royce—the living one—and he's standing only five feet away from me. He's watching the scene in the cube, not me. His hands are unbound. The dried blood flaked around his wrists appears black.

Glass Royce hits glass Ember again. Her head snaps to the side.

He pulls down her pants.

There's a rock in my hand. I know I picked it up; I know it's big and heavy and I know I'm going to cut myself again and I don't care. Without a word, I smash the rock against the cube wall, as hard as I can. I create a spiderweb of fresh cracks but it doesn't break, so I smash it again, and again, and finally I punch a hole through it, but that still doesn't stop the program.

The scene melts. It resets from the beginning; I'm back in the chair with my chai. Royce is skulking past the door.

I switch the rock to my other hand, shake the blood from my fingers. "We're leaving soon," I say, "and we're not taking you. You can stay here and suffer."

Living Royce laughs. "You're leaving soon, all right. You're leaving because we're kicking you out. No one wants your disease, *November*. It's already been decided."

Decided? By who? But I know. Of course, I know.

Shadow figures appear over his shoulder, grubby and eerie and bathed in the pale light. Four men, five. Glitter Carousel. Paloma. The women are watching the scene in the cube, but the men are all watching me. They're monsters emerged from the dark, their features gone flat as the face of the moon.

Were they there all along, lurking? Were they waiting for me to wake up and come here? Did they program the cube to show me being beaten over and over?

The coyote pack screams again, even closer. *Yip-yip-yip!*

"So go on," Royce taunts. "Leave me behind. But you're the one who's going to *suffer*. You and that TB-3 brat, you'll be nothing but fresh meat out there in the woods. Drag Castaneda with you, and pretty boy. You can use them as fodder for the beasts while you run."

"Now, hold up," begins one of the men, sounding uncomfortable, but that's all he says. He scowls at me, his lower lip protruding, then drops his gaze to the ground.

"Go on," Royce repeats, very soft. "Run away, bitch. Better run before we make you run."

"You think you can?" I'm trying to sound confident, but let's face it, I know they can. There are eight of them and four of us. Eight adults against three kids and one feeble old man who can't even stay awake.

"Oh," Royce says, grinning his yellow grin, "I think so."

I find Glitter Carousel's eyes, lift my hand with the rock. "You'd choose him over us? Even after seeing this?" I indicate the cube.

Her face hardens. "You're a danger to us. I'm sorry. We can't allow you here any longer. When help arrives, we'll tell them about you. Tell them which way you went."

"Because you want us rescued, or because you hope they'll kill us for you?"

Royce laughs again. Glitter Carousel shoots him a look before narrowing her eyes at me.

"We'll tell them," she repeats, frosty. "So go."

I draw myself up as tall as I can. I'm glad I still have the rock in my hand, even though it's not much of a weapon against all eight of them. I want to argue with them, to inform them that we're not going anywhere (despite the fact that I'd already decided we were), when something streaks out of the dark and hits me in the face, right above my eyebrow.

I'm stunned into silence. It takes me a full three seconds to realize it was another rock.

"This is all your fault!" Paloma screeches. She grabs a second stone and throws it too but her aim's off this time; it soars over my shoulder. I duck belatedly anyway. "Everything is your fault! If you hadn't stopped the train we'd still be *fine* up there, we'd be *fine*, and someone would have found us and brought us down when it was *safe!*"

"Babe!" Brecken peels away from the shadows, tries to take her hands. "Babe, calm down!"

"No! I won't! I hate her! I hate all of them! They're disgusting, diseased little *pigs* and I *hate* them! We're stuck here in this dreadful place because of *her*! She has to *pay!*"

My head pounds where the rock hit. The pain spreads out in a bullseye, rings and rings of it thumping through me. I look at Paloma and the others but weirdly what I see are those kids from school so many years past. The captain of the softball team snarling at me (*TB-3 bitch!*) as she hurls her stone. The jeers of the other students surrounding me, laughing at me.

How it feels when the rock strikes my skull. How the impact reverberates all the way through my bones until I go numb, and the school nurse telling me, *you're lucky it wasn't worse, it could have been your eye, go home now, you go on home.*

I back up. I bump into someone. It's Drew, who steadies me and says nothing, only stares at the attack scene playing in the cube.

"You need to go," says Glitter Carousel. "Today."

"Cowards," I spit, but it comes out fractured, and then I'm mad *and* ashamed.

"Come on." Drew's arm is around my shoulder. He's trying to pull me away but my legs are robot legs, stiff and unyielding. "Ember."

I don't let go of my rock; it feels heavy and light at once in my hand. I'm dividing in two, rage and offense and possibilities and consequences rippling through me, and just when my body decides a split second before my mind—*yes, do it, hit them back*—a small, girlish voice quivers from behind me:

"Ember?"

Followed by a long, wet cough.

I'm poised to throw the stone. "If you touch her, I'll kill you," I say, and this time I don't sound fractured. I sound ferocious.

Glitter Carousel sighs. "We don't *want* to hurt you." She's speaking calmly, reasonably, as if she's only trying to explain to us how to activate a FlickSlip, or how to smear caviar on a cracker. "We just want you to leave the train. Collect your belongings and leave."

"Ember," says Drew again against my ear.

"You'll all die here," I choke out, the only thing left in me to say. I don't know if I mean it as a warning or a curse. Probably a curse.

Yip-yip-yip-AAAooooo!

"Yeah, we might die here," Royce agrees lazily, scratching his stomach. "But you're definitely gonna die out there."

THEY GIVE US UNTIL dawn. It rolls over us in heavy black clouds and thin gray light and brings with it the gathering storm.

Royce and his pack are in the shelter of the car nearby, practically standing guard over us, like we're going to rise up and overcome them if they don't monitor our every move. So I ignore them, regally, disdainfully, even as I feel their gazes boring holes in my back.

I hope they drown in the rain. I hope they get ripped to pieces by coyotes and crimson-eyed squirrels. I hope the med bots malfunction and crush them into goop.

Drew and Haven and I huddle around Javier on the mattress. We're trying to decide what to do about him. He's slept through this whole ordeal and part of me wants to just slip away before he comes to. But I can't bring myself to do it. He won't care if the reason we leave him behind is because there are med bots and morphine for him here, and nothing for him out there but a much slower, more agonizing end.

He will care that his friends have abandoned him. Have been chased off. And who's to say that this group of oh-so-benevolent people who are doing the chasing will even allow the bots to treat him? I wouldn't put it past them to hoard all the remaining pain meds for themselves.

Bastards.

"You don't have to come," I mutter to Drew. "You know that, right? They only want Haven and me gone. You're not contagious. You could stay."

I don't want him to stay, though. It's selfish but I don't want to leave him behind, any more than I do Javier, because two teenagers versus the wild has got to be better than just one.

Drew answers without looking up. "Shut up, already. I'm only trying to figure out the best way to move him."

"Fireman's carry," I suggest. "We can take turns." I attempt to sound like I believe it, which isn't easy since I'm tired and I don't.

He sends me a sideways glance. "Right. Except that Javier's—what, six-one, six-two? And you've got the approximate muscle mass of a kitten."

"Looked in a mirror lately?" I flash. "You're not exactly in peak physical condition yourself. But do you have a better idea?"

Drew lowers his lashes, then shrugs. It's a slight shrug and there's mostly frustration behind it, but at least it means he's willing to give it a go.

I turn to Haven, tattered and glimmery in the gray leaky light. "Can you carry the rest of our stuff? Our meds and . . ." I try to think of what else we have left, but there's only the shard. "Our meds and your book and the glass piece?"

A raindrop splashes between us. Then another. A microsecond later, it's pouring. We're drenched at once but none of us try to escape it. The nearest dry spot is where the other passengers stand.

I step closer to Javier, tent my hands over his nose and mouth. The fireflies crawl down inside the collar of my shirt.

"I can," Haven says, wiping the water from her eyes, "but why don't we just put them with Javier?"

"What do you mean?"

She points to a couple of long, flat pieces of wood on the ground, perhaps the railings from the bed, that somehow escaped the astute attention of the signal fire brigade. "We put those together, tie a blanket around them to make a middle. Then we put Javier on the blanket, and carry him like that. Like a hover stretcher, only it won't hover."

The rain is coming down so hard it stings, smashes itself into vapor against everything around us.

"Did you know that you're a genius?" I have to almost shout it because the storm is so loud.

"Yes," she shouts back.

I give her a hug. Javier begins to sputter because the rain's hitting him square in the face. Drew pulls the cryo blanket up over him and holds it there so he has air to breathe. I'm relieved to see that the blanket's waterproof; the drops only bead along it, slide off.

The clouds press low and ominous, crackling with thunder. The forest is already hazy with mist, hiding anything and everything lurking within. The pack clustered in their dry shelter stare at us and say things to each other that I can't hear beneath the sibilance of water striking land and train.

"Okay," I say. "Let's get out of here."

Drew asks the obvious. "Where are we going?"

I think of the Unknown Structure, the 3.21 miles stretching between us and it. Of how that sounds like an eternity of distance, even if I'm lucky enough to pinpoint its exact coordinates again.

"Anywhere away from here," is what I say.

But before I do anything else—get the planks, tie the blanket, move Javier, pray for luck—I tilt my face to the sky and close my eyes and open my mouth.

The raindrops smart my bruises, but they taste as sweet as nectar.

It's hard to imagine that I was ever thirsty. It's hard to imagine that I was ever dry. The best thing I can say about this downpour is that I can see the color of my skin again. The itchy, filthy layers of blood and grime that have coated me ever since the crash have washed away. I'm shiny with rain, and shivering with it, too.

I wonder what season this is. I thought it was summer but now it feels more like autumn, even though the grasses and trees are still mostly green. Occasionally I spot leaves the color of flame between the patches of mist. Not merely the *color* of flame—they look like genuine flames, burning and dancing in the wet, which is absurd, and I assume some sort of consequence of the force of the storm. But I didn't see anything that color even a couple of days ago. Maybe I just wasn't paying attention.

We trudge along the scarred path of our landing, heading for Main Controls. It's slightly out of the way from where I think the Unknown Structure might be, but it's the safest place I can think to go right now. The ground along the scar has been scraped level, so it's easier to walk and since we're basically following a straight line, I'm not afraid that we're going to get lost. The shard, useful in clear weather, can only tell us that we're looking at water right now. If we can shelter in one of the cars up ahead, we may be able to wait out the storm.

Javier is gangly and heavy and frankly too tall for our makeshift stretcher; his heels bump along the ground as we go. The wooden bed railings are rectangular and not designed for a comfortable grip, so my fingers keep slipping. The same thing is happening with Drew. We have to pause every few minutes to readjust. In no time at all, I'm exhausted.

Haven slogs along beside us, every now and then anxiously checking under the blanket we've draped over him to make sure Javier's still breathing. I found a walking stick for her and told her it would help her keep pace, but the truth is, I think at least one of us needs to have some sort of potential weapon at hand. I figure I can grab it from her in a hurry if I have to.

Because the woods go on and on, and the storm is choking, and most of the time we can barely see ten feet ahead of us.

Or behind us, where the other passengers supposedly stayed.

Everything about this new world is spooky and cold and sodden.

There's a scent hanging around us that I don't quite recognize. It's not only rain, it's almost salt. I'd think *blood* but I've tasted enough of that lately and that's not quite it, either. It's the smell of caves. Of minerals and raw dirt—and that's saying something, what with all the water washing down. Whatever it is, I don't like it. I can't actually hear anything (*breathing, the woods are breathing*) past the rainfall, but my skin is crawling anyway.

On top of that, I keep thinking I glimpse lights through the mist.

Topaz sparks, small and round, glowing and floating. Bobbing. There and gone and there again.

If my life were a fairytale, those lights would belong to trolls. Wood sprites. Terrible tiny creatures with sharp dagger teeth that lure you in close so they can devour you.

Just keep walking, Ember.

I tell Drew we need to go faster. The smell of dirt follows us all the way down the burn scar.

The divided hulk of the Quiet Car looms over us suddenly, mist one second, jaggy metal the next. We clamber up into the closest half, Drew hauling the stretcher up by the top, me pushing from the bottom, until Javier is flat on the floor. There's a rug rumpled against a wall and I drag it to us, then flop it over a lopsided table and the one chair I can find. It becomes a tent, and we are campers hunkered inside it, and I'm still shivering and the mist is still slithering and I'm afraid, truly afraid, that if I look outside I'll see those topaz lights shining at me through the trees. Observing us. Measuring our meager defenses.

"I'm hungry," Haven whines.

I cup her knee. "I know."

"We can forage in the woods," Drew offers. One of his eyes has gone bloodshot, the other hasn't. "Berries and things."

"No," I say instantly. "Not yet. Not till the storm stops."

We settle in. I don't smell dirt any longer; my nose is filled with the pungent stink of wet wool. We sit shoulder to shoulder and eventually I get a little warmer. I work at the ring Haven gave me, twisting it around and around to get it off, but my finger's too swollen from carrying the stretcher and it won't budge. Finally, Drew grabs my hand and I give up and let him, and we all slump into rest.

The rain hits the rug like someone's tossing pebbles at us. The material pitter-pats with it but it's super thick and the sound becomes almost soothing. Before I know it, Haven's head is on my lap and, just like Javier, she's asleep.

"Sooo," Drew whispers.

I turn my face to his. In the gloom, the damaged veins of his one eye disguise the pupil and iris; he is a cyclops. I think I should mention it, then I think I shouldn't. Either way, we can't fix it.

He leans in very close, so close our lips nearly touch. "What do you want to be when you grow up?"

I can't help my puff of laughter. "Alive."

"Good answer."

His lips brush mine, and they're soft and cool but that's all; I'm the one who ends up pulling away. He studies my face but doesn't protest.

"Sorry," I whisper, but I'm not certain exactly what for. I suppose . . . for not feeling like being kissed right now. For feeling grungy and stressed out and beat up and mostly what I want is some space to *not* feel these things. To be left in peace.

Is there ever a polite way to say that?

Drew hesitates, then shrugs. He slips back into the gloom.

The rain pitters and pats. Eventually, it's a lullaby without words. It sings me into a state that isn't quite sleep but isn't quite awake, either.

I'm slanted against Drew's shoulder. I'm drifting inside myself, gliding through this daybreak of wet shadows and pebbled rain until I hear this:

Humt?

I start.

Huh-huh-huuumt?

The sound is so deep and close that whatever made it must be just beyond the rug.

Humt? Humt? Huuuuuh . . .

It sounds like a call and a question and an answer all together. It sounds breathy and rumbling and eager.

Haven's eyes are open, though she doesn't move. Drew and I stare at each other. My hand gropes carefully, carefully, for the walking stick on the floor at my other side.

Huuuuuuh.

The stick is slender in my hand. Why didn't I pick a bigger one? This one feels like it's going to crack apart beneath my fingers.

Huuuuuuuuh.

Despite all the moisture in the air, my mouth's gone dry as dust. When I swallow, my tongue makes a small clicking noise and the rug in front of my face slowly dents inward.

Something on the other side is pushing on it. Testing it.

I smell dirt again, suddenly and swoopingly strong.

I don't have any room to retreat. My body is screaming at me to move my feet, to pull them under me to get ready to jump up, but Haven's still on me and she feels like she's turned into iron. I'll have to shove her off. Drew is watching the dent and his fists are clenched, but I've got the stick because it was closest to me so that leaves nothing for him. Maybe the rug. Maybe, if I can get him to look back at me and I can communicate this with my mind, we can flip the rug up over the thing out there and—

Something pokes through the weave, about two inches from my nose. I think it's a knife at first, the narrow curved blade of a knife, but then I realize it's a claw. It's followed by four more claws, all of them large, curved, sharp as scythes. They retract while simultaneously curling deep into the rug. It's being tugged off of us.

I have time to exhale once and then the rug is all the way gone, and I'm leaping up (sorry, Haven) and yelling and brandishing the stick, and the—

—horse—

—giant cat—

—spotted—

—soaked—

—jaguar—

—crouches back in surprise and spits at me, its massive front paw still hooked in the rug.

I *think* it's a jaguar. It looks like one, but I've never seen a feline so big—it's a monster, a colossus—

I hit it before I think to hit it. A little piece of me—a faraway watching piece of me—is sorry for that, because the jaguar is beautiful and terrifying and can't get its leg free, so I hit it again to let it know I mean business.

Haven is shrieking and scrambling backward and Drew—I don't know what Drew's doing because all I can see is this enormous cat, its reflective lime eyes and the spots on its coat that are swirling, swimming over its body in dizzying patterns that are unquestionably and absolutely not possible.

But they are.

It tears its paw loose. I hear that, even past Haven screaming and me gasping and the thundering of my heart in my ears. I hear the threads of the rug go *snip-snip-snip* and the jaguar crouches even lower on all four legs and prepares its death launch.

Drew leaps between me and the creature. He's holding the chair in front of him with both hands and staggers back when the cat hits him, barely missing crushing Javier in the chest with his foot.

I hop to catch my balance because I'm about to crush Javier too, but I manage to land beyond him; the jaguar pushes off of the chair and swerves back to me. Its ears are pinned flat against its head and the spots are spinning over it so strangely and nauseatingly that I can't look, it makes me sick to look. I focus on its eyes and lift my stick.

When it snarls at me, I swear the rain parts between us.

I swing the stick through the air, a warning, hard and fast. Drew's yelling at it but the cat's recognized me as the bigger threat. It yowls, opening a mouth so wide that its jaw must come unhinged, and I see that all of its teeth, fangs and *all*, are doubled and serrated.

It's the mouth of a shark, not a cat.

I raise the stick higher. I'm preparing to swing again, and this time I'm going to club it over the head, this cat-shark-spinning-spots thing, I'm going to kill it, but the jaguar shifts its gaze from me to Haven, who's shrunken back against the far wall. Who, in her fear, has retreated too far away for me or Drew to reach her in time.

I'm shouting *No! No!* and my feet are trying to pull free of gravity so I can protect her. But I'm a girl and this is a feline, and there is no chance that I'm faster.

It coils, springs. It is a blur of motion.

Out of nowhere, a beam of cobalt light burns through the mist. It highlights the jaguar, twists it in midair, and the cat slams against the wall beside Haven. Drew gets there before I do and yanks her away by the arm. The light returns and hits the cat again until its fur is smoking and there's this high-pitched screaming sob coming from it that I've never, ever heard any living being make before, and which will surely haunt my nightmares for the rest of my life.

"Stop," I cry out, but I don't even know who I'm pleading to. "Stop hurting it!"

I was ready to kill the cat myself but now, watching it smoke and thrash, all I feel is horror over whatever the cobalt beam is doing to it.

The beam disappears. The jaguar cringes on the floor, panting, its throat working to produce small, whimpering *mew*s. Then it lurches up and reels off into the woods, and the smell of burned flesh and fur is even stronger than that of dirt.

I'm quaking. I can't unwind my fingers from the walking stick; they're glued to the wood. I only realize that the rain has stopped completely when I see, in the foggy distance, the figure of a woman who looks like a movie star standing at the rim of the only other car in sight.

She says, just barely loud enough to make out, "Laser ablation sequences complete."

CHAPTER THIRTY-FIVE
Ember

WE STARE AT EACH other in shock. The mist twines itself into long, looping ribbons that caress the remains of the car and the ground, that open pools of clarity around our ankles and legs and close them again. The air smells singed.

The fireflies decide they've had enough of the inside of my shirt. They crawl out and use me as a springboard, jumping into the air.

"You guys saw that, right?" I clutch the stick to my chest. "You saw the spots on its coat moving, right?"

Of course not, Drew and Haven are going to answer. *You imagined the whole thing, Ember. That was an ordinary jaguar, trying to kill us in a perfectly ordinary jaguar way. Nothing abnormal there.*

"I saw it," says Drew. He's breathing hard and wiping a hand down the side of his face, the side with the bloodshot eye. He's blinking rapidly, too, maybe to clear his vision.

Haven is on her knees with all of her fingers stuffed against her mouth, but when she meets my gaze she snaps a nod.

"The teeth," I say helplessly. I'm struggling for other words, for some sort of other explanation, something I can say that makes this whole thing less surreal. Yet all I can manage is, "Those *teeth*."

"Those," Drew says, "I saw goddamned clearly."

I'm shaking my head. "Maybe this isn't Earth."

Haven says from around her fingers, "Maybe we're dead."

Over on the stretcher, Javier lets out a moan.

"Come on." Drew gestures to Main Controls. "It'll be safer for us over there."

Which seems a spectacular understatement.

So I have to relinquish the stick. I offer it back to Haven, make certain that she pries her hands from her face to accept it, then grab my end of Javier's stretcher.

None of us speak on the walk over. Our footsteps crunch along the glass-glazed path; we're moving as fast as we can but it feels like we're never going to get there, we'll never reach it. The air is sopping still, difficult to breathe. I don't see the floating lights following us any longer but I do hear something flapping above the trees. I tell myself that it's only the bats, confused by the storm into thinking it's night instead of day.

Bats. Day bats. Those could be real, couldn't they?

The mist is stubborn, reveals a silvery blank nothing.

The avatar watches our approach, so out-of-place glam and lovely she seems even less plausible than anything that's happened so far.

There's not as much room inside the wreckage of this car as there was in the Quiet Car, mostly because of all the tech that's remained attached to the walls and ceiling and floor. A few of the screens still emit a dull radiance, but the majority are dark. As soon as we're grouped together inside the cabin, I turn to the avatar.

"Laser ablation means you cook something alive?"

"It's a cleaning program, actually. It resolves issues of microscopic particles—dust—in the machines."

I don't want to think about what it would have done to my fireflies. To me.

"How far out can you shoot the laser?"

"Unfortunately, there is no longer enough power to activate that particular program again."

"Excuse me?"

"As we previously discussed, Miss Duval, the train is dying. Engaging the laser to deter the animal threat to you has significantly drained my battery source. Laser ablation will not activate again."

She flickers. Stabilizes.

"But you have other programs you can run, right?" I ask, desperate. "Other defenses?"

"I fear I was not designed for this environment."

Yeah, I fear we weren't, either.

"So, we're defenseless," Drew concludes.

"Intelligent minds . . . are never defenseless."

It's Javier, awake at last, staring around the car with his usual bright and canny look. He fights to sit up; Haven and I are there at his sides, pulling at his arms to help.

"Judging by . . . things . . . a lot's happened . . . since last night," he says.

"They threw us out." I point back down the burn scar. I'm annoyed to see that my hand is still shaking. "Afraid we're *catching*," I sneer.

"Well, hell, honey." Javier puckers his lips and sips in air, thin and steady like it's liquid. "Told you before . . . they were jackasses."

ONCE UPON A TIME, right before Mom left, our parents took Mason and me for a drive all the way to the mountains, just for fun. Taking the mag-train there would have been too expensive (even at that age, I understood that most things other people did were too expensive for us), but the truck still had working solar conversion panels, so we all four crammed in and went. A Sunday drive, Dad called it.

(It was the last time we went out together as a family. I think now that it was maybe Dad's final attempt to show Mom how well we all fit together, to keep her nestled in our group. Too bad it didn't work.)

Anyway, up until that day, I'd only ever registered the mountains in the distance as this smudgy, bumpy, purplish line that rose above our fields of wheat and corn. Sometimes it was a smudgy, bumpy, snowy line. It had always seemed more like a picture, a background from a vid game, than anything from real life.

But as we drove closer and closer, I found that line changing. The mountains weren't really solid purple; they were purple and green and brown and blue and white. They had trees and roads and houses and people, very much like where I lived.

I was astonished. This constant fact of my life that I'd thought I'd understood had completely, bafflingly altered. The more I studied it, the less I recognized. I sulked the whole ride home because I felt like I'd been tricked, though I couldn't figure out by who or what.

I bend my knees now and find my footing on what's left of the roof of Main Controls, arms wide out. I gaze around me and I see a land that wants to trick me into thinking I know it. I'm surrounded by damp hills, treetops, the mist that's burning leisurely away.

Clear sky teases me in winks. When I look straight up, it's as if I'm back in orbit, gazing down upon the world. Blue ocean between clouds.

In the distance is a smudgy, bumpy, purplish line. I have seen this line before, the line of the Sangres, albeit in reverse. I do know it. But

I don't trust it because right now it's hard to put my faith in anything my eyes are showing me.

I look at the far-off line of those mountains, and it's normal. I look away, look back, and it is upside down. The tips of the peaks point downward. The bottom fades into sky. A few minutes later, it reverses again.

I don't want this planet to be my planet.

But what else could it be?

If Haven is right, and we're already dead, I wouldn't be able to say if this was heaven or hell. It seems some of both.

When I turn my back on those mountains, I see a desert stretching beyond the hills. I think it's a desert. It might be instead a sea of quicksand. Or pudding. Or some other unknown oddity I can't explain. It looks like a standard desert, though, at least from the top of this car. Sand dunes. Scrubby strands of brush that gradually wind down into stubs the further in they go. The storm is blowing over it, erasing all the firm edges wherever it touches.

Unknown Mountain Range, the glass shard informs me. *Unknown Desert Terrain.*

What I can see of the dunes glistens with anomalous details. Like the mountains, those details are always changing. From certain angles, I imagine I view battered buildings, listing silhouettes of dilapidated towers. A boneyard of sandswept carcasses. A tree composed entirely of machetes. A waterfall pouring up into the sky. But at least when these images disappear, I can tell myself they were only mirages. Totally normal desert stuff . . . even if I did detect them through the pragmatic science of the shard.

Right.

"What do you see?" Haven calls from below me. She and Drew and Javier—and the Brain, of course—are still down in the car. I'd had to climb up Drew's back to get up here (I was the only one both tall enough and light enough), so no one else has been able to follow.

What do I see? A whole lot of weird.

"More woods. Maybe a river not that far off, though it's hard to tell through all the leaves. Some kind of—mountains—to the northeast. Desert to the west. The shard can't identify any of it by name."

"What about that cabin?" Drew asks.

"I can't see it from here. But it's probably shorter than the trees."

"Life?" Javier's voice barely rises to me. "People?"

"No," I say, a word that feels heavy and final as it falls from my lips.

A chickadee watches me, almost eye-to-eye with me from its perch on an oak at the front of the car. It bounces along the branch, cocks its head at me inquisitively. Clicks its beak. Bounces closer.

Why are all the birds here so fearless? Maybe it only looks like a chickadee. Maybe it's a pterodactyl in disguise. Anything seems possible.

The Sangre de Cristos go upside down. Right-side up.

The chickadee says, *"Kaaaaaw!"*

I sit down at the edge of the roof, hand the shard back to Drew, who accepts it gingerly. Before he can catch me, I slide down the edge and land on my feet, then on my butt. It knocks the breath out of me for a minute but that's okay. It gives me time to think about what I want to tell them next.

They gaze down at me, three pairs of apprehensive eyes, one pair of flat green (we've got the nanny avatar again). It doesn't help that whatever truth I can offer isn't going to make them any less worried.

"The good news," I begin, "is that I think the cabin I saw is on the way to the river. So we'll be closer to fresh water there."

"What's the bad news?" Drew asks.

"Everything else," I admit. "No cities, no mag-line tracks or power lines or anything. I did see some buildings far out in that desert, old factories or refineries, but they're ruins. Nothing habitable. And . . ." I rub at my forehead, trying to think of how to phrase this. "And I think the mountain range might be the Sangre de Cristos, which is where I used to live. That would put where we are now somewhere either in southern Colorado or northern New Mexico. But I can't be positive because they kept inverting as I watched."

"Inverting?" repeats the nanny, since the other three only stare at me.

"Yes."

"That is scientifically impossible, Miss Duval."

"I *know*." I drop my hand. "But it happened. Also, there's a chickadee up there that sounds like a crow."

Drew's eyebrows are practically to his hairline. Haven scrunches her lips into a rose and Javier goes *hmm*.

I climb to my feet. "You guys don't have to keep looking at me like that. Remember the jaguar? *That* wasn't my imagination. I'm telling you exactly what I saw. This world is . . . haunted, or something. Altered from what it used to be. If we're even home."

The nanny says, "I can assure you all that this planet is indeed Earth. Whatever you witnessed, Miss Duval, there will be a rational explanation for it."

"Fantastic," I say. "I am a thousand percent reassured."

But as I mentioned before, the Brain is immune to sarcasm.

"What are we going to do?" Haven asks.

"You must keep going," the nanny replies. "All of you. Remaining at the wreckage of the train without food or water reduces your chances of surviving the upcoming week to less than thirty-three percent. It is less than one percent for Doctor Castaneda. Use the fragment of the Observation Car glass to find your way to the cabin structure you know is nearby. Water and shelter will be essential to your continued existence. In addition, a manmade structure indicates a human presence, no matter how far removed from this moment in the timeline. It is more than you will find here."

She's right. I can see the truth of what she says sinking into them, changing them. Drew seems to shrink but Haven grows, and Javier nods and looks wise, as if he knew this was coming all along. Which I suppose he did, since it's the most logical course of action available to us, and to a tech guy, logic is life.

I suppose I knew it, too. Deep down, however, I was hoping I was wrong about us being stranded here. That there was going to be some sort of miraculous, New Earth rescue coming for us soon, after all.

That the purple line in the distance would stay purple.

That my disease was never invented.

That none of us were trapped in this future.

"I predict a temperature drop of twenty-seven degrees Fahrenheit in the next eight hours," the Brain says. "I suggest you depart now to locate the cabin in time to shield yourselves from it."

Drew, even though he grew smaller, is the first to take a step toward the edge of the car. His eyes find mine, one a blot of scarlet, one regular white.

"So let's go for a walk," he says.

THE FIREFLIES FIND IT before the rest of us. I told them what to look for, had them scout ahead in pairs. I was worried a bird or bat might try to eat them, but they're fast and they're wily, and it turned out all right.

The human half of this group is much, much slower than the 'flies. Javier still can't walk so he's back on the stretcher; I can tell he feels bad that we're having to carry him, but there's no other choice. Without the level ground of the burn scar to follow, we are struggling along.

The woods are sun-dappled, beaded with water. Every step we take is fragrant with pine and muddy earth, springy with needles and leaves.

The fireflies zip ahead, turn back, zip ahead. They communicate with each other in blinking lights, figuring out which path to lead us down.

Not that it's an actual path. More like a meandering direction.

Haven's got her walking stick back, but we've got two more on the stretcher with Javier. I'm not taking any chances on shark-jaguars or wood trolls or anything else sneaking up on us. Yet the strangest thing we encounter the entire journey is what I can only describe as a meadow of spotted mushrooms, an entire *meadow* of them, that visibly shudder as we plod near. The air above them clouds dark with a sickly, rancid scent. Their spots flush from drab pink into solid jet.

We circle *wide* around that meadow.

All in all, our three-mile trek takes hours, and Haven and I are both staggering by the end of it. No matter how many times we stop to rest, I can no longer pull in a clean, deep breath. I feel like I've been running uphill for days. My palms are covered in blisters and blood.

But then the 'flies are twirling, twinkling, and we're there.

In my head, I'd been calling it *the cabin.*

We're going to the cabin now. We're going to find the cabin. Just a few more steps and we'll be at the cabin, and I can let go of this stretcher. A few more steps and I'll be able to breathe better. A few more. A few more.

But it's not truly a cabin, and it's not truly a hut, either, which was my second guess. It's more like someone's extremely rickety old house, small and quaint with a sharply pitched roof, and plain square windows, and a flight of warped wooden stairs leading up to a covered porch that drips with tawny-dry pine needles. With a heap of money (and even more hard work), you could sand it down and clean it up and maybe give it a new roof, and then you'd have a cute little home in the middle of the woods in the middle of nowhere.

But as of right now . . .

If my life were a fairytale, this would be the house of a wicked witch. No question.

All seven 'flies have landed on the ledge above the door, our own personal welcoming committee. The house is an enigma of shadows and scoured wood; the 'flies are practically garish against it.

Without saying anything, without even looking at each other, Drew and I both put down the stretcher at the same time. Well, he puts his end down. I more or less let go of mine, not on purpose, because my fingers refuse to hold on any longer. Javier had drifted back into his doze but now, since I dropped his legs, he wakes some. I double over and sink to sit on the bottom step of the stairs.

"Just . . ." I mean to finish *give me a second*, but I'm panting too hard to say the words. Neither Drew nor Haven mentions it; they only come to sit beside me. The buckled steps creak as if we're torturing them.

Anyway, it's obvious that I need more than a second.

At some point soon, perhaps very soon, my lungs are going to give up. My disease is blossoming inside me, waiting to steal my final breath. Even without all of this unanticipated exercise, I've felt its rising burn. The doctors warned me that stress was a trigger for an attack, and they were only talking about my regular old life, where *stress* would be failing a class in school or something. Missing Homecoming. *Stress* now has a whole new meaning, most of it to do with avoiding being eaten by mutant wildlife.

I honestly don't know if I have enough meds left to counter a severe TB-3 spasm, so the next one may be my last.

But none of that changes *this* moment, which is the only moment ever that counts. In this moment, Drew's on one side of me and Haven's on the other, and they both lean into me enough so that our sides touch, so that we're all connected, and apparently I am their heart.

Their courage.

Their leader.

And I am going to keep my new family nestled together and control my breathing and climb these stairs and lead us inside to safety. I hope.

No, I *am*.

"Okay," I say, when at last I'm able. "Here we go."

Drew takes one of the walking sticks and hands me the other. We test each step with them before trusting them with our weight, but they all hold. The front door of the house is just as battered as the steps; it's a wonder it still fits the jamb. The knob's missing, so I push it open with my stick. The hinges creak even more savagely than the stairs.

Inside is dust and dark, the scent of forgotten things, like old paper or faded violets. I pause, because although I can't yet perceive the details of the room in front of me, I can feel the uncertainty of the wood beneath my feet. Then my eyes adjust and I see it: the hole in the middle of the living room floor. The vine composed of green leaves and curlicues that coils merrily out of it, dotted with ruby-throated flowers. The vine's already consumed an end table and is headed for one of the windows, for the murky shaft of light that cuts through the gloom.

There are no light fixtures; no lamps, hovering or otherwise. Decaying furniture slants this way and that, and a cupboard hangs crooked and empty, doors open, on a wall. A pair of paintings (actual paintings, not FlickSlips) flank the front door. They're so thick with cobwebs that I can't tell if they're portraits of people or perhaps sheep.

But the windows have glass. The door is able to close behind us. There's a shallow staircase leading to a second story that I didn't notice from the outside, but even if the roof's rotted up there, we can stay down here.

It's better protection than what we've left behind us.

"Creepy," decides Haven, right behind me, and I have to agree.

I enter the kitchen. It's tiny, crowded with a corroded pot-bellied stove and a table for two with a cracked plastic top, but only one slatted chair. The window above the sink has a ruffled eyebrow of yellowed eyelet lace. When I reach up to touch it, it crumbles apart.

Beneath its impressive layer of dust, the table is still set for a meal. There's a chipped plate, an empty glass, a fork. A black smeary stain on the plate that might have once been food. A salt shaker, encrusted in crystals, lays on its side against the fork. The chair is pushed slightly away from the table as if the person eating had only briefly gotten up to grab something they'd forgotten.

Beyond the window grow more of those ruby-throated flowers. They tip and nod and tap against the streaky panes.

Who could have lived here? In this lonely house without computers, without electricity, solar panels, holo pads, anything? *When* did they live here?

In my right ear I hear murmuring, words too swift and hushed to make out. When I flinch and turn my head, it's only the flowers, their petals tap-tapping the glass.

"Let's get Javier inside," I say. My instinct is to whisper but instead I say it loudly. I want to drown out whatever spirits might be lingering here. To let them know that our living blood makes us stronger than they are. "Then let's go look for something to eat."

WE FIND NO EDIBLE food. We find no drinkable water. And that night, Javier dies.

That's not even the worst thing that happens next.

CHAPTER THIRTY-SIX
Ember

I DON'T KNOW WHAT TIME it is. Late. The house is dark, and all four of us are stretched out on the living room floor wherever we've found space around the hole and its vine. The forest outside shivers with broken bits of moonlight, with the restless path of a breeze that clatters through its leaves, but neither the light nor the breeze reach us in here. Still, I'm awake, and I can tell by his breathing that Javier's awake, too.

We wrapped him in the two blankets we carried with us, but the floor's splintery and hard and I bet the blankets don't help that much. I wish now that we'd thought to bring along one of those flashlights from the wreckage, or a FlickSlip, a light tile—anything that would provide a hint of illumination to push back the night.

But all we have is that distant moon and my fireflies, clinging to a support beam directly above my head.

There was no time for it, I console myself. *No time to save anything from the Time Train but ourselves.*

The upstairs of the house is even more depressing than the downstairs. There's nothing left up there but junk-filled rooms and dangerously sagging ceilings, which is why we're down here, even with the hole.

I'm cold. I'm starving. This is my existence now, this forgotten place, my sleepless hunger, the uncomfortable floor. I've got only weeks left to live and this is how I'm going to spend them.

This.

I'm gazing up at the 'flies and feeling sorry for myself when Javier whispers:

"I apologize if I made a mistake."

I lift myself to an elbow, find him in the shadows. His face turns toward me. His eyes gleam.

"What are you talking about?" I whisper back.

But I know.

His voice wavers, thin as a thread. "Life is . . . best lived when we serve the greater good. Help others. Mentor genius. Change the world . . . for the better."

"You have," I assure him. "You've changed the world."

"Queenie," he says, but nothing else. I sit all the way up, scoot over and find his hand. Despite the blankets, it feels icy in mine, so fragile. His fingers are knobby stiff twigs.

"I'm here."

I follow his respiration, rough shallow breaths, until he speaks again. "Caught him in the hack. He was brilliant. Once . . . in a *generation* brilliant. Saw . . . all that potential . . . what good he could do, with just . . . a little help. Institutes. Investors. *You* were . . . his only price."

My skin feels fiery compared to his. I want to hold on tighter, tighter. He's old and I don't want to hurt him, but I don't want to let go.

"Sorry if it was a mistake," my friend Javier sighs. "But I'm still glad you came along."

It's okay, I want to tell him. *It'll all be okay.*

But my lips won't shape the lie.

I am a selfish, vile person. I am cold and angry and afraid and I won't lie, not even to offer him a better goodbye.

I count four more breaths. Five. Then they're done.

I FALL ASLEEP SITTING up, still holding Javier's hand. I'm not aware of it, though, until I feel a short tug on my fingers. I lift my head and can't think for instant of where I am, what's going on, then there's that tug again only stronger, and whatever it is I'm clasping (cold, knobby) is suddenly absent from my grip.

Watery light surrounds me; the windows bathe me in a clouded sunrise. I'm in a shabby room filled with odd shadows, Drew and Haven passed out nearby, and Javier—

Javier!

I snatch my empty hand to my chest, wide awake and ill with fright. Javier *died*, he *died* in the dark just now so—where is he? Where did he go?

Shhhhhhh . . .

My hair stands on end. My face jerks left, toward the sound. Something large and long is sliding away from me across the floor-boards. Is being *dragged* across them. It's Javier. His body. His arms are up by his ears and his hair trails pale beneath his head and his eyes and mouth are open, but he's dead, he's *dead*, and there is something dragging him by his feet toward the center of the room. Toward the hole in the floor.

It's the vine. Wrapped around his legs, all the way up to his knees, flowers jiggling. Pulling him into that black maw.

I scream.

I mean to scream; it comes out so high-pitched and whistle-thin it's barely a noise, so I do it again, and this time I'm shrill and loud and Drew lunges up and Haven starts screaming too, even though she's looking panicked at me and hasn't seen anything else yet.

I'm on my feet. I want to be moving backward but instead I'm going forward, toward the hole and the sinuous plant that is stretching out eager new feelers toward me.

The universe narrows. I see everything, *everything*, with the pixel-sharp clarity that only comes from absolute terror.

Javier's legs are already gone. His palms cup upward, fingers curled into claws as his knuckles bump along the wood. I leap for them and get hold of one. As I'm pulling, I feel a tightness winding around my ankle. Around my calf.

The vine that had been so motionless before (*waiting, it was waiting for us to fall asleep*) is squirming and growing and erupting from the chasm in the floor with unholy speed. It's got both of my legs now, and I have to release Javier to stay upright, because it's pulling me, too. It wants me in its maw, too.

Drew's got an arm around my ribcage and he's digging his heels into the wood to keep us both aboveground. Haven hasn't stopped screaming. I'm screaming as well, but Haven's screeching, "The door! The door is gone!" and I don't have time to see what she means because Javier's body teeters at the edge of the void.

He doesn't make a sound as he vanishes, not a thump or anything. The vines and flowers have devoured him completely as they suck him down.

Drew and I are losing ground. The tendrils are high up both my legs, waving and searching and feeling their way to my waist. A flower pops open on my thigh.

"Let go," I scream at Drew, another something I don't mean, because the last thing I want is for him to let go of me, to release me to the silent, lethal glee of this plant.

He grunts in response, still pulling. A stalk wraps itself into a sinewy green cuff around his bicep.

"You have to," I cry, and now I *do* mean it. I can't bear to have him to die, too. Not here, and not like this.

"No, no," Haven is sobbing, and then, damn it, she's hurled herself at both of us, yanking and sputtering and howling.

"Get out of here, both of you!" I gasp. But neither of them are listening.

Quick as a whip, the vine cinches around Drew's chest. It gets Haven by her hair.

I'm slammed to my knees. There are stalks around my chest now, too, squeezing; spots in my vision and Haven's pure soprano wail in my ears, and I can't wrench enough of the shoots off me fast enough—they lash back twice as strong, up into my mouth, over my eyes, and this, *this* is how I lose my final breath—

Chapter Thirty-Seven
Taza

THE HOUSE WAS SICK. It shimmered with it, like the cast of heat from a fire that rose and warped the air before anything else could disperse it. The sickness had leached the place nearly entirely of color; the house crouched gray and dull in a forest composed of deep emeralds and violets, of browns and freckles of gold. It was as though something had sucked the life from it.

Or, was *still* sucking the life from it, Taza amended. The house wasn't wholly dead yet, because as he stood there and watched, the front door switched places with an upstairs window. The river rock chimney tilted alarmingly first to one side, then rearranged itself to tilt alarmingly the other way.

So, all right, *some* magic left.

All the same, he wavered about venturing inside. He'd been hiking half the night and could definitely use some sleep, but Taza couldn't help feeling that there was something rotten about the entire situation. Something vampirish. The house not only lacked color, it lacked texture; it lacked its *face*. Even the light around it seemed wrong, washed-out and fuzzy. There was no indication of any other creatures nearby, animal or insect.

Bad juju, his old Primary Spells tutor would have said.

A clear warning for halfwits, Kai would have said.

And that spy from the tavern. *The monsters out there will keep you in your place.*

But where is my place? Taza thought tiredly. He'd been breaking the law for days now, and still no sign of the girl. He was sure he was near, he had to be near, but the magic that thrived out here in the Forbidden Zone was so predatory and skewed, none of his locater spells seemed to function.

Success had been such a habitual part of his life until now. He was, Taza had to acknowledge, a tiny bit discouraged at the lack of it.

So when he'd spotted the house through the trees, he'd been looking forward to closing his eyes for an hour or two, monsters or no. It was the first genuine refuge he'd encountered this side of the border. He'd mapped out this journey fully believing his bike was coming along, but now his shoulders burned from the weight of his pack and his legs were beginning to feel like rubber.

The front door creaked higher, higher, creeping upward to kiss the bleached and bowed edge of the roof.

It's a house made of bones, he thought now, and that was enough to make him turn around to go.

He hoisted up his pack. He'd taken just three steps into a slick of shadows when he heard the first scream.

It was a girl's scream, high and piercing. It was followed instantly by another, even higher and more terrified.

Both had come from inside the bone house.

He dropped the pack and sprinted back, kicking up needles and mulch. The door was now well out of reach but the window that had taken its place was still there. It reflected a phantom forest, a phantom runner, rushing toward him.

Taza pressed against the glass. He saw at once that it wasn't the kind of window that opened, that had hinges. It was a solid pane and as deeply and firmly a part of the house as the wooden planks, as the lichen-covered stones that composed the chimney.

He crashed an elbow into it. His arm bounced back, repelled. Magic still lingered here, too.

Behind the glass he glimpsed frantic movement, figures struggling, at least two of them, maybe three. But it was murky inside and what he couldn't see was probably much worse than what he could, so Taza stepped back and threw his hands up to the pane, only this time he incanted, *"Shatter!"*

And the window exploded.

Wooden frame destroyed. Glass rendered to powder, glittering outward and away.

His mind roared, *Get in! Get in! Get in!*

Before the spell had finished wrenching through him, he'd launched himself inside.

Rational Taza felt the splinters of the wall as they dug into his palms, then into his knees. Felt the inconvenience of pain, the heat of fresh blood. But Irrational him—the rougher, better him, composed of sorcery and potency and all the incredible, tangled-together events that had propelled him into these woods, into this second—soared past it. Past the jagged hole that was now the window. Past the glittering glass dust. Past the blanched light of the new day outside and into the depths of a room that echoed with cries.

His feet hit the floor. Something dark and swift rose up in front of him. He thought it was a person because it was person-shaped, but it writhed, twisted: a million green snakes pretending to be a person.

He slashed a palm at it, amazed and not quite unafraid. *"Undo."*

The snakes—vines—went motionless, then the entire shape

tipped to the ground. A hand, very human, shoved out from the green, scraping desperately at where the head would be, and when Taza bent to help another set of vines raced up his spine and wrapped around his neck. He was towed backward, garroted, abruptly and entirely unable to breathe. Dancing black monsters burst behind his eyes.

It all happened so fast. He was moving one second, and now he was on his back, and the vines—snakes?—were crushing him, and the ceiling was a confusion of dark and flowers and someone was still shrieking—

He didn't need words to kill this, whatever *this* was. Words worked; intent worked; touch would work, too. His head was choked with blood; if he didn't do something soon, he wouldn't be alive enough to do anything at all.

His fingers dug a space between his windpipe and the tough snakeskin of the vine. It had already captured his torso, was sneaking up his nostrils to stab into his brain.

Die, Taza thought hazily. *Die now, you thing.*

And the silent power in him, dim and strangled as it was, flooded up. It seared into the plant, crackling, an inferno without heat.

The vine recoiled. Singed. When Taza could move again, it broke into pieces and crumbled to charcoal along his skin.

He sat up, coughing, then crawled to the person-shape. The lone hand had been joined by another. *Female* hands.

The vine concealing her hadn't crisped all the way yet. She was wheezing and still tearing at the tendrils; he could see a single sea-colored iris and the pale jut of her chin. He brushed his fingers over the coils that ensnared her, and then she, too, was covered in charcoal.

But alive. Free.

For a heartbeat, they locked gazes. Then she collapsed into the cremains of the vine and a puddle of sooty hair, her eyes rolled back.

Blood marked the corners of her lips. Her chest wheezed, *heeeeeeeee, heeeeeeee, heeeeeeee.*

"Girl," Taza said in a voice that wasn't his own; deeply hoarse, rusted. "Girl, it's dead. The plant's dead. You're all right now."

Her lips were turning blue. The bruises on the side of her face were a yellow-purple sunset against the ashen rest of her.

heeeeeee. heeeee.

"Girl," Taza said louder, dismayed. His fingertips painted her in Dalmatian spots. "Girl!"

heee—hee—

he—

he—

She wasn't supposed to die. That's not what he saw in the vision. He saw her *alive*, talking to him, and he'd *felt* that and she couldn't die—

"*Mend,*" he rasped, with both palms over her heart.

he.

. . . he.

"Get out of the way!" someone shouted, shoving past him.

A set of nervous green lights buzzed around his head, bugs of some ilk. Taza lifted a hand to them but didn't swat, preoccupied with this new person—male—who was doing something to the girl, pushing up one her ashen gray sleeves, pushing a metal needle into her ashen gray skin, depressing a plunger—

He'd seen something like it before, although he didn't know where. It was an old thing, an old-fashioned thing—

Medicine, supplied his mind, surprising him.

And then: *She's sick. Like the house.*

A slighter shape pressed against his other side. A much younger girl's hands thrust a small, clear, curved thing against the base of the sick girl's nose.

"Ember," the younger girl pleaded shakily, fumbling with the curved thing, holding it in place. "Ember!"

That's her name, Taza's mind informed him slowly, grandly. He felt like he was a dozy beat behind everything that was going on around him; at the same time, he felt like he was only remembering things he already knew.

Ember. Of course, that's her name.

"Ember," Taza tried out loud in his rusted and broken voice, and it sounded musical and foreign to him, and her eyes rolled open again.

CHAPTER THIRTY-EIGHT
Ember

As you've probably realized, I've spent a huge chunk of my life alone. I've never been the type of person who makes friends easily, and the few kids I could even call friend*ly* always either moved away or drifted away, maybe due to lethargy or just lack of common ground.

Dad called me *prickly*. Mason said *choosy*. However you slice it, my natural inclination has always been to hold myself apart. I mean, hello, the one boy I ever even had a crush on got exploded by lightning.

Then came the TB-3, and our shift to the mountains, and my confinement to our cottage. And that basically mashed flat any chance I ever had of meeting more people or finding new friends.

By and large, human connections—I mean the deep, transformational, revolutionary kind—have been a mystery to me. I don't think of myself as *entirely* antisocial, but . . .

Boyfriends and girlfriends who constantly cling to each other like barnacles? Couples who claim they recognized their soulmates at first glance? Even classmates who swear they'll be best friends forever and a day—

Stuff like that always secretly bewildered me.

Perhaps I was too comfortable with how I was anyway: secure with my twin; content in the wheat or the corn or the snow. Perhaps I never really understood what I was missing, being so at ease by myself.

So I never thought I needed to work harder to earn anything more.

I was wrong.

I OPEN MY EYES. There is a boy above me. Not Drew.

This boy is smudged and scruffy. His cheeks are blue with stubble he hasn't shaved, and his black hair (*long, really long*) drapes down to graze my cheeks.

His eyes are pale and reflective.

Twin moons. Twin skies.

He touches my face. His lips form my name, though the sound of it reaches me low and distorted.

Oh, I want to say, but my body no longer seems to be connected to my brain. My thoughts go like the Sangres, upside down, wrong way up. My ears ring.

The boy checks the pulse at the side of my neck. There are seven small green fireflies crowning the top of his head.

My life is not a fairytale. I don't believe in magic or fairy god-mothers or in princes coming to my rescue.

But . . .

Oh, I would say to him, if I could. *There you are at last.*

EPILOGUE

IT WAS WIDELY ACKNOWLEDGED that Taza Sullivan had been born with a hole in his heart. And even though no one had been able to foresee what, exactly, was needed to fill that gap within him . . . she did exist. She had existed for ages, locked in a sleep without dreams.

She had tangled gold hair and eyes that echoed the sea. She was a gift from the stars, from a time and place that no one—not even the son of a sovereign—could touch.

And everything about her was forbidden.

END BOOK ONE

About the Author

Shana Shaheen lives in Colorado with several rescued house rabbits, two loudly opinionated cats, about three dozen giant, surly goldfish—and a very handsome and patient husband.

www.shanashaheen.com

www.ingramcontent.com/pod-product-compliance
Lightning Source LLC
Chambersburg PA
CBHW021207250626
47155CB00008B/2710